NOVA DESCENT

David Kimberley

First published 2020
Published by GB Publishing Org

ISBN: 978-1-912576-48-7 (hardback)
978-1-912576-49-4 (paperback)
978-1-912576-50-0 (eBook)
978-1-912576-51-7 (Kindle)

A catalogue record of the printed book is available from the British Library

Cover Art © Wendy Kimberley Art

GB Publishing Org
www.gbpublishing.co.uk

'It is often a long, difficult road to releasing a second book. However, with the right people making the journey with you, it makes the road less bumpy. All my thanks go to those people who believed in Galahad Suns and have now made this journey with me on Nova Descent. I hope you are all strapped in and ready for the rest of the series!'

CONTENTS

Prologue

The galaxy is in a state of political turmoil as the five corporations vie for power across the known systems and within the unexplored regions of space.

Davian Kurcher, a Taurus Galahad enlister reliant on drugs to forget his past, is chasing down serial killer Edlan Rane on Kismet when a series of unforeseen events results in his reassignment.

Tasked by Commander Santa Cruz with finding and bringing back alive seven priority criminals who were for some reason released by another enlister, Kurcher is told only that one of them is unknowingly carrying a data implant that Taurus desperately want to retrieve.

Together with his pilot, Frost, he locates the first criminal and persuades him to help find the other six. However, whilst apprehending the next, Kurcher is unexpectedly helped by Rane, who has his own reasons for tagging along.

As they make their way across various systems and worlds in search of the criminals, Kurcher's dependency on drugs grows to dangerous levels as he battles to silence the voices of the dead from his past, and the dynamic of the enlisted criminals on board changes as they reluctantly begin working together.

When Rane exposes the truth behind Kurcher's mission, the enlister begins doubting Santa Cruz's motives and it is only Frost's quick-thinking that rescues the situation.

When a murder on board reveals the location of the data implant, Kurcher and Frost make the bold decision to view the information they had been sent to safeguard. Confused by what they see, Kurcher demands answers from Santa Cruz, who reveals the most startling discovery in the history of the human race before entrusting the enlister to set in motion the next part of his plan.

Kurcher takes his ship and its restless occupants on a high-risk journey outside their galaxy, realising too late that his drug supply has run out. When ships from rival corporation Sapphire Nova track them down in an attempt to claim the mysterious prize first, Kurcher hands himself over but is wracked by withdrawal symptoms.

To his surprise, he is rescued by the criminals and Frost, fighting their way off the ship which results in the demise of some. Before his brain shuts down from the withdrawal, Kurcher makes a rash decision and carries out Santa Cruz's orders, resulting in the unprecedented death of millions back in known space.

The screams of the long dead return, this time accompanied by the crushing weight of regret from his recent actions, and Kurcher falls into a depressive state. Frost and the remaining criminals are forced to take action and flee when Santa Cruz orders them executed, having used them to set in motion his plan to seize control of the galaxy.

When they are tracked down in orbit of a quaran world, the ship is damaged beyond repair and the ultimate sacrifice allows Kurcher and the criminals to escape to the surface.

They make the decision to try stopping Santa Cruz and seek the help of other organizations in doing so, calling in old and new favours alike before confronting the rogue commander and his fleet as they head to Sapphire Nova's homeworld to commit further genocide.

As battle rages, Kurcher fights back the growing darkness within himself to right his own wrong and destroy Santa Cruz's murder weapon. When the commander tries to stop him, the resulting deaths are fair payment for saving Nova's homeworld. However, revealing his own ruthless agenda, Rane commits one last crime and is responsible for the death of an entire planet.

Now a wanted man himself, Kurcher makes the only sensible choice and flees, opting to ally himself with those he once hunted.

However, unbeknownst to him, his actions have awoken an even greater threat from the darkest corner of unknown space.

MAP

Farrin
Coldrig
Krondahar
Milky Way Galaxy
Scutum-Centaurus Arm
Orion SPUR
Perseus Arm
Elrian
Drakan
Hest
Henning
Kember
Sanctus
Columbus
Clark
Barclay
Karstad
Miller
Galen
Freeman
Meddian
Ulrich
Jura
Vaughn
Bridge
Geraint
Reynold
Lincoln
Vega
Wagner
Genesys
Callyn
Sol
Berg
Tassel
Narwhal
Oralia
Daedalus
Almaz
Brittia
Ixxis
Atalanta
Weisman
Kalbrec
Iridia
Pendium
Pegasus
Haskell
Benedict
Griffin
Dalton
Achon
Ross
York
Alscion
Tacit
Purnell
Flint
Phoris
Yardwell
Colborn
Labris
Armstrong
Bastion
Valen

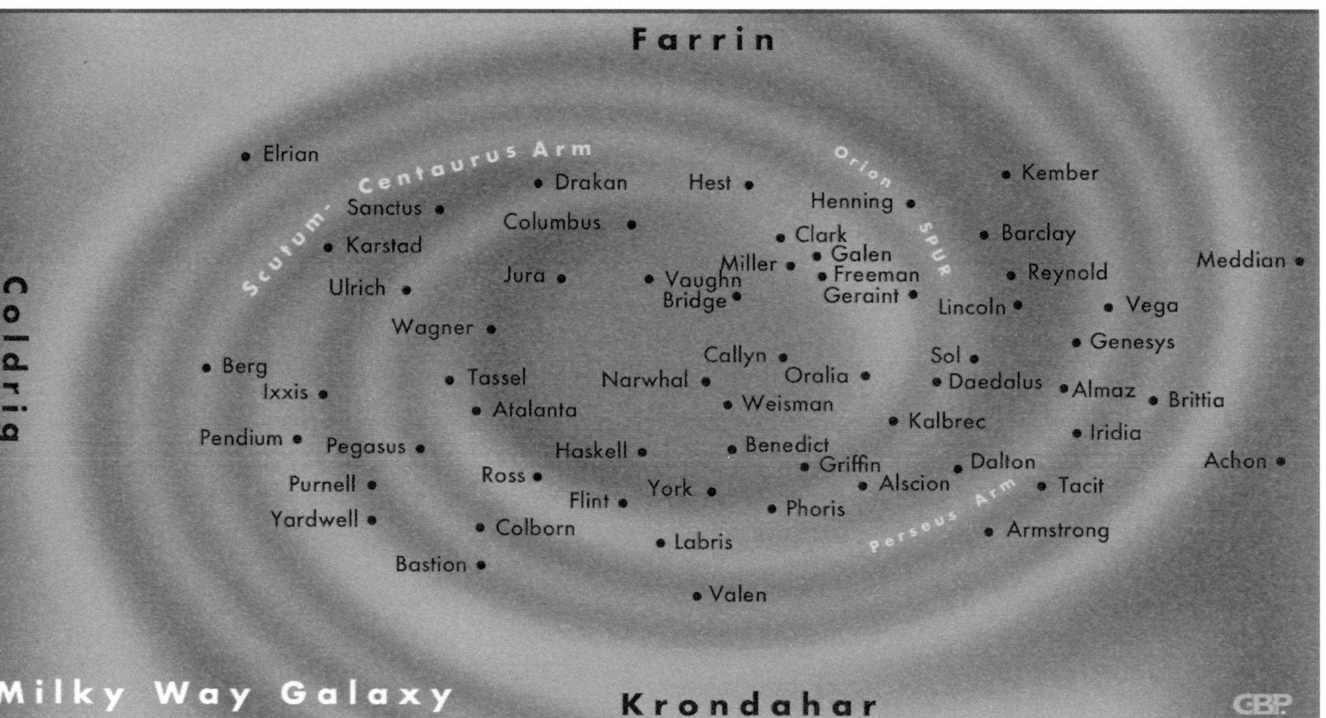

Corporations

Taurus Galahad
Sapphire Nova
Libra Centauri
Sigma Royal
Impramed

Factions

Echo (pirate)
Fortitude (merc)
Jericho's Bold (pirate)
Knights Templar (merc)
Schaeffer's Nine (pirate)
Cobb Resistance
The Kindred

Echo

Davian Kurcher - ex-Taurus enlister
Jaffren Hewn - leader of Echo
Sieren Broekow - ex- Taurus sniper
Shannon Drake - pilot of the Falcata
Tariq Masami - pilot of the Crius
Vance Fischer - Jaffren Hewn's second
Jos Chaplin - head of operations on Tempest

Taurus Galahad

Karin Hayward - judicial officer
Gen. Mitchell - head of military operations
Gen. Garrett - military officer
Cmdr. Neri Ishlan - military officer
Cmdr. O'Brien - military officer
Cmdr. Byrne - military officer
Dr. Samuel Li - lead scientist at Hayes
Dr. Lynn White - lead researcher at Hayes
Akeman - agent
Fraser Lenaghan - senior board member
Exec. Kort - senior board member
Exec. Tench - senior board member
Exec. Pavleachenko - senior board member
Exec. Marris - senior board member
Exec. Chaldevert - senior board member

Prakhad Culman - junior board member
Exec. Billings - junior board member
Joseph Dant - head of the LDCR on Mars
Lt. Tolbert - military officer
Gotzer - Shard scientist
Jacobs - rescue team leader
Ablett - rescue team medic
Surimoto - rescue team medic
Oberman - rescue team medic

Sapphire Nova

Cmdr Tomas Klein - military officer & board member
Cmdr Kam Bavelli - military officer & board member
Cmdr Arys Fletcher - military officer & board member
Mikan Rist - agent
Devlin - head of Harper security
Manders - exploration team leader

Additional Characters

Coyle - Fortitude merc
Morton Hurst - leader of Fortitude
Ruck - Fortitude merc
Flynn - leader of the Knights Templar
Suren - Knights Templar merc
Cal Fuller - leader of the Cobb Resistance
Marie Butler - member of the Cobb Resistance
Dale Rettin - member of the Cobb Resistance
Monk - member of the Cobb Resistance
Cho - member of the Cobb Resistance
Leeson - member of the Cobb Resistance
Trystan Hengeveld - Libra Centauri officer
Hedmun Oakley - commander of the Oakley fleet
Erric Keening - trader
Harz - Jericho's Bold pirate

Straunia
Flint system

His lungs were burning but fear gave him the adrenaline to keep going.

Behind him, there was one final burst of fire from an assault rifle. The sound gave him hope that others in the team had managed to break through and were following him back to the *Cognis*, but he didn't dare look over his shoulder.

Manders made the decision to veer from the main road and head through some of the side streets. The abandoned buildings were just a blur as he sped past and he nearly tripped on a child's bike that was lying at one junction.

Static hissed suddenly in his ear, giving him a fright he could have done without. Against his better judgement, he came to a halt in one claustrophobic alley and caught his breath before trying the ship again.

'Vik, you there?' Even the whisper was too loud. 'For fuck's sake, answer me.'

What if those things had managed to get onto the *Cognis* somehow? The thought chilled him to the bone.

'If you can hear me...'

A woman's scream echoed through the streets of Brandt, further shredding his nerves. He knew immediately it was Pelia but there was nothing he could do for her now. There was nothing he could do for any of them.

Manders clutched his pistol tightly. He wouldn't part with the weapon as easily as he had the rest of his equipment, which was probably still lying where he dropped it all back among the outskirts of the settlement.

'Vik.' He doubted the pilot would hear him but it made him feel better speaking to someone. 'I'll be back at the ship shortly. Prep for launch as soon as I am on board.'

Luckily, Brandt had not been designed with the complicated layout other colonies had been, so he knew the quickest route back to his ship. In fact, it felt as though the place had been constructed in a hurry. It was the total opposite of Credence, which he had always considered to be one of the best-designed cities on any Nova world. That was over 2,000 miles away though and, like Brandt, was just a husk now.

The daylight was waning as Manders emerged back onto one of the main streets. Even in the twilight haze, he could still see the fallen *Grail* to the west resembling some bizarre titan that loomed over Brandt. He recalled his initial surprise when the team landed. Not surprise at the ginormous alien vessel that lay derelict on Sapphire Nova's late homeworld, but surprise that the buildings of Brandt hadn't been shaken apart when it crashed onto the surface. Then again, the *Grail* itself was relatively intact. It didn't break apart as it entered Straunia's atmosphere and hadn't split asunder when it hit the ground.

As he pulled his eyes from what had been their primary mission, he recalled the chatter that had broken out among not only his team but also the soldiers who had been sent with them. For a while, there had been an anxious excitement until Lieutenant Emberson had reminded them all what the *Grail* was capable of. Of course, nobody needed reminding. Vik had constantly referred to Straunia as the *Poisoned Planet*, despite the fact oxygen levels had returned almost to normal swiftly after all life was extinguished. Manders himself had believed it to be more of a dead planet considering there was no ecosystem left, just ruins.

Then there were the arguments over the name of the alien weapon. Some refused to call it the *Grail*, which was a moniker given to it by the late mass murderer Santa Cruz. It was unfortunate that the title had stuck. Again, it was down to Emberson to point out what a waste of breath it was trying to debate such a topic. In his eyes, Sapphire Nova had endured a severe loss but would rebuild. The three members of the new board would guide the corporation through such a devastating time and ensure it prevailed.

Manders had wanted to ask the officer just why the board had seen fit to send them to investigate the fallen leviathan. He had expected Straunia to be marked as a quaran straight away and avoided, as Meta had, but the pull of the alien structure was just too inviting. The explorer in him could appreciate that, but millions had been killed by it and he didn't want to be added to that tally.

As he headed back into the ghost town in search of his ship, the air began tasting stale and he found himself struggling to take a deep breath. At the corner of his vision, the oxygen readout was slowly dropping. It seemed Straunia truly was dying. It was as if their arrival had prompted a critical change.

As all traces of the Flint sun vanished and a clear canvas of stars appeared overhead, Manders finally saw the *Cognis* ahead. It was just where he had left it and looked secure enough. There was a dim light emanating from the cockpit, where Vik was likely kicking back with a cigarette and one of his dirty mags. The pilot would be blissfully unaware of what had just happened to the rest of his team.

Manders would be haunted by what he had seen and heard for the rest of his life. The looks of disbelief on the faces of Emberson and the other soldiers as they opened fire. The sound of the assault rifles and the dull thud as bullet after bullet hit their intended targets. The eerie silence from said targets as they refused to fall and continued to shamble towards the team. Those fucking eyes. Pelia's final scream.

He tried clearing his mind as he made for the ship. The data he had recorded in his library app needed to be sent to Klein or Bavelli as soon as he was on board. The rest of Sapphire Nova needed to know what was happening on Straunia, although he still wasn't quite sure himself.

There was a movement ahead and he instantly froze, watching in horror as something slowly detached itself from the hull of the *Cognis* and dropped quietly to the ground, slivers of blue and silver glistening in the darkness.

Manders had no idea what he was seeing. The dark spectre moved in the shadows close to the ship, occasionally stopping. Whenever it did, he was afraid it had spotted him and so he instinctively began taking small steps backwards, his knuckles white as his grip on the pistol tightened. When two more forms crawled into view over the top of the *Cognis*, Manders' remaining courage drained from him completely and he turned to run for the cover of the nearby buildings.

Fear was now firmly in control. He had no other thought than to flee and hide where nobody could find him, to wait among the ruins until the board decided to send a rescue team.

The darkness ahead suddenly came alive, writhing and reaching out for him. Manders slid to a halt and leapt back, nearly losing his footing. All around him, something stirred in the night and he caught glimpses of silver or flashes of soft blue.

'What do you want?' he found himself yelling.

Maybe Vik would hear and come charging out of the *Cognis* with guns blazing. That might buy him time to get back to the ship. Then again, maybe Vik was already dead, just like the others.

Manders looked down at his pistol then out into the darkness at the shifting silhouettes. With a shaking hand, he raised the weapon and considered firing into the murk until the clip was spent, hoping to drive off whatever was closing on him. Instead, he placed the cold barrel against his temple and cursed the day he had agreed to take his team back to Straunia.

Echo vessel Falcata
Iridia system

He hated the silence.

There was a time when being alone with his own thoughts had been bliss. That was when the Parinax had been surging through his system, numbing his brain and making even the mundane seem so fucking amazing. The drugs had kept the dead at bay too, of course.

He tried to focus on the distant thrum of the *Falcata*'s engines holding them in a steady orbit and started flexing the digits on his right hand. His index finger and thumb were still numb but at least they were moving. His eyes lingered on the angry scar across his wrist. *Consider it a gift to make sure you never forget*. Santa Cruz's mocking tone echoing in his head made him flinch. If the commander had been present, at least Kurcher could have silenced him with a bullet to the brain.

He stood and walked to the window, staring out at Tempest and wondering what was taking so long. The transport should have docked with them by now.

Just be patient, Frost said. *It's not like you're in a hurry*.

'I don't feel like being patient.' He looked around at the empty room. 'Fuck's sake.'

At least this time there wasn't someone else there looking at him like he was a lunatic. Still didn't stop him from feeling like an idiot though.

Pain lanced through his skull and he reached into his jacket pocket for one of the tablets Hewn had given him, hoping that he wouldn't need them much longer. He had been told that the after effects of Echo tampering with his app implants would eventually calm down but that was six months ago. He accepted that incapacitating the Taurus tech was wise, to stop the corp tracking him, but the discomfort was making him wish they could have just cut them out.

'Good news.'

It took a moment for Kurcher to register the fact that the female voice was real. 'Impress me.'

'If you take a look at the guardian, you'll see our guest is on his way.'

He peered down to where the oval silhouette of Libra's watchful protector stood out starkly against the planet. A tiny ship glistened alongside it as the transport made its way up to the *Falcata*.

‘I only want him on board, Drake. Nobody else, understood?’

‘Your wish is my fucking command.’

Kurcher allowed himself a brief smile as the comms link was cut abruptly. When Hewn had given him the *Falcata* to use, one caveat had been that Drake had to be the pilot. It hadn’t taken long to realize why that was. One less pain in the ass for Hewn to deal with.

A sharp jolt reminded him he hadn’t taken the tablet so he quickly swallowed it, grimacing at the shitty taste. Using the comms app often resulted in a dull ache pulsing in his temples. Again, he had Echo to thank for that after they altered the tech to allow only their own signals to be picked up while burning out the Taurus chip in the process.

When the transport from Tempest finally docked, he returned to his seat at the table and watched the door.

I hope she checks him for weapons, Frost remarked.

Any doubts about whether or not the new arrival would be armed were quickly snuffed out as Drake marched him into the room, giving him a gentle shove when he saw Kurcher waiting for him.

‘I don’t understand,’ Chaplin blurted out.

‘Sit down.’ Kurcher waved at the chair opposite. ‘We’ve got a lot to talk about.’

The bespectacled pirate looked back at Drake. ‘Shannon, what’s the meaning of this?’

Drake pursed her lips. ‘Oh, I don’t think we’re really on first name terms yet. Take a seat.’

As Chaplin slowly lowered himself into the chair, Kurcher nodded to the pilot who replied with a middle finger before leaving. She may have been wild, with her half-shaven head and painted blue lips, but he liked her attitude.

‘Jaffren sent *you*?’ asked Chaplin, incredulously.

‘Enough with the questions.’ Kurcher recalled beating the man before on his last trip to Tempest so was surprised by his boldness. ‘Hewn is a very busy man, as you well know, and I’ve become someone he sends to deal with certain...matters.’

Chaplin sniffed and crossed his arms. ‘So you’ll be wanting a report then on the production. After your sabotage set us back drastically, it’s taken up til now to get back on track. We’ve had to replace vats as well as the ingredients your men destroyed, which meant waiting for them to be transported from one of the Libra colonies.'

'All very interesting but not why I'm here.' Kurcher noticed the corner of Chaplin's mouth twitch. 'Hewn received very troubling news that someone from Libra Centauri visited his production facility and was given intel on a number of Echo ops, trade routes and colony locations. Echo's alliance with Libra means only the need-to-know info is given out. The intel they now have means they can fuck Echo over whenever they like, which doesn't make for a healthy relationship.'

'So you're here to find out how they received this information,' Chaplin stated.

'To start with.'

They stared across the table at one another for a moment before Chaplin shrugged. 'Why not just send me a message then? No need to drag me off planet.'

'So you know who gave Libra the intel then.'

'Well no, but I could've been looking into it. When Jaffren's not on site, it's down to me to run the place after all.'

Kurcher leant back. 'See, that's the problem. You seem to think that you're the one in charge here.'

A frown furrowed Chaplin's brow as he pushed the glasses back up his nose. 'Jaffren trusts me.'

'He did, until you betrayed him.'

The pirate's reaction was almost comical, puffing out his chest and wagging a finger. 'How dare you come here and make such an accusation. It's quite the joke considering that it was you who had a gun to Jaffren's head just nine months ago and whose men were killing both Echo and Libra personnel at whim.'

'A lot of things have changed since then,' Kurcher told him calmly. 'But refer to them as *my men* again and I'll jettison you into orbit.'

It was your idea, chuckled Ercko. *Take some of the fucking credit.*

'I don't recognize you as part of Jaffren's operation,' sneered Chaplin. 'Now let me get back to my job and I'll find out who is actually to blame.'

Kurcher sighed as he placed his revolver on the table. 'I'm not guessing here. We already know it was you. What we want to know is who this Libra officer was and what exactly you told him?'

Chaplin eyed the gun nervously. 'I'm telling you, you've got the wrong man.'

Your interrogation skills have much to be desired, enlister, scoffed Santa Cruz.

'Let me tell you about this revolver,' began Kurcher, picking up the weapon as he stood. 'I lost my old one several months back and Hewn had this specially made so I could easily use it with either my injured right hand or my stronger left. It packs more of a punch than my previous revolver and holds more bullets in the clip, plus they fashioned a silencer for it. Instead of the loud crack, the last thing people hear now is a swift hiss of air as the bullet blows their head off.'

Chaplin was starting to sweat. 'So you're an assassin now then.'

'Not really.' The barrel of the revolver swung to face the pirate. 'The point is that either you tell me what it is we need to know or you'll get to hear that hiss of air before your brains get spattered all over the wall. You know me. I don't like waiting, so what's it to be?'

'His name is Trystan Hengeveld.' Chaplin was shaking as he crumbled. 'He came to Tempest looking to find his brother's killer.'

'So you just decided to give him intel on Echo instead?'

'I told him that you and the others came here to apprehend Jaffren; that Lars was killed by them when they infiltrated the facility. He decided to lean on me heavily to make sure I was telling the truth, then he told me he wanted details on how to locate Jaffren too. I just wanted him to leave and, before I knew it, I had given him more than I had anticipated.'

'Seems you just have a face begging to be beaten. All you had to do was lie and give him false information. Now Hewn knows just how weak you really are.'

Chaplin held his hands up. 'Wait, you need to understand who this man is. He isn't some grunt in the Libra military. Trystan is an officer with serious backing from his board and with enough firepower behind him to make him a real threat to Echo. He demands justice for Lars' murder.'

I'd like to see him try, Ercko said.

'Tell me what intel you gave him,' Kurcher ordered the trembling pirate. 'Hewn may still be able to make changes to his plans so he doesn't have any run-ins with this fucker.'

As Chaplin began listing everything, it became apparent that he really had sold Echo out. In fact, Kurcher doubted that someone based on a planet like Tempest would know so much. Perhaps Chaplin had been accumulating information for years just in case he ever needed a bargaining chip when working so closely with Libra. The man certainly wasn't stupid.

'Hewn has always paid you well from the Eidolon profits so what was in this for you?'

'Trystan would have killed me. I had no choice.'

Kurcher lowered the revolver. 'Hewn can forgive a lot of things, believe me, but not this. He sent me to determine what Libra now knows and to express his disappointment to you. He also wanted me to tell you that your replacement is already on his way.'

'This is all your fault.' Chaplin's fist slammed onto the table. 'You do realize that? Jaffren made a huge mistake trusting you to do his dirty work.'

'Do you know the problem with diseases?'

The question caught Chaplin by surprise. 'What?'

'You can treat the symptoms of a disease, keep an infection at bay and stop the production of bile. Trouble is, it can come back and next time it might just finish you off.'

As Chaplin gave him a perplexed look, Kurcher raised the revolver again and fired a single shot that took the pirate through the forehead and sent his glasses spiralling into the air.

Was there any point to that little pre-execution speech? asked Frost.

Moronic considering the man was about to die, added Santa Cruz.

As he holstered the weapon, Kurcher peered over the table to see that most of the blood and brain matter from the exit wound had sprayed across the floor.

'Time to head back to the Expanse, Drake.'

'Already?' came back the slightly muffled response. 'I thought you'd be a lot longer. I've hardly had time to take a piss.'

'Need to dump the body and clean up.'

'It's your mess.'

You'll need to jettison Chaplin when you're well away from Tempest, D'Larro stated. *There is also the matter of his transport.*

'Tell the transport pilot Chaplin is coming back to the Expanse with us so he can leave.'

Drake was taking a drag on a cigarette. 'Fine. You'd best get cleaning.'

There was no denying that she was more of a handful than Frost ever was but there were still some similarities that made him smile. Then again, Drake's cigarettes tended to be packed full of substances Frost would have shied away from.

He found himself thinking about the *Kaladine*'s pilot, remembering the look on her face whenever he had done something she didn't like, which was most of the time. She always liked to play it as safe as possible. He also remembered her face as she had said goodbye to Broekow and the way she whispered into her lover's ear before pushing him away.

He was right, you know, she told him. *Taking Rane and Ercko down to the surface was too rash. They murdered Lars Hengeveld and now you have to face the consequences.*

'How was I to know they would kill him?' Kurcher yelled. 'They were there to cause the distraction.'

You let yourself be manipulated.

Kurcher glanced at Chaplin's shocked-looking corpse. 'One more dead pirate doesn't matter.'

Ercko's dead, D'Larro reminded him. *Rane has disappeared. Who do you think Trystan Hengeveld will go after?*

Fuck him, boomed Angard. *He isn't about to wander into the Expanse and take on the whole of Echo.*

Kurcher turned his eyes to the window, catching sight of the transport disappearing back down to Tempest. A moment later, the *Falcata* broke orbit and headed for the jump point. As the dead continued to voice his thoughts and concerns over the situation, he watched the stars and wondered when exactly the galaxy would implode.

Temple
Lincoln system

Despite his lust being sated, Lenaghan still couldn't sleep.

Lifting his head, he looked around at the four naked women sprawled across the ginormous bed. They had no problem sleeping. Then again, they didn't have to worry about the threat of war or governing an entire troubled corporation.

Throwing the silken sheets back, he swung his legs off the side of the bed and stretched. When he took a deep breath, he almost choked on the smell of sweat and alcohol lingering in the processed air. It had been a good night though.

Checking the time, he was pleased to see that there was still another ten hours before he was due to leave the hospitality of the Knights Templar and return to Galt. Ten hours before he had to face that harsh reality. It wasn't long enough.

'Leaving us so soon?' asked one woman as he began pulling on his clothes.

Jet black hair, pouting lips and an incredible body. He wished he could recall her name. 'There are people just waiting to be fleeced by a professional gambler such as myself,' he grinned. 'I take a shitload of money from Taurus so I might as well go blow some.'

'Well come back later,' she purred, wrapping herself in the soiled bedclothes. 'We're pretty good at blowing things.'

Lenaghan knew that, as soon as he walked out the door, all four would be heading for the shower to wash his stench off. Once or twice he had caught them exchanging disgusted expressions during their session so he knew exactly what they thought of him. Having an overweight, ugly bastard thrusting on top of you couldn't have been a nice experience but he had paid a small fortune for their company, so fuck it.

After combing his hair and applying some pungent aftershave, the executive was ready to face the other businessmen and mercenaries in the gambling dens of Temple.

'Sounded like there was some alarm going off among your gear,' the raven-haired temptress mentioned. 'Messages from your wife?'

Lenaghan tutted. He didn't want to check his HDU but curiosity got the better of him. Only fifty-three new messages. 'Christ.'

He swiftly scrolled through them, checking who sent each so he could tell whether to ignore or not. Most of them were from lower-ranked execs in Taurus sending through reports on the activity of the other corps. Sapphire Nova assault ships roaming the edges of Taurus systems, Libra Centauri skulking in the shadows as per usual, Sigma Royal still reeling from the attack on Meta by Santa Cruz's *Grail*, Impramed confirming they would not take sides for the hundredth time.

There was a note from Mitchell among the reports, reminding him that the *Victory* was heading out to Berg soon to check on the Minerva science teams. The general had been very vocal following the events in Flint and had been quick to set up defenses of the Taurus systems, knowing that Nova would retaliate despite Santa Cruz operating under his own jurisdiction. Lenaghan was not sure why Mitchell saw a need to visit Minerva personally but he wasn't about to question the motives of the man keeping Taurus safe.

The only other message that caught his eye was from Karin Hayward, calling for yet another meeting. The new judicial officer was certainly tenacious but he didn't like the fact she had been instantly promoted to a seat on the board after Rees was killed. Her eight months in the role had seen her delve into every nook and cranny of Taurus, looking for ways to stamp her newfound authority. She had already had eleven junior execs arrested on corruption charges and Lenaghan knew that she was keeping a close eye on senior personnel too, including himself. Let the bitch try and take him on though. At least she was based on Earth while he ran the Galt headquarters.

'I expect my luggage to all be here when I get back,' he told the sleepy women, shoving the HDU back among his possessions.

The corridors of Temple were quiet as he made his way toward the gambling hub. The occasional person would stagger past, inebriated or high, and once or twice he caught sight of men eagerly heading to their rooms in the company of some bored-looking woman. The Knights Templar were certainly raking in the money though and he wondered just how much of it was from Taurus.

As he passed one of the broad windows, his pace slowed. He enjoyed watching the tormented Kalvion, the dark grey quaran always shifting as the constant storms danced across its surface. From the relative tranquility of the station, the planet was silent, but he could imagine how different it must be below the clouds.

'She's quite entrancing.'

Lenaghan had not heard the man approach and it took a moment for him to recognize the weathered face of Flynn. 'How do you move so quietly in that armour?'

The leader of the Knights Templar gave a laugh that echoed along the corridor. 'I didn't expect to find you wandering our halls. Have you grown bored of the company already?'

'Of course not. I just wanted to get in some gambling too before I left.'

'Fair enough.' Flynn nodded at the view. 'It's hard not to appreciate the fierce beauty of Kalvion. I often spend time here myself.'

Lenaghan raised an eyebrow. 'Why do I get the feeling you have something else on your mind?'

'I do,' admitted the mercenary. 'I wanted to speak to you about the agreement between ourselves and Taurus.'

'Right now, I'm not wearing my business suit. Besides, I don't really have much to do with our working relationship. I just enjoy your facilities.'

'Listen, there's a high stakes poker game going on behind closed doors. I'll take you there now if you hear me out on the way.'

'If they're professional players, count me out. I'm not going back to Galt empty-handed.'

Flynn smirked. 'Rich amateurs who have paid for the VIP treatment. Someone talented at reading people would stand to make a lot of money.'

Lenaghan tried to look nonchalant. 'Lead on then.'

Flynn led him away from the view of Kalvion and back into the gloomy artificial light of the station. Lenaghan noticed the occasional amused glance from passers-by who saw the stark contrast between the two men. He must have resembled a pudgy dwarf next to Flynn, who was tall, broad-shouldered and looked as though he had just returned from some medieval battle.

'I'm thinking of moving Temple again,' the mercenary told him. 'I'd appreciate your thoughts.'

'You haven't exactly been in orbit of Kalvion long. I would've thought this to be the perfect location.'

'Ever since Santa Cruz executed Cairns, our business with Nova has diminished and the other corps are too frightened to come here in case something like that happens again.'

'Santa Cruz is dead,' Lenaghan stated bluntly. 'I'm not keen on Nova being in our system anyway. There is a war going on, you know.'

Flynn shook his head. 'Don't remind me. War is very bad for business.'

'So what is it you want to do? Leave Lincoln?'

'No. When we were closer to Shard, we made more money from the arena. Since we made the move here, we have only had a handful of fights. I propose we orbit Shard for a year or so.'

The idea made Lenaghan nervous. 'You used to have a presence on Shard and that didn't really end well for the Templars.'

'My predecessor ruined that venture. Besides, I'm not asking to go to the surface. Just give us a year in orbit and then we will move again.'

'It could work.' Lenaghan shrugged. 'I'd have to run it past a few others though.'

'If it helps, you can always arrange to have a military presence close by to ensure everything runs smoothly.' Flynn pointed him at a nearby junction. 'Shard is always well-protected though.'

Lenaghan tried to get his bearings, but this part of Temple was unfamiliar to him. 'The military has their hands full keeping Nova at bay.'

'It's that bad?' asked the Templar.

'Unfortunately. War tends to stretch resources.'

'Lincoln's worlds are always well-defended so no need to worry, right? It's not like Nova are about to pay a visit to Galt or Shard. I'd rather not get caught up in a firefight.'

Lenaghan remembered that the Knights Templar were one of the only absentees in the battle to stop Santa Cruz's fleet. 'You'll be safe. We may not be able to spare any assault ships but Shard will always have guardians in orbit.'

'Plus soldiers on the surface.'

'Yes, although most of them are fresh from training. We need the veterans elsewhere.'

Flynn fell silent for a while as they traversed the corridors and Lenaghan wondered whether the merc was having second thoughts about the move. However, as they reached their destination, Flynn placed a hand on the executive's shoulder and smiled as the door opened.

'We'll make it work.'

Lenaghan stepped inside, expecting to walk into a smoky atmosphere with several fresh-faced execs seated around a table pretending to be experienced poker players. Instead, he saw just two people. A man dressed in a long black coat was standing before the only window, his face shrouded in shadow. The woman however...

'You?' Lenaghan couldn't mask his confusion. 'What the hell is going on here?'

The black-haired temptress from his bed looked up from a HDU screen and gave him a wicked smile. 'I work fast, just like you in the bedroom.'

Flynn gave him a shove forward and closed the door behind them. 'I've got what I need,' he said to the window gazer. 'He's all yours.'

Lenaghan felt dread start gnawing at him. 'I demand to know what this is about.' He realized then that the woman's HDU was actually his. 'You thieving whore.'

She ignored him and instead turned the screen towards Flynn. 'Lots of tasty information in here.'

'You can't just steal Taurus intel like this.' Lenaghan's voice was strained. 'My associates will hunt you down and...'

'Do shut the fuck up.' The man turned from the window to stare at the executive with cruel eyes. 'Several months ago, Commander Rolan Cairns was murdered by a Taurus operative. Sapphire Nova want to send a message to Taurus Galahad that actions such as this will not go unpunished.'

'Santa Cruz was a rogue officer who was not acting on Taurus orders.' Lenaghan felt like he was going to puke. 'You're from Nova?'

'Very astute. My name is Mikan Rist.'

Lenaghan took a step back, his eyes narrowing. 'Rist was killed nearly a decade ago. I saw his profile and you aren't him.'

'In a way, I'm not.' There was a deep sadness in the response.

'Flynn, you need to think about this,' Lenaghan yelled at the merc leader.

'Oh, I gave it all great thought.' Flynn kept his eyes firmly fixed on the HDU. 'Including the rewards we can reap if we work with them.'

Rist pulled a strange-looking weapon from beneath his jacket and held it up for Lenaghan to see. 'I need your undivided attention.'

The executive's eyes widened when he recognized that the gun was a customised boomer, clearly designed to be held in one hand. 'What do you want from me?'

'You're going to help us send the message to Taurus Galahad. Now, take off your clothes.'

Rikur
Almaz system

An air of discomfort had fallen over the Harper Sec office but that didn't bother Klein. What pissed him off was being dictated to by some jumped-up security guard with a Napoleon complex. Devlin wasn't even that short but all three officers still had a couple of inches over him.

'Has your head been shoved firmly up your ass for the last few months?' Bavelli asked the head of security angrily. 'We don't have the resources to send someone after these men. Besides, is this a priority when you consider what has happened to Nova?'

'Don't treat me like some wet-behind-the-ears rookie.' Devlin hadn't seemed intimidated by their presence from the moment they had arrived. 'I'm talking about bringing three extremely dangerous individuals to justice, and not just for the murders they committed here.'

Klein glanced at his partners. Whilst Bavelli looked as though he wanted to punch Devlin square in the bullish face, Fletcher had remained strangely calm throughout their time in the office. Even after working together for so many years, he still found it hard to read the latter.

'You're asking us to send operatives out with no idea where these men are,' Bavelli said slowly yet firmly.

When Fletcher finally spoke, his tone was menacing but measured: 'He's hardly asking.'

Klein didn't want the conversation dragging on much further. 'Listen, we could go round in circles here for some time. The cold facts are that these men are long gone and are either dead or hiding out in some dark corner of the galaxy. Either way, they aren't a major concern for Nova at this time.'

'Maybe not to you but...'

'Not to the corporation as a whole.' Klein made sure he cut Devlin off quickly. 'Straunia is gone. Millions died, including the rest of the board. Our priority is to make sure the other corps don't take advantage of this situation and to avoid any problematic ripples across our other worlds. Your crims will be brought to justice but we have to secure our future first.'

Devlin looked down at his monitor, a sour expression plastered across his face. 'I'm not an idiot. I understand how fucked up everything is. All I'm saying is that the board gave me this position to watch over Harper and I don't want history to repeat itself. The rig is too important, not only to Harper but to Nova *as a whole*.'

'Yes, but *we're* the board now,' Fletcher stated, offering a half-smile. 'So that position can be taken away.'

'We don't want it to come to that though,' Klein added, wishing that his colleagues would stay quiet sometimes. 'So until such time as we can deal with these crims, we'll raise the bounty on their heads. Not a huge increase but enough for greedy colonists or freelance pilots to take note.'

Devlin shrugged. 'Unless I hire some mercs to do the job instead. Plenty come here trying to sell their shit or looking for other bounties.'

'No mercs.' Bavelli leant across the desk and tapped a finger on the top of the monitor. 'We just said that these men can wait, so rein your impatience in.'

Klein decided to move things on again. 'So, to return to the reason why we came here in the first place, we need that upload of Harper's data files.'

'I'll ask the same question as when you first arrived then.' Devlin crossed his arms. 'Why do you need trading reports with the mining and security files?'

Bavelli gave an amused snort as he looked across at his colleagues. 'Remind me why this guy was put in charge of such an important operation.'

Klein ignored the remark. 'This isn't a request. It's an order. Show these two to the data though, and I will gladly explain our reasons to you privately.'

Devlin flashed a suspicious look across all three of them but eventually nodded solemnly before calling one of his team in. The woman looked nervous as he explained she would be taking Bavelli and Fletcher to the data archives to collect everything they had on file.

'We don't bite,' Fletcher told her, giving her his most dashing smile.

When she led the two officers from the room, Klein nodded at Devlin's vacant chair.

'Please, take a seat.'

'I prefer to stand.' Devlin rubbed at the stubble under his chin. 'So I'm guessing that you want to use Harper as the base for the new board.'

'Is that the impression we've given?'

'Why else would you be here?'

Klein hated it when people answered a question with a question. 'We don't plan on having a fixed abode yet. For now, we'll keep moving so that the other corps never know our location. Having all of the board together on one planet has always been a crazy idea and I don't intend on making that mistake.'

Devlin's brow furrowed. 'So the three of you will just flit from one system to the next on an assault ship? Surely there wouldn't be another attack on one of our worlds, especially with that weapon ending up as a relic on Straunia.'

'Just let us worry about that.' Klein wanted to slap the man across the face but that was more Bavelli's style. 'Your job is to watch over Harper and ensure the rig keeps on working. We need trade to remain strong here and keep the funds rolling in for Nova. I'm not going to insult your intelligence by saying that we weren't affected financially. We have to rebuild the facilities that were active on Straunia and are selecting where best to do this.'

'I see.' The sour look finally melted from Devlin's face. 'It would've been simpler to just say that when you walked through my door. The other two clearly haven't had much experience dealing with people.'

To a degree, that was true. Klein had known Bavelli and Fletcher for years, as he moved up through the military ranks alongside them both. When they were all selected for duty on the *Harbinger*, he had been the one who quickly rose to the rank of commander while the other two were best suited for the muscle work. They seemed more comfortable with a gun in their hands and that suited him just fine.

When the attack on Straunia came, Klein had been mere days from joining the military arm of the board. He doubted that the other two would have had the initiative to step forward themselves once the board was wiped out but he needed someone to stand alongside him. They had their uses after all. Some of the junior board members who were not on Straunia at the time would have seized control had it not been for Bavelli and Fletcher paying them a visit. Now the board was three-strong and that made sense. Nova didn't need more than that to become the power it had once been.

'As for those crims you're so keen on finding, I guarantee that we will look into their whereabouts just as soon as we can but the raised bounty will hopefully do the job for us.'

'Very well.' Devlin finally sat, casting one last glance at the images on his monitor. 'But I would like them brought here so I can deal with them in my own way.'

Klein nodded. 'Fair enough. I'll make the arrangements and get the bounty update sent out galaxy-wide.'

'Will you stay in orbit long?'

He knew just what Devlin was getting at. 'No. Having a large fleet in one location for too long will only draw attention so we will be on our way as soon as we have the data. The fleet needs to redeploy anyway to make sure all our assets are protected.'

'Well if you decide to build any facilities here, all I ask is you keep me informed.'

'Again, fair enough.' Klein headed for the door but hesitated. 'Oh, one last thing. In the future, you will recognize the authority of the board. If you receive an order from Arys Fletcher, Kam Bavelli or myself, you will not question us again. Is that understood?'

Devlin was taken aback by this and struggled to utter a response, simply nodding once.

Klein didn't hang around after that and met up with the other two at the airlock to the landing pad. They didn't really talk until they were on board the transport and heading back up to the *Harbinger*, which sat patiently waiting with the other fifteen assault ships above Rikur.

'Did you tell Devlin the truth then?' Fletcher asked him.

'Of course. At least, the small amount of intel I gave him was true anyway.'

'What about Kurcher?'

Klein was tired of questions, even when they came from his closest friends. They knew that he wouldn't tell Devlin the full story behind the crims the sec head was seeking.

'As far as he knows, Kurcher is a Taurus enlister who has to answer for killing some of the sec team whereas Broekow was an accomplice in finding and removing Edlan Rane from Harper. I don't really care about finding Broekow but the other two...' Klein gave them a knowing look. 'I don't need to remind you how important it is we get to them before Devlin or anyone else for that matter does.'

'Fuck Devlin,' sneered Bavelli. 'He can have what's left of them once we've finished.'

'And once we've extracted the information we need,' Klein reminded them.

They sat in silence for several minutes, watching the haze of Rikur's atmosphere change to the black of the void. An alarm chimed somewhere on Fletcher and he checked his comms app.

'No unusual movement from Sigma,' he told the others. 'Still licking their wounds and mourning Meta. Libra activity has been focused lately in the systems out near the Echo Expanse and beyond, towards Farrin.'

'Keep a close eye on them.' Klein really didn't like the fact that Libra assault ships were being fitted with new conflector tech. 'Something is happening and I wouldn't put it past them to be planning an aggressive takeover of systems they consider to have been weakened after the attacks.'

Fletcher gave a slight nod. 'Impramed are their usual selves, staying out the way of everyone else. But Taurus are being a lot bolder than I expected, keeping themselves out in the open.'

Bavelli gave a derisive snort. 'Let them. They probably think they are untouchable after issuing a statement saying Santa Cruz was not acting on their orders.'

'Arrogant bastards,' grunted Fletcher, the unnerving half-smile on his face again.

'They won't be able to resist the temptation of the *Grail* for much longer,' Klein said, rubbing at his eyes. He hadn't realised how tired he was, moving the fleet from one system to the next in order to make them a moving target. 'What about the rest?'

Fletcher's eyes flicked across the reports scrolling in his vision. 'Fortitude are remaining under the radar for the most part, apart from their insistence on letting the whole fucking galaxy know how well trade is doing on Sullivan's Rest. We know what is happening with the Templars. Schaeffer's Nine and Jericho's Bold are still causing unrest wherever they visit but have been keeping away from our systems.'

'Echo?' Klein's eyebrow raised inquisitively.

'No reports of them operating outside the Expanse lately but that doesn't mean they aren't. After what happened, it doesn't surprise me that Hewn is in hiding.'

Klein knew that Echo had much more going on than any of the corps were aware of but they would be crazy to go looking for Hewn and his accomplices in the Expanse.

'What about the Cobb Resistance and the Oakley Fleet?' Bavelli asked, taking the words from Klein's tongue.

Fletcher gave a bored shrug. 'They're hardly going to be a problem. They took casualties during the battle with Santa Cruz's fleet and didn't have that many ships to lose in the first place.'

'We need to account for all organisations before the next phase, Arys.' Klein was getting pissed off with the flippant attitude of his partners. 'Take none of them for granted.'

This time, it was Bavelli's comms alert that warbled and they all knew what that might mean. Klein and Fletcher leaned forward anxiously as he read the brief report.

'Mission complete on Temple. Rist is moving on to the next target.'

As Fletcher and Bavelli shared a joke about a new moon now in orbit of

Kalvion, Klein sat back and closed his eyes. Using Rist in such a way was something the previous board would never have considered but that one man's actions would help to lead Sapphire Nova into the new era, forging new alliances and destroying old ones. By the time they had finished, five corporations would become two or, better still, one.

Echo flagship Glaive
Clark system

They were still looking at him like he was a corp enlister.

'They can smell Taurus on you,' Drake said, picking up on Kurcher's body language each time they passed one of the crew. 'They can also smell the residue of betrayal.'

He glared at the next pirate to give him a look of disgust. 'Don't know why. I had no choice but to join Echo.'

Such a load of bullshit, chuckled Frost. *You could have gone anywhere you wanted. You could have even stayed with Taurus. They wouldn't have wanted you dead after bringing down Santa Cruz.*

'They're just waiting for you to fuck up.' Drake pushed the half-fringe from her eye. 'Or for you to go running back to your previous life when you run out of money.'

He wasn't planning on running low on funds any time soon. The money Santa Cruz had transferred to him prior to that fateful trip out beyond the Milky Way was still waiting for him. He had moved it quickly before Taurus could cut off his assets, which oddly they hadn't done.

'Anyone ever told you you're a mouthy bitch?'

'Of course. I just say it as it is.'

Kurcher turned to give her his darkest scowl but wasn't surprised to find her looking elsewhere, chewing something that gave her breath a flowery scent. He watched her blue lips moving for a moment and wondered whether she would taste the same.

That wouldn't be a smart move, Frost told him. *She's likely to bite your tongue off.*

'Or worse,' he smiled, taking his gaze off the pilot.

At this, Drake looked over at him. 'You're a weird fucker. Later.'

With that, she veered away from him and disappeared along one of the adjoining corridors, no doubt off to get drunk or laid, or both. Tempted as he was to join her, he had to report in.

Hewn was in the usual position, standing over his map trying to work out what Echo's next bold move should be or keeping an eye on reports from various operations. Around him, the *Glaive*'s command crew were busy at their stations and their voices formed a steady white noise in the small room.

Still doesn't feel right, muttered D'Larro. *Hewn may be Echo's creator but you shouldn't have to answer to him.*

You should if you want to stay alive, Frost countered.

'I didn't expect you back so soon.' Hewn didn't even lift his eyes from the star map. 'Can I assume that means there were no unforeseen incidents?'

'I didn't want to hang around too long. Not with Libra sniffing round.'

At this, the pirate glanced up. Every time Kurcher returned from a mission, Hewn gave him the same look, as though he was weighing him up for any sign of dissent.

'Good. Last thing we need is you getting in trouble with them.'

Kurcher approached the map, recognising the Echo Expanse and wondering just why Hewn was studying his own systems. There were eleven in total but intel had always been very limited on all but three. Clark, Freeman and Miller had been highlighted decades before Echo was even conceived due to their worlds having mineral-rich landscapes and hospitable atmospheres. Supposedly named after famous explorers, the three systems were targeted for colonisation but, thanks to a series of delays, the corps were beaten to the chase by Echo. Several failed attempts to retake them followed, showing the likes of Taurus Galahad and Sigma Royal that the fledgling pirate operation was a force to be reckoned with.

'Do you know that people still think the Expanse is named after us?'

Kurcher realised his gaze had lingered too long on the map. 'Does it matter?'

Hewn smiled beneath his well-trimmed beard. 'Matters to me. There's some satisfaction knowing we took the name after a group of corporate bigwigs came up with it.'

'Has there been another trespasser in the Expanse then?' Kurcher asked, nodding down at the screen.

'No.'

He's probably keeping an eye on his family, Frost suggested.

Kurcher knew that Hewn's wife and young sons were hidden somewhere in the small cluster of stars. As far as he was aware, only the pirate leader knew their location. After rumours that Jericho's Bold were planning on finding and kidnapping his family, it was likely Hewn would keep a close eye on what was happening across the Expanse.

'You want this report then or shall I go join Drake and get wasted?'

'I always thought it was the Parinax withdrawal that made you so impatient,' Hewn said, lifting his mechanical arm and jabbing a metal finger at Kurcher. 'As you've been off the drugs for several months now though, I realise you're just a cantankerous bastard.'

The mere mention of the substance made Kurcher's jaw clench. He still missed the high he felt from the Calmers or from the boost app. They always made his shitty life seem that much better.

'It's more the headaches from these fucking implants.'

'Well we can always stop the blockers and let Taurus or Nova track you down,' Hewn told him nonchalantly. 'Of course, we would have to turf you out of Echo so it didn't bring a shitstorm down on us.'

Careful, warned Frost. *He won't take your moaning like I used to.*

'So, the report.' Kurcher thought it best to get the debriefing over with.

'Come with me.'

Hewn turned the map display off and headed for the door. Kurcher fell into line behind him, noticing the amused looks on the faces of the command crew as he trudged after their iconic leader.

It wasn't long before he found himself seated at the polished black circular table in Hewn's quarters, where the pirate often conducted his meetings. A glass of strong-smelling brown liquid was placed in front of him before Hewn took a seat opposite.

'Fresh from the brewery on Warren.'

Kurcher gave an obligatory sip, finding the beer surprisingly sweet. 'Not bad.'

Hewn gulped half of his drink down in one go. 'Good. Several thousand batches are being shipped out to Libra colonies shortly. It's our own take on honey mead.'

'Leaves a bitter aftertaste.' Kurcher took another sip. 'Broekow on board?'

'I sent him to Summit on a recon mission,' Hewn replied, studying his beer. 'Impramed have been pretty quiet since Espina paid Tidewell a visit.'

I like to leave my mark, as you well know.

Kurcher flinched at the sound of the Nova officer's sultry voice. His more torrid dreams quite often featured Trin either interrogating or fucking him, sometimes both at the same time. The dream always ended the same way though, with her pulling back her fringe to show off a bloody bullet wound in the centre of her forehead.

'Seems a mundane task for someone with his talents,' he said finally, noting that Hewn was watching him.

'When was the last time you saw Broekow?'

The question threw him somewhat. 'Couple of months ago, I guess.'

'You must've seen how fucked up he was then.'

Kurcher sat back and took a long swig of the strange beer. The medics had barely managed to save Broekow's life after he was shot by Santa Cruz. Twice he had flatlined as they worked to stop the bleeding but the sniper was brought back both times. His recovery had been slow and there was a definite change to his demeanour.

'Why not just let him go his own way?' asked Kurcher. 'It'll only be a matter of time until he self-destructs.'

Hewn wiped a droplet of beer from his beard. 'He knows too much to cut loose, and I don't just mean about Echo.'

There are a lot of people out there who would kill to get their hands on Sieren, Frost said, sadly. *Just as they would for you and Rane.*

'There is always another option,' Hewn continued, seeing Kurcher gazing down into his glass. 'If his depression and general attitude becomes a serious liability, Broekow would have to die.'

That jolted Kurcher from his thoughts. 'That's more like the Jaffren Hewn I remember. I suppose you're going to ask me to do it too.'

'No. Tariq would see to that.' Hewn saw Kurcher's blank expression. 'The pilot I assigned to babysit him.'

'Not just a pilot then.'

Hewn leant forward, resting his contrasting arms on the table. 'Tell me about Chaplin.'

As Kurcher relayed the information, a dark cloud settled over the pirate, his expression becoming increasingly harsh. When the room fell silent, Hewn simply glared across the table, anger roiling behind his eyes.

'No wonder Libra are edgy,' he growled. 'If they know about our ops and the fact that I'm protecting you, it won't make for a pleasant alliance.'

'Chaplin was a cowardly little prick. You must've known that he would buckle if anyone ever put pressure on him.'

'I didn't think anyone would dare.' Hewn flinched, as though in pain. 'I have to act quickly to stop there being any more violence.'

Kurcher nodded. 'Kill Trystan Hengeveld.'

'Absolutely not. If we start icing Libra officers, things will turn ugly fast. Unfortunately, this will need diplomacy for once.'

Kurcher smirked. 'Well that's not a job for me then, thank fuck.'

Hewn tapped the table surface with a metal finger. 'No, I've got a different job for you. I'll brief you and Drake once you've had a chance to rest.'

Great, muttered D'Larro. *Another mission to clean up Echo's mess.*

Another chance for those fuckers from Nova or Taurus to capture us, added Ercko.

Why do you think Hewn keeps sending you outside the Expanse, enlister? Santa Cruz asked. *He wants you dead, just like the rest of the galaxy.*

Kurcher tried to imagine which old haunt he would be sent to next. There had been a lot of talk before about a small Echo fleet heading to Cradle or Cobb for another bout of talks with their newest allies but that wouldn't suit his skill set. Besides, he didn't really want to lay eyes on the Oakleys again or to visit the remnants of the Resistance. He had only just started to silence some of the ghosts from his past.

He downed the final mouthful of beer. 'Can't wait.'

Earth
Sol system

Smoke was rising several miles to the north, beyond the compound wall. It was a thick, oily plume that marred the otherwise calm blue sky.

Hayward bit at her bottom lip, as she often did when she was this nervous. She knew exactly what that smoke meant and it terrified her beyond words. If the Revenants managed to breach the walls of the Taurus site, it would spell disaster for the skeleton crew who were left behind when the board fled their homeworld for the safety of Galt. Of course, said crew still consisted of several hundred people, including the security teams patrolling the perimeters.

She glanced down at her HDU and read through the brief report again. Revenants had never been seen in any of the central states, just those coastal regions where they had washed ashore following their sinister pilgrimage from Europe. Now here they were in Montana, emerging from over the Saskatchewan border.

She looked up once more and scanned the horizon. To the west rose the mountains, like huddled giants. They had always made her feel secure, especially when she was growing up in Great Falls. To the east, the blue sky gave way to billowing white clouds that moved swiftly with the breeze.

Despite all of the other people working inside the compound, she felt alone and helpless. The citizens going about their daily business beyond the walls were starting to understand just why so many others had either fled across the oceans or sought refuge on Mars or Titan Station, or dared to go even further afield. How long before Earth was classified as a quaran?

Before being sworn in as a member of the board, Hayward had made sure she read up on the entire history of the Revenant scourge, dating back to the Holy Revolt in 2589. Even that name was unsuitable though for what had happened. Cult fanatics were not true holy men and women, especially when they started their *cleansing* of the disbelievers. It hadn't taken long for them to brainwash more to their cause and their cult spread out from Central Europe like wildfire, indoctrinating the weak-minded and burning those who refused to follow them.

At that time, they had been known as *The Children* but it was the actions of the military that saw them become Revenants. Killed in their thousands during bloody skirmishes, the survivors of the cult quickly rose again, emerging from hidden lairs across the known world. They swarmed towns and cities, killing or kidnapping. Bizarrely, every time the military fought back, it just seemed to create more of the wretches, as the lesser members of the Revenants came to be known.

During the last decade, it was as if the corporations had realised Earth was doomed and slowly began to withdraw soldiers, focusing instead on the new worlds beyond Sol. Now, the Revenants were a very different beast altogether. Senior cultists known as *Prophets* had claimed territories across the globe, each with his or her own followers who protected them ferociously. It was the Prophets who had been a focus of the recent Taurus excursions into Revenant-run areas, the aim being to cut the head off each snake and hope the rest of the body died. With the infighting among the wretches increasing recently, Taurus had hoped they would start wiping themselves out but there were always more lurking in the ruins of the old Earth.

Her eyes shifted to the smoke again. There was a decision to make and the burden of command rested firmly on her shoulders. If she sent the sole squad of soldiers within the compound out to repel the Revenants, she ran the risk of losing the only protection they had. If she kept them close instead, more innocents would suffer but the Taurus staff would feel safer. There was always the hope that one of the militia groups formed by the public would deal with the threat themselves but success depended on how many of the fanatics had crossed the border. Reports said there were three Prophets with approximately fifteen wretches each but she didn't trust the intel.

Another wisp of smoke began to rise just to the east of the plume. Hayward opened a comms link directly to Lieutenant Tolbert.

'Yes, ma'am.' The soldier's voice was a deep growl.

'We can't just ignore them. Take your men and deal with it.'

There was a couple of seconds' silence before he answered. 'Understood.'

'If the situation becomes dire, get back here immediately.'

'Yes, ma'am.'

She remained at the window until she saw the forty-strong squad board their transports below and head for the north gate. She was certain Tolbert wouldn't take any unnecessary risks but her stomach still twisted when the transports disappeared from view.

Deciding to take her mind off the situation, she moved to her desk and scanned all the documents strewn across the surface. It was a complete mess, just like Taurus Galahad's entire administration. She pulled open one of the drawers, aiming to sweep some of the papers out of sight. Solomon Rees' name leapt out at her from a HDU she had forgotten about; the late judicial officer's personal device.

Hayward lowered herself into the uncomfortable seat. Rees' desk, Rees' seat, Rees' fucking office. The ghost of her predecessor was always present and she hated it.

Placing her own HDU on the desk, she opened up the most recent reports from the rest of the Taurus board and read them one more time before requesting a link to the *Victory*.

It wasn't long before Mitchell's craggy face appeared. 'I thought I would've heard from you sooner.'

'There have been urgent matters to attend to here, general. The Revenants are getting closer to us.'

'Can your men there handle it?'

'Let's hope so. It's not like we're about to welcome reinforcements from the military any time soon.'

'We've been through this.' The topic always touched a nerve. 'Nova are the pressing threat and all military resources are to be used to defend Taurus space against them.'

Hayward considered her words carefully. 'Except so far there has been no full-blown attack. Nova are resorting to terrorist tactics instead of sending their assault ships against us. Do you really think they would risk what's left of their corporation after the *Grail* incident?'

Mitchell's face loomed menacingly on the screen. '*Terrorist tactics*? They admitted to blowing one of the senior Taurus board members out of an airlock, and in *our* system. That hardly sounds like the actions of a corp who want to play it safe.'

Hayward wanted to tell him just how pleased she was that Lenaghan had been disposed of. A few more months and she could have brought the corrupt son-of-a-bitch up on a number of charges, just as she had some of those who had been working beneath him. She needed to remain wary though, as there was no telling just how far the corruption had spread within Taurus.

'They were making a point, general,' she told the brooding image. 'An eye for an eye, even if it did come several months later than expected. But security has been ramped up for other members of the board, just in case.'

'Just remember what happened to your predecessor, Miss Hayward. He got too involved with matters outside his jurisdiction and ended up as debris in orbit of Straunia.'

Was that a threat? 'I am the judicial officer for Taurus Galahad. My jurisdiction covers all known systems and worlds belonging to us. That's quite the reach.'

Mitchell was beginning to lose patience. 'So did you get in touch just to teach me about Nova's plans?'

She drew a quiet breath, calming herself before continuing. 'I am going to travel to Galt soon. The board needs to gather in order to discuss all matters regarding the security of Taurus. That includes Nova, the Revenants and even the Knights Templar.'

'There is no reason for you to come to Galt yet. Earth needs you to continue monitoring the Revenants as well as keeping them at bay.' He paused for a moment. 'The Knights Templar?'

'Yes. Lenaghan was on Temple when he was taken, as was Cairns. They need to be questioned. Temple must also be moved out of Taurus space. The longer we allow these mercenaries to remain in Lincoln, the more chance they have of infiltrating operations on Galt or even Shard.'

Mitchell's sigh was audible even across the deep space link. 'They're hardly going to try that. Temple is neutral and have just been unfortunate to play host to some copycat killer wanting revenge for what happened to Cairns.'

'I don't trust them and neither should you,' Hayward said through gritted teeth. 'I will still come to Galt though, as I need to continue the recruitment of our new enlisters and there are suitable candidates there.'

'That is not a priority. Just because Rees led the other enlisters to their deaths doesn't mean we need to replace them straight away.'

She couldn't help but laugh. 'With all due respect, general, we need to continue the enlister process now more than ever. We need new blood desperately. Besides, I hardly class eight months as *straight away*.'

'Let me put this another way.' Mitchell's anger was barely contained. 'You are *not* to come to Galt yet. You *will* remain on Earth and continue your duties there overseeing Taurus headquarters, rather than trying to expose conspiracies where there are none. Is that understood?'

'General, if the rest of the board are on Galt then...'

'I'm on my way out to Berg,' he announced impatiently. 'The others have their own jobs to do, just like you.'

Hayward frowned. 'And can you share the reason for your visit to such a distant system?'

'That's classified. You have your orders, Miss Hayward.'

The screen went blank and yet she continued to stare at it, a storm of thoughts whirling through her mind. Mitchell couldn't have made it clearer that he didn't want her anywhere near Galt and that rang a number of alarms. The corruption within Taurus went much deeper than she had anticipated and, if the general was part of it, how exactly would she discover his secrets? The fact he was heading out to Berg concerned her greatly too. Santa Cruz had visited that particular system on numerous occasions, giving official reports that he was overseeing the shipyard being built there.

Mitchell had also taken Lenaghan's death very well. The late board member was universally disliked but she would have expected to see more anger in the general's eyes when talking about it.

She turned the chair to peer back out of the window, wondering whether Tolbert and his men had reached their destination. She hoped they all returned from their encounter with the Revenants but something told her there would be casualties. There always were.

Her eyes shifted to the two visible corners of the compound, where the heavy defense turrets kept watch, waiting for something to finally shoot at. Even the Revenants wouldn't be so stupid as to attack the compound head-on.

She opened comms to her contact in the air traffic control office, ignoring his attempt to engage her in small talk. 'Get a shuttle ready. I'm leaving shortly for Galt.'

Mars
Sol system

Pioneer City was nothing but a blur of neon. Every now and then, he caught sight of a building or a faceless citizen, but the train moved too fast even for his sight app.

Rist took a look around the sterile carriage, finding he was alone. He was the only one riding it to the end of the line, and that suited him just fine. The Pioneer colonists all looked at him like he was a member of The Kindred, stupidly trying their best to distance themselves just in case he had a bomb strapped to his chest.

Outside, the illuminations of the city began giving way to standard street lighting; the occasional blip of white in the darkness of the outer districts. No matter which colony he visited, the outskirts always felt cold and uninviting. All the corporations built them this way but Taurus were particularly unoriginal. Housing for the workers and maintenance structures were a mundane necessity, so they saw no need to bother making them enticing.

Rist focused on the data scrolling steadily across his vision. The train was almost at its final destination. Turning his head slightly, a marker appeared and he accessed the district map briefly, checking on the directions once he left the transport. Satisfied that he was taking the quickest route, he used the remaining time to make sure the targets were logged into his sight app for fast recognition.

When the train came to a halt and the doors opened, Rist stepped out into the processed air and his breath suddenly became visible. It was the only way he could tell it was cold. Over a decade had passed since he had last felt the sensation of cool or warm air on his skin, when his body had been his own.

Most of the working class living on Mars had retired for the night, although the odd inebriated colonist was seen staggering home. There were many bars in Pioneer City, from the fancy ones in the centre of the colony to the seedy dives in the outer districts. Rist had lost his taste for those kind of establishments a long time ago.

The structure highlighted by his app looked mundane. However, beyond the ordinary security door lay a network of corridors reaching deep into Pioneer's perimeter wall. On the top level, the long distance comms relay waited for him. Outside the wall, exposed to the Mars atmosphere, the booster dish slowly rotated. It was a typically drab operation.

As Rist approached, lifesigns appeared with a resounding ping. The security team guarding the entrance were lurking just inside, although they would not be expecting any visitors this late.

The streaming data pointed him away from the door and he followed the directions to a small sewerage station. The door lock was easy enough to hack and he soon found himself inside the narrow chamber, staring down at the chugging processor. The foul air would have choked others but Rist's only concern was that it would seep into the very fabric of his clothing.

The hatch next to the processor dropped him into the tunnels below Pioneer and he began making his way along the slippery walkway. Occasional shapes flowed past in the waste water below but he kept his eyes firmly focused on his route through the maze.

The left side of his body felt strange as the deep thrum of the sewer machinery made the metal skeleton vibrate. Even his artificial eye felt like it was rattling in the socket. He just hoped the tech inside it remained in place.

He was relieved when he finally climbed the ladder and emerged into a claustrophobic maintenance room inside the perimeter wall. He hoped his targets wouldn't smell him coming.

It was relatively easy locating both his primary and secondary targets, as they had stuck closer to the LDCR than he had anticipated. The only problem he might have would be bumping into patrolling guards but his sight app gave him ample warning and he managed to bypass the issue simply enough as he negotiated the corridors and stairwells.

The LDCR itself was watched over only by the shift crew, which consisted of a handful of exhausted-looking individuals staring for hours at their monitors. It seemed that the only alert person in the comms office was Joseph Dant. Typical, considering he was on the hit list.

Rist paid close attention to Dant's lifesigns as he crouched in wait by the office entrance. While the other staff were stationary, the head of the LDCR moved around erratically from one end to the other. With no discernible pattern to his movements, Dant would be difficult to corner. Perhaps it would be easier to deal with Culman first.

Shifting his attention to the lifesigns on the edge of his app's range, Rist could make out several sleeping forms nearby: Prakhad Culman was one of them. The primary target information scrolled once more at the side of his vision and he studied the smiling face.

Culman had worked under Lenaghan for three years and was the Taurus board's link with the LDCR, having spent time in Pioneer City with Dant before becoming a junior executive. It made perfect sense that Taurus would send him back to Mars after Lenaghan's death, to hide from Nova's assassins.

Rist moved quietly, giving the offices as wide a berth as possible, and slipped inside the sleeping quarters. Ignoring the workers who were no doubt dreaming of a better life on some verdant world, away from the drab existence they led on the red planet, he found he had no need to hack the door to the room Culman occupied. The exec clearly felt secure and was lying on his back with one arm behind his head, soft snores emanating from his open mouth.

Rist found his hand reached for the boomer instinctively and there was a brief crackle of static as the tech in his brain reminded him that there was a time and place for such a violent weapon. Instead, he pulled the silenced pistol from beneath his jacket, placed the barrel over Culman's brow and fired twice. Both bullets passed through the skull and into the mattress beneath. Before he moved on, he put a final bullet through the dead man's heart, as per his specific orders.

When he stepped back, reholstering his pistol, he noted that Culman had not even moved from his sleeping position and looked positively peaceful. Rist gazed down at him for several seconds, feeling jealous of the young exec. He had never had the chance of a peaceful end, thanks to Sapphire Nova.

An image of the flames erupting all around him shot through his mind, catching him by surprise. The human part of his brain usually subdued memories of what happened on Thorn but something had wormed its way through. He could see the toxic brambles burning; smell the sweetness in the air as the fire reached the poison inside. He also heard the dying screams of those who had trusted him, cursing Nova for betraying them.

As quickly as they had arrived, the memories of Thorn were gone, replaced instead by the blurred faces staring at him through reinforced glass. He recalled talk of phantom limbs and a constant feeling he was floating. Surgeons plucked at the torn or burnt skin, blood specks across their gowns and masks.

Clarity was suddenly restored as his biomechs took back control. It was a disconcerting experience having such intense memories swept from his mind but it meant he could focus once more on his task.

Dant proved trickier to reach, as he had expected. Rist couldn't just walk into the manned office and open fire, no matter how much time it would save. The countdown to his deadline was ever-present in one corner of his vision. If he missed his transport off Mars, he would have to find his own means of escape and Taurus grunts would be on his trail.

The opening he was waiting for finally revealed itself as Dant's signature slowly ascended to a position above his staff. The head of the LDCR had gone up to a walkway that looked out at the booster dish. There wouldn't be a better chance.

Rist peeled away from the shadows and made his way quietly into the main office. The five shift workers were sharing some joke about their superior, taking advantage of his being out of earshot. Rist employed his disruption app and all of the monitors fizzed with static as the data momentarily vanished, startling the workers. It had the desired effect though as they all simultaneously turned back to their respective stations to study the apparent malfunction.

Rist slipped past them, heading swiftly up to the walkway. Dant was standing in front of an enormous window, staring out at the dish while furiously tapping at his HDU. Data began scrolling vertically up the left side of Rist's vision as it began the all-important hack. A timer appeared too: three minutes, fifteen seconds.

'Fucking piece of shit.' Dant spun on his heel and hesitated when he saw he wasn't alone on the walkway. 'Who the hell are...?'

'Quiet.' Rist's pistol appeared in his hand. 'One more word and I'll put a bullet through your brain.'

Dant looked him up and down before glancing around. 'If I shout for help, security will be here before you got to the bottom of the stairs.'

'You'd still be dead,' Rist stated. 'Then I'd be forced to kill them too.'

Two minutes, twenty-five seconds.

Dant's eyes narrowed. 'What're you waiting for then?'

Rist could see the drastic increase in the man's heart rate, betraying the brave face he was wearing. Dant had been a military man once, formidable in close combat and with an exceptional penchant for all things tech. He had clearly learnt to hide his fear a long time ago.

One minute, fifty seconds.

'Ah, I see,' said Dant, holding up the HDU. 'You're here for data. Who are you working for? Nova? Libra?'

His voice was too loud for Rist's liking. 'Doesn't matter.'

'Sure it does. You've been hired to steal Taurus comms data so your employer knows all their little secrets.' Dant waved the HDU at him. 'It won't do you any good hacking into this. All it does is control the booster level for the dish.'

A voice came from below. 'Everything okay, sir?'

'Call for help and I'll kill them all,' threatened Rist.

Dant could tell there was no bluff. 'I'll be down in a moment,' he yelled.

'You've saved a lot of lives today, Joseph.'

'Look, like I said, there's no value in hacking my HDU or any of the machines here.'

Rist nodded. 'I know. What I needed was in your personal data app.'

Realisation spread across Dant's face. 'The codes?'

The pistol fired a lone shot that took Dant through the right eye. He crumpled to the walkway instantly and Rist stepped forward to examine the body. As he put a second bullet into the heart, he could only feel respect for his target. He knew Dant was a good man and he had made the right choice in the end.

With both primary and secondary objectives achieved, Rist considered his exit from the LDCR. There was no dwelling on his orders to kill Culman or Dant, nor was there any curiosity as to why Bavelli had told him to take the communication codes.

With one last glance down to Dant's corpse, he headed for the stairs with pistol still in hand. He didn't anticipate further casualties but humans were unpredictable animals. Hopefully none of them would get in his way.

Echo vessel Falcata
Callyn system

This is such bullshit.

Angard's voice bounced around his head just as he was about to drift off to sleep, making him wish he could just reach beneath his pillow for a Calmer. They always helped him rest and gave him vivid dreams. Since coming off the drugs, all Kurcher dreamed about was a gigantic black monstrosity belching its sickly breath onto helpless worlds and the deafening death rattle of those who perished.

They will not let you sleep, enlister, Santa Cruz told him. *Might as well put a bullet through your own brain.*

That was one solution.

Kurcher sat up and checked his HDU. The *Falcata* was already deep inside Callyn, meaning it would not be long before Drake woke him with her usual verbal slap across the face. Angard was right though. The mission Hewn had sent them on *was* bullshit. Just another way to keep him out of the way of Echo's more important operations.

A lot of people in this system would love to get their hands on you, Frost reminded him. *Best be careful.*

'For fuck's sake.' He jumped from his bed to stand in front of the small window. 'All of you need to shut the hell up.'

We're simply voices for your thoughts, D'Larro explained.

Kurcher banged his forehead against the cold window. He needed to find a way to stop his own thoughts manifesting in this way. Maybe drastic surgery was needed, or a reinitialisation of his app implants. Maybe a fucking lobotomy.

He tried thinking of something else as his eyes scanned the dark of Callyn. He wondered how Broekow was faring on Summit and whether the sniper was just spending his time getting drunk in the bars of Tidewell. He wouldn't have blamed Broekow for just walking away from everything. In fact, he was surprised he hadn't already.

Would Rane resurface at some point? He wasn't the sort to stay skulking in the shadows too long. Perhaps the man who had watched with satisfaction as Straunia died was already living in some colony under a new identity. How different things would have been if Kurcher had just executed him when he had the chance.

He was a very clever man, said Santa Cruz. *He had a plan for the Grail and used me to see it through.*

Fucking bastard got me killed, Ercko snarled. *Promised me some of that sweet Oakley bitch if I helped him on Tempest. Even persuaded me to take the Eidolon.*

You deserved everything you got, Frost snapped.

Kurcher shook his head. Now the dead were arguing among themselves.

'Fuck this.' He activated his comms. 'How long, Drake?'

There was a noticeable silence before the pilot replied. 'Hour or so. Surprised you're awake. Did you piss the bed?'

'Yeah. I need you to clean my sheets.'

'Burn them, more like. Did you actually want something?'

'Some civility would be nice.'

'You get what you paid for, and you paid fuck all. Now, can I get back to my alone time?'

Kurcher just felt glad to be speaking with someone living. 'I'll be up to keep you company soon.'

'I'll roll out the red fucking carpet.'

As he began dressing, memories of his last visit to Callyn plagued his mind. He recalled the meeting with Kopetti, who introduced him to the more potent Parinax hits but didn't warn him of the ramped-up side effects. That old scumbag had set him on a bad road. In a way, Trin had done him a favour killing Kopetti.

You should have been there, Davian, she purred. *I know how much you enjoy hearing people beg.*

Callyn was also where they had found Ercko, hiding among his victims like the deranged psycho he was, and with him came that fucking data implant.

You're welcome, Ercko laughed.

As he headed to the cockpit, all Kurcher could think was how much he hated the layout of the ship. The *Kaladine* had been basic but efficient, with all rooms off the main corridor. The *Falcata* was sleeker and yet the chambers were all interconnected, with the cockpit squashed into the upper prow, accessible only by the narrowest set of stairs he had ever seen in a ship.

He also hated the fact the only other seat in the cockpit was clearly an afterthought by the designers, positioned at the back of the room. He didn't like sitting behind the pilot.

'Had any ships sniffing around?' he asked Drake, leaning on the back of her seat.

'Plenty. None of them fancied tangling with us though.'

'Probably backed off the moment they saw you glaring at them.'

'Wise move.' She turned her head slightly. 'Wanna get the fuck off my chair?'

He wondered what would happen if he didn't comply. He had seen Drake give men warnings before and she more often than not followed through with her threats. Probably best not to get on her bad side.

'Run into any factions more than the others?'

'A lot of freelancers,' she replied, checking scrolling data on a screen to her right. 'A few of the Bold roaming around too but they kept their distance.'

Kurcher glanced down at the data and noticed several coordinates, bringing an unwanted memory to the surface.

All well within the Milky Way, Frost reassured him.

'Have you had a chance to study Keening's file?'

Drake gave a casual shrug. 'No point. The guy's dead as soon as we get close enough.'

'Hewn wants to know just what he has been supplying. If Schaeffer's Nine want Keening dead, something must be spooking them. They wouldn't just ice some random trader without good reason.'

'*They* aren't,' Drake pointed out. '*We* are.'

'Even so, I will have to talk with him first. He won't just let me onto his ship so it'll have to be via comms.'

'Fine. When he runs then – which he will by the way – *then* I'll open fire.'

Kurcher gave an amused snort. 'Don't get too trigger happy.'

'That's fucking rich coming from you.'

The *Tradech* was loitering in a region of Callyn frequented by Fortitude ships and that made Kurcher nervous. Then again, just being in the merc-owned system made him nervous.

'I've tracked those other ships and they are moving away fast,' Drake told him. 'All belong to Fortitude but are making a quick exit. It's almost like they know what's coming.'

'Just keep an eye out for any others approaching while I'm dealing with him.'

The sweet scent of whatever Drake was chewing filled the air as she laughed. 'He isn't going to tell you shit. Might as well just hit and run.'

'That's why you're the pilot and I'm the...' What the fuck was he exactly?

'Just stay alert.'

The trader's ship was much smaller than the *Falcata* and had been fitted with a number of antennae that, at distance, resembled spines. It reminded Kurcher of an image he had once seen, of a creature native to Valandra's oceans. Maybe Keening had based it on that.

Up close, it was just another customised piece of crap.

'I thought he would have had a much better ship,' Drake said, voicing his own thoughts.

Less likely to draw attention, Frost added.

If Erric Keening was nervous about being approached by an Echo vessel, he certainly didn't show it as his broad, heavily-bearded face appeared on the monitor.

'Howdy. Can I be of assistance?'

Kurcher weighed him up for a moment. 'For your own sake, I hope so. We've come a long way just to find you.'

'Anyone from Echo is a friend of mine,' smiled Keening. 'Is it tech you're after? Apps maybe?'

'We'll get to that. As you know Echo so well, you'll be aware of their alliance with Schaeffer's Nine.'

There was a short pause. 'From what I hear, it is tenuous at best.'

'Nevertheless, some intel has come to light saying that you're selling something new to those organisations who see the Nine as something of a blight on the galaxy. Word is you have even sold this product to Fortitude, who in turn are supplying it to Sigma Royal. There's no love lost between Sigma and the Nine either.'

Keening gave an apologetic shrug. 'Ah, well that is an exclusive deal that I can't possibly discuss. Besides, I am all out of that product now. Believe me though when I say that it is not something designed to be used against Schaeffer's Nine so they can rest easy.'

Lying cocksucker, said Ercko.

'You specialise in mech tech, right?' Kurcher asked him. 'Hardware, software, apps.'

'I do.'

'So I can assume this is something along those lines.'

'You'd be wrong.' Keening glanced down to his left briefly. 'Sorry that I can't be of more help.'

'Let me put this another way then, so you understand.' Kurcher gave Drake a nod to fire up the fusion beams mounted on either side of the *Falcata*. 'Tell me what you're supplying them or we'll destroy your ship and sift through what's left.'

The colour drained from Keening's face. 'That would upset a lot of people.'

'It wouldn't upset me. I'll give you five seconds.'

He reached three before Keening gave in. 'I'm selling on someone else's product, at their behest. It's a new app implant called Link.'

'What does it do?'

'It allows fluid control of mechs, from pursuit through to assault, meaning that people no longer have to rely on the AI. They are in full control all the time.'

No wonder Sigma were buying it, but why would Fortitude be acting as the go-between? 'And who is it creating this app and giving it to you?'

'I don't know who they are. Comms are limited to text only.'

Kurcher raised an eyebrow. 'You must know more. I doubt you would agree to sell the wares of someone you never met.'

Keening gave a slow nod. 'My contact refers to themselves as *The Luminary*. Sent me some of the tech to examine and it blew me away. Never seen anything like it. It's unique.'

'Someone clearly thinks highly of themselves with that title.' Kurcher watched Keening's face closely as he pushed again. 'Were you lying when you said you didn't have any of the products left?'

'No. Fortitude just bought the last ones.'

Drake glanced up and Kurcher noticed the glint in her eyes as she waited to fire on the *Tradech*. She would take great satisfaction in seeing the ship blown apart.

'I'm going to need your customer data.' He saw that Keening was growing more uncomfortable by the second. 'Who you sold these apps to, where you pick up your stock and details on just how it all works.'

'I can't do that,' snapped the trader, looking away from the screen again. 'Nobody would ever trade with me again if I gave away such confidential intel.'

'I know. Not my problem.'

He's going to run, said Santa Cruz.

'Maybe we can come to some deal.' Keening's tone was desperate. 'I would be happy to give Echo a discount moving forward and give them priority over stock.'

Kurcher shook his head. 'I'm sure you'd do anything to save your skin right now but what I want is...'

At that moment, Keening's image vanished and the helium-3 drive on the

Tradech engaged, jolting the smaller ship forward suddenly. It moved quicker than expected.

'Fucking told you,' Drake smirked.

The *Falcata* fired both weapons. One beam grazed the hull of the *Tradech*, whereas the other struck it directly inside the exhaust port. The resulting explosion tore the stern of the vessel apart, obliterating the engines and sending it into a violent spin.

'Wait.'

Drake chose to ignore Kurcher's shout, issuing the command to fire again. This time, both beams struck the *Tradech* and Keening's ship broke apart like a dropped glass, pieces spinning away into the void.

'I didn't give the fucking order to fire,' yelled Kurcher, slamming his hand down on the back of her seat.

Drake shot up and spun to face him. 'Firstly, I don't take orders from you. Secondly, touch my chair again and I'll cut off your hand and shove it up your ass.'

As he stared into her harsh yet strangely captivating eyes, he realised that there really were no similarities between Drake and Frost after all. There was an intense wildness behind those eyes that appealed to him.

'Just get us back to the Expanse. I don't want to linger here any longer than we have to.'

He left the cockpit and returned to his quarters, wishing he could take a hit of something to negate the fears plaguing his mind. He forced himself to record the details of their encounter with Keening, knowing that Hewn would want to know every tiny detail.

He'll want you to go after The Luminary, Frost said.

That was inevitable, but there would probably be more intel to glean before they could even hope to locate the new player in the tech market.

Do you really want to be an errand boy for Schaeffer's Nine? asked Santa Cruz.

He didn't like the alliance that Hewn had manufactured but could understand the benefits, especially in keeping Jericho's Bold at bay. It would all collapse one day and he didn't plan on being anywhere nearby when that happened.

Run away again, coward, growled Ercko.

Kurcher accessed one of the public news streams on his HDU and started reading through the random reports. Continuing supply wars on Kismet, Revenant activity on Earth, some colony out in the sticks looking to hire a new medical team. He wasn't interested in any of those stories and soon found his way into Sapphire Nova's specific news feed. Seconds later, he was staring at his own face. Alongside his rough-looking visage were Broekow and Rane. It pissed him off that the image of Rane had that same infuriating smile he had seen so often.

He read the report beneath and could feel his heartbeat getting faster. So Nova had increased the bounty. He wasn't surprised in the slightest. He knew they were still looking for him but had hoped they would give up considering Nova's unusual situation.

Even though their homeworld was poisoned and millions died, they're still relentless in hunting you down.

D'Larro was right, although something felt different now. He had expected the Nova fleet to strike out in retaliation, blaming anyone and everyone, but they were relatively subdued. Perhaps those who had taken over the running of the corp were more level-headed than their predecessors. If so, he had no doubt they would be planning something. They wouldn't stay quiet long.

He turned the HDU off. Rane should have been top of their most-wanted list, not him. It was the killer who had murdered all of those people after all. Perhaps he should contact Nova and explain what really happened.

You still killed Nova sec on Rikur, Frost reminded him.

'Fuck it.' Those two words often helped him refocus his mind. Not much he could do now but stay where he was.

As he turned back to check his report for Hewn, he saw a silhouette in the doorway of his quarters and instinctively reached for his revolver, fumbling at it slightly in his haste.

'Smooth.' Drake stepped into the light, her arms folded. 'That old wound still causes problems then.'

The reminder of Santa Cruz's knife biting deep was almost as painful as the injury had been. 'Knock next time, for fuck's sake.'

The pilot approached and he was struck by that same flowery scent, albeit much stronger than usual. He also noticed that her pupils were dilated.

'Whatever you're taking, I don't want any,' he told her, aiming to brush past.

Drake caught his arm and kissed him violently, biting his lip. 'You sure?'

'What the hell are you doing?' He considered pushing her away but instead stayed dangerously close.

'Counting your teeth with my tongue,' she replied.

The sarcasm just made him want her more. 'You hate me.'

'I dislike you,' she corrected. 'You're the only man here though and I have needs, so go take off your clothes like a good boy.'

He looked into her drugged-up eyes. 'Bad idea. You'll want more.'
Drake gave a mocking laugh. 'I doubt that.'
Kurcher smiled as he realised just how turned on she had gotten from blowing up Keening's ship. 'Just don't go soft on me.'
'That's what I was going to say to you. Just in a whole different context.'
Kurcher knew it wouldn't end well but he didn't care. He felt human again and wanted to hang on to that for as long as he could.

Summit
Benedict system

He didn't recognise the man staring back at him. Once-steely eyes were now tired and dull, the beard that he had hidden behind for so long had grown wild like a thick brown weed and, beneath that, the face was narrow and drawn.

Broekow turned away from the mirror, finding it difficult to gaze for too long at what he had become. As he plunged his hands under the taps, wringing them in the tepid water, he noticed how they were both trembling. Masami would say it was down to the drinking but Broekow hadn't been able to keep a steady hand since waking up in that Echo medbay. He still recalled the intense burning in his chest; side effects of the damage done extracting the bullets.

Someone entered behind him and he glanced at the newcomer in the mirror. Old habits died hard. He expected he would be watching his back for the rest of his life.

Leaving the men's room, he headed back into the bar and returned to his table by the window overlooking Tidewell. As the sun slowly dipped behind the surrounding hills, only the tops of the nearby buildings still gleamed white. Below, automated street lights were beginning to blink on.

'Seems a shame to be leaving.'

Broekow downed the remnants of his last beer before shrugging at the pilot sitting across from him. 'Don't then. We might as well stay here a while longer.'

Masami's smile was more out of politeness than amusement. 'Hewn wouldn't like us taking the piss. He won't fund us to sit around getting drunk.'

'Then Hewn can go fuck himself.'

Broekow's words were loud enough to make the other patrons look their way and Masami leant forward, lowering his own voice.

'I think there are some on the other side of Tidewell who didn't quite hear you. Look, my friend, we've been here for days and people are going to start thinking we're not just here for a break.'

Broekow signalled to the waitress that he was ready for another round.

'Just relax, Tariq. We were sent here to find intel on what Impramed are up to and I just need another couple of days. What I have isn't enough yet.'

'That's an understatement. You've spent most of your time here getting drunk. I read your report so far and it contains information Echo are already aware of.'

'And that's why we need to stay here longer,' snapped Broekow, slamming one hand down onto the table.

Masami noted the same disapproving looks aimed at his colleague. 'You need to stop drawing attention to yourself.'

Broekow's drink arrived but he was too angry to even thank the waitress, who was eager to go serve someone else. He was only on his fifth beer. Two nights before, he had downed at least twelve.

Nobody else could possibly grasp how much pain the alcohol actually numbed, not even Masami. He had explained to the pilot on several occasions what had happened to him eight months ago but often forgot that, not only was the man an Echo pirate, he had also fought against Santa Cruz's rogue fleet and lived to tell the tale.

He had never told Masami about Frost though; never told him the agony he felt as he watched the *Kaladine* plummet to the surface of Cerberus. He hated Hewn for persuading them to head for the quaran, hated Rane for manipulating everyone to get what he wanted and hated Kurcher for leading them all down such a dangerous path. Those three had gotten Frost killed and he would never forget that.

'I need to get back to the ship,' Masami announced, standing. 'Instead of drinking yourself into another stupor, you should do some more digging.'

Broekow stared down into his beer. 'I will. Just quit mothering me.'

Five minutes after the pilot had left, Broekow was ordering his sixth.

Tidewell lit up as night fell and the noise of evening revellers began drifting up. More patrons appeared in the bar too. Believing that there must be off-duty Impramed workers among them, Broekow looked for a possible source.

'You on your own?'

He had seen the man approaching out of the corner of his eye but it took a moment to register that the question was aimed at him. Looking up, Broekow saw a broad ugly face, broken nose and crooked smile. He also noticed there was no drink held in the large hands.

'Expecting company soon,' he replied, hoping that the man mountain wasn't looking for a new friend to play with.

'We'd appreciate you vacating the table.'

Broekow glanced around the stocky frame and could see a group of men lurking near the bar. 'There's plenty of other places to sit.'

'Not with such a good view.' Off-white teeth appeared as the man grinned. 'We'd rather you relocated to one of those *other places*.'

'Well *we* can piss off, big man.' Memories of Angard always came flooding back when he used that moniker.

'Let me put this in a way you'll understand then. Fuck off.'

Broekow looked across at the lurkers. One of them stood out for some reason and seemed familiar, but perhaps the beer had dulled his senses too much to remember why.

'You want to get your heavy out of my face before he goes through this window?' he asked sharply.

'Not a clever move,' the brute muttered.

'It's okay, Ruck.' The familiar lurker stepped alongside his thug. 'I can speak for myself.'

'Yes, sir.'

Broekow met the glower from Ruck before studying the second man. Tall and slim, well-manicured and an air of arrogance about him.

'Merc or military?' he asked the ex-sniper, narrowing his dark blue eyes.

'Both. Neither. Take your pick.'

'Ruck here is sometimes abrupt. It's just he knows that my team and I always sit here when we visit. Sort of a tradition.'

Broekow's brain was desperately trying to place the narrow face. 'Good for you. I just want to be left alone to finish my drink.'

'You don't know who I am, do you?'

'Only people who think they are important say things like that. To be honest, I couldn't care less.'

The man slipped into the seat opposite before continuing. 'I'm Morton Hurst.'

Even under the influence of alcohol, Broekow knew he needed to be very careful what he said next. Now that the name had been given, it sparked his memory and he recalled seeing news items with Hurst's face plastered all over them. Then there was the fact that Kurcher had killed the man's nephew, which Frost had told him about as they lay together one night.

He almost laughed at the absurd coincidence they were in that bar at the same time. What were the odds considering the number of systems and worlds in known space?

'I wouldn't have expected Tidewell to be high on your list of holiday destinations,' Broekow said, sipping his beer.

‘It’s the perfect place to mix business and pleasure.’ A curious expression appeared on Hurst’s face. ‘So what do I call you?’

Broekow considered his reply, his inebriated mind struggling to act as fast as usual. Would it be so bad to tell him his name? After all, Fortitude did help them fight Santa Cruz’s rogue fleet and Hurst must have given the order to do so. Then again, that alliance might have been a simple necessity at the time, with Fortitude using it as an opportunity to ingratiate themselves with Nova. If so, Hurst would be more likely to see Broekow as a valuable trading commodity.

‘You can call me bored.’ He downed the last of the beer as he stood. ‘Have the damned table.’

The fresh evening air made him dizzy as he stepped into the busy street. As he waited for it to pass, he didn’t have the usual urge to find another bar. Meeting Hurst and his cronies had put paid to that. What business would bring the most influential man in the Fortitude hierarchy to Summit? He wished he could have stuck around longer to glean more information but the sober part of his brain was screaming at him to get out.

Masami’s pride and joy – the *Crius* – was at the southern end of the city and Broekow knew the direct route back was through the main streets. Something pulled him towards the eastern edge of Tidewell though and he was soon walking along the promenade parallel to the ocean. Light buoys hovered over the water, their reflections shimmering on the gentle waves. Above them, the sky was clear and Summit’s moon, Chaukan, shone brightly. The planet really was another Earth, just without the insane fanatics and burning cities.

He stopped and gazed thoughtfully out across the waters. How easy it would be to just wade into the depths and vanish. Nobody would miss him and nobody would care.

A ship passed quietly overhead – but it was enough to jolt him back to reality. After watching it accelerate and ascend into the upper atmosphere, he continued along the promenade.

Despite the serenity of Tidewell and all of the resort locations, Broekow knew that Summit’s darker side was lurking just out of sight. Every world had something to hide, even the most popular vacation destination in the Milky Way. Beyond the final light buoys, large predatory creatures moved silently through the water, kept at bay by the great barriers Impramed erected between the shallows and the deeper trenches further out to sea. Most of those visiting Tidewell had no idea they were that close to such dangers as they cavorted and swam in the safe zone.

It was the same in the city itself. Mercenaries, pirates and killers stalked an unseen underworld as the holiday makers lounged around blissfully unaware. He wondered whether Impramed themselves knew just how many cut-throats were skulking below the surface of their utopia.

He eventually made his way back into the streets, aiming to cut through one of the quieter parts of the city. To his annoyance, a number of people had gathered to hold an impromptu party and he pushed past them, trying his best to ignore the smell of alcohol. A group of women called to him from a doorway but he kept his eyes down. Their combined perfume threatened to choke him so he held his breath until he could escape into one of the narrower alleyways. He dared to glance back as he headed away from the revellers and could see just how scantily-clad the temptresses had been. Impramed would label them as *escorts* but Broekow knew what everyone else called them, and more were appearing every week on Summit. Another sign that the underworld was taking over Tidewell piece-by-piece.

Ahead, he could see the familiar junction which meant the *Crius* was just around the corner. This time, he would have something worthwhile to tell Masami.

As he approached the intersection though, he came to an abrupt halt. Were those footsteps he had heard behind him? He listened for a moment but all he could hear was the rhythmic hum of distant music. He noticed that his hand had reached down for a weapon that wasn't there. Ever since Sapphire Nova goons killed several guards during Kurcher's extraction of D'Larro, Impramed had increased security. Those found with a weapon of any kind were more likely to get a few thousand volts through them before the guards asked questions.

A light breeze whispered along the alley, bringing a hint of that damned perfume with it. Broekow had always liked how Frost preferred a more subtle scent, the sort you couldn't detect until you were up close. Whenever he had entered the cockpit of the *Kaladine*, a blend of that perfume and smoke had always hit him. It was just another thing he missed about her.

There was something else on the breeze too and it wasn't the scent of a woman.

'You on your own?'

Broekow ran for the junction as the ominous figure emerged from shadows nearby. He never saw the other man waiting to pounce and a fist struck him hard on the cheek. The alley spun as he stumbled and fell. He tried to get straight to his feet but a large boot pushed him back down.

'I wouldn't bother.' Ruck's voice came from above, his amusement clear in his tone.

Broekow cursed himself for being so stupid. There was a time he would have made sure nobody could follow him, working out his escape route before taking out a target. He had insulted Morton Hurst. Of course he would send his heavies to teach him a lesson.

'So here's what happens next.' Ruck applied more pressure. 'We're going to take you back to Sullivan's Rest, where you'll gladly tell us everything you know about the *Grail* and the whereabouts of Davian Kurcher.'

Broekow had to wonder whether the alcohol had destroyed his common sense completely. Naturally Hurst would recognise him.

'No idea what you mean.' It was hard to speak with Ruck's weight crushing the air from his lungs.

Someone else's boot kicked him hard in the side, sending an agonising spasm through his torso. The old burning sensation returned in his chest too.

'There's no point pretending,' Ruck snapped. 'We were ordered not to beat the shit out of you, but there's always room for interpretation.'

'Listen.' Broekow's synapses needed time to start firing. 'You don't want to be hauling me off to that shithole of a station.'

'Why is that?'

'There's nothing I can tell you. I don't know where Kurcher is and I know fuck all about the *Grail*.'

Broekow found himself being lifted by both arms and came face-to-face with Ruck's smirking visage. 'I expected more from such a notorious criminal.'

One of the mercenary's bear paws slammed into his stomach, knocking all of the air from his lungs. The fresh wave of agony would have made him cry out if he had not been trying desperately to draw a breath.

'What was it you said back in the bar?' Ruck asked, not expecting an answer. 'That you'd put me through the window?'

Broekow wondered whether he could get the brute to hit him harder. One of those fists driving the nasal bone into his brain would end it, and get Ruck in trouble with Hurst at the same time. A small consolation.

'By the looks of you, I doubt you could even lift your own dick to take a piss.' Ruck's disappointment was clear as he glanced at his colleagues. 'Bring him.'

As the Fortitude mercs started dragging him away, a familiar voice called out to them. Broekow didn't know whether to be relieved or disappointed.

'I'm afraid I can't let you take my friend there.' Masami was standing at the end of the alley, pistol in hand.

Ruck was quiet as he weighed the pilot up, then laughed. 'Tidewell security won't like you waving that piece around. If one shot goes off, you're finished.'

'The benefits of a silencer.' Masami waved the weapon so they could see he wasn't bluffing. 'And I doubt you're unarmed.'

As he began walking slowly towards them, Ruck nodded to two of his colleagues and they moved to intercept. Masami gave the subtlest of shrugs.

'It's only fair to give you the chance to walk away. Please take that chance.'

Broekow had managed to finally catch his breath and the feeling was returning to his limbs. As the two men holding him were focused on Masami, he could turn slightly to see the stand-off. They didn't know Masami was an Echo man. They also didn't know what he was capable of. The pilot came across as a gentle soul, softly spoken and placid, but Broekow knew there was more to him than met the eye.

'Who the fuck are you anyway?' Ruck asked, growing impatient as his men approached warily.

Masami ignored the question, swinging his pistol up and firing twice. Both the advancing mercs stumbled and fell with a bullet lodged just below the knee. As they yelped in pain, the pirate aimed the gun at Ruck.

'Take the chance to walk away or you'll be crawling like these two.'

Broekow glanced at the Fortitude thug and could see the fury in his eyes. Masami had put his men down in the blink of an eye and there was no doubt he could do the same to the remaining mercs. Plus, Masami had no fear of the authorities. He had planned on leaving Summit anyway.

Reluctantly, Ruck gave the signal and the men holding Broekow released their grip.

Masami gave a grateful smile. 'Good choice. Now, I suggest you be on your way.'

As the mercs scooped up their wounded colleagues and slowly moved away, Broekow staggered alongside the pilot.

'You have impeccable timing,' he muttered.

Exchanging one last meaningful look with the withdrawing Ruck, Masami ushered Broekow away through the alleyways without another word and the two were soon boarding the *Crius*.

As the pair took their seats in the cockpit and Masami guided the ship swiftly away from Tidewell City, Broekow had time to reflect on his brush with Fortitude. Were the mercs working with Impramed? Perhaps the corporation had been so shaken by the deaths in their beloved Tidewell that they had asked Fortitude to act as peacekeepers of a sort. Surely Hurst wouldn't have been there unless some important deal was going down. Then again, someone could have tipped Fortitude off that Broekow was on Summit and that was the only reason they were there.

'Good job I decided to keep track of you.'

Broekow gave Masami a sideways glance. 'You'd better not have implanted me with some beacon.'

'There are simpler means of spying on you. You're welcome, by the way.'

'Yeah, thanks.'

Masami shook his head. 'You're going to end up getting yourself killed if you keep on like this.'

Broekow gazed out into the darkness ahead of them. 'With luck.'

Echo flagship Glaive
Clark system

'I don't give two shits about your facility or your men.'

Hewn could see he would have to change tactic. Trystan Hengeveld may have been similar to his younger brother in appearance, but Lars had always been ready to listen. The man before him seemed driven only by anger and vengeance.

'I wanted to meet with you in person to discuss the situation,' the pirate explained calmly, pointing to the seat on the other side of the table. 'Let's have a drink and...'

'I didn't come here to play nice.' Hengeveld's left hand brushed the pistol at his side. 'I came here to find my brother's killers and bring them to justice.'

Hewn glanced at the men and women standing behind the Libra officer. All looked ready to pull their weapons at any moment but their nerves were clear. After all, they were standing on the largest ship in the Echo fleet. Even though their own vessel waited nearby, they were alone in the Expanse and if a firefight broke out it would only result in their deaths.

The handful of pirates he had chosen to accompany him were also showing signs of discomfort at the way the conversation was going. His second, Vance Fischer, had insisted on being present for the meeting and Hewn was glad to have him there. Not only was Fischer handy in a fight, he was also a calming influence on most of those around him.

'I understand your need for vengeance, Trystan. You also have to understand what happened after I left Tempest.'

Hengeveld's smile was devoid of warmth. 'True, I want to find those who murdered Lars. The thing is that he was an officer of Libra Centauri and I have full jurisdiction from the board on this matter. I'm not going rogue just to dish out my own revenge. I'm here on corporation orders.

Also, I don't like you using my first name. I'm a commander and will be referred to as such.'

'Fair enough, *commander*. As I say though, you have to understand what happened after Lars was killed.'

As Hewn paused, he recalled the report he had received from Chaplin once

Santa Cruz had been put down. They had all hoped Lars survived the sabotage of the machinery but the clean-up crews found his burnt body down in the maintenance tunnels below the destroyed vat, nearly exactly where Hewn had last spoken with him. He had not divulged to many people that Lars was already dead when the vat blew but those who discovered the charred remains had no doubt talked.

Realising Hengeveld was waiting, he continued. 'He was murdered by Rane and Ercko. Shortly after, Ercko himself was killed and his body jettisoned into space. As for Rane...' He could still see Straunia covered with the sickly aura. 'He disappeared. Nobody knows where he went or if he is even still alive. My suggestion would be for Libra to send scouts to some of the outer systems and see if he surfaces. He would likely steer clear of Taurus, Libra and Nova worlds though, so Sigma or Impramed would be the best bets.'

'I'm not a betting man,' Hengeveld growled. 'We'll find Rane eventually and, for your sake, I hope Ercko is dead. In their absence though, I'll settle for Davian Kurcher. He was after all the one who took those two psychos down to your facility.'

Hewn saw another similarity then between the Hengeveld brothers. Grim determination to see a task through no matter what.

'Kurcher didn't kill Lars.'

Hengeveld straightened his green and white uniform before crossing his arms and regarding Hewn with untrusting blue eyes. 'He is the one responsible though. He made the call. I suppose you'll tell me next that he isn't here.'

'Why would he...?' Hewn hesitated. Try lying to a senior officer of Libra Centauri and it could wreck the alliance he had worked so hard to set up. 'Yes, Kurcher joined Echo after what happened in the Flint system. He was wanted by all of the corps. He isn't your man though. Rane manipulated pretty much everything that happened.'

'Give me Kurcher and we'll be on our way.' It wasn't a request.

'No.' Hewn heard the sharp intake of breath behind him from Fischer. 'Even if he was on the *Glaive*, which he isn't, I wouldn't hand him over to you.'

Hengeveld looked genuinely perplexed. 'Why would you protect someone like him?'

'I'm not protecting him. He's conducting important business for Echo and needs to see it through.' He was also one of the only people to see what was inside the *Grail*, so there was worth in keeping the enlister alive. 'Lars was a loyal man and I liked him. He didn't deserve to die the way he did, but Kurcher didn't order Rane to kill anyone. That fucker took it upon himself to start murdering both Libra and Echo men alike.'

'You don't have to tell me what my own brother was like,' yelled Hengeveld, his face reddening slightly. 'When Kurcher returns, hand him over.'

Hewn looked back at Fischer, who was trying his best to remain stoic. 'Libra Centauri and Echo have been allies for a while now. Despite the setback, Eidolon is generating increasing revenue for both organisations and it would be a pity to damage the relationship now.'

'And you think I care about that poison you're cooking up?' Hengeveld's mouth gave the subtlest of twitches. 'This *alliance* you speak of was with a very different arm of Libra and I'll happily blow that agreement apart to get what I need.'

'If you're going to start throwing threats around, commander, then this meeting is over.'

An uncomfortable silence fell over the room as the two men exchanged ferocious glares. Hewn hoped nobody had itchy trigger fingers.

'I guess it is,' said Hengeveld finally. 'I'll give you some time to think on what I have said but I'll be back for Kurcher. I also expect Echo to help in finding Rane. I'm not about to send our entire fleet out into the dregs of space on some wild goosechase.'

'I'll spare some ships to look for Rane but I've already told you we're not handing Kurcher over.'

Hengeveld shot a look to his soldiers. 'We'll see, Hewn.'

As soon as the Libra entourage had left the room, there was a collective sigh of relief.

'I don't understand, Jaffren,' began Fischer, who had clearly been waiting to blurt out his feelings. 'Kurcher isn't one of us and he never will be. Why not just agree to hand him over and save the ballache that Libra twat will give us later on?'

'I have my reasons.' Hewn gave a nod for his people to leave the room, knowing that his second would remain. 'Kurcher found a way into the *Grail* before and my hope is he can do so again.'

An uncertain smile appeared on Fischer's face. 'You actually want into that thing? I knew you were fucking crazy.'

'When I first found out about the *Grail*, it struck me just how much of an advantage Echo would have if we could somehow harness the tech inside. Unfortunately it ended up lying on Straunia so getting into it now would be impossible, if it weren't for the fact we have two of the three survivors working for us.'

'Now it makes sense why you send them both out on relatively safe missions.'

Hewn shrugged. 'Kurcher tried making the crims he gathered feel like part of the team, to keep up the facade of enlisting them. I'm just doing the same to him and Broekow. If I kept them here all the time, they would know something was up.'

'You'd risk the alliance with Libra to get inside the *Grail*?'

'Absolutely. Libra don't plan on being friendly with us too long. They're using us like we're using them and it's only a matter of time before it all comes to a bad end, especially with Trystan fucking Hengeveld getting involved.'

Fischer chuckled and shook his head. 'You're right, as always. So when does this expedition to find the *Grail* happen?'

'Once it's safe to do so,' replied Hewn, taking out his HDU and checking some of the latest reports coming from the corps. 'Sapphire Nova are buzzing around Straunia and will be for some time. No doubt they're trying to gain access to the *Grail* too, but I know the others will just be waiting in the shadows like a pack of mawhounds, getting ready to pounce on the carcass once Nova have had their fill.'

'You think they haven't got inside yet?'

'One of our contacts said Nova are hesitant for some reason. We'll bide our time and use a Libra conflector to get us in under their radars when we do decide to act.'

Fischer waited patiently while Hewn scanned over the reports, finding nothing of real value. 'We need to be careful of Hengeveld, Jaffren. The *Erudite* is one of the most dangerous ships I've ever laid eyes on and we don't want him sneaking around the Expanse without us knowing.'

'I doubt he would sneak anywhere,' Hewn stated. 'These Scandinavians are direct and cold. He's clever though so he wouldn't attack Echo unless he had no other choice. He has other things to attend to which will keep him occupied for a while. Sigma Royal for one.'

Seeing Fischer's confused look, he continued. 'Meta being wiped out has opened the way for Libra to start taking control of Sigma's outer worlds. Hengeveld has orders to lead this campaign.'

'Is there anything you don't know?'

'Unfortunately I don't know what he is actually thinking. I don't know whether the grief over losing his brother will make him do something rash. I don't know whether Libra will hold him back if he does. The alliance is important to them right now, just as it is to us.'

'Not sure how the others in the alliance are going to react to this,' Fischer noted.

Hewn realised that his second probably wasn't the only one with concerns as to the direction Echo was heading. There had been several changes to his organisation over the recent months and those under his command were bound to have doubts over the choices he had made.

'The only other members with any real clout are Schaeffer's Nine but the agreement with them is based on a mutual hatred of the corps so the fact Libra are involved doesn't make it easy.' Hewn flexed his metal fingers, looking along the flat edge of the bionic arm. 'We don't need to worry about the Cobb Resistance. They lost a lot of people fighting Santa Cruz so giving them the chance to set up a base on Seko will keep them busy. Eventually we'll integrate them into Echo.'

'Not sure Cal Fuller will go for that.'

'Well he's still on Cobb overseeing the clean-up of their old site, which will take a while. Gives us the opportunity to sow the seed with his people on Seko.'

Fischer had been the one chosen to show the members of the Resistance to their new home so he knew what was coming. 'You mean it gives *me* the opportunity.'

'Yeah. The only other ones to worry about are the Oakleys. Like the Resistance, they suffered heavy casualties and didn't have that many ships in the first place. Their fleet will remain at Cradle licking their wounds and trying to rebuild so don't expect to see them any time soon.'

'Apart from the fact Hedmun Oakley is helping Fuller clean up Cobb,' Fischer reminded him. 'Acting like some big saviour to the downtrodden.'

Hewn recalled the one time he had met the captain of the Oakley fleet. The man was charismatic, just like his murderous niece, but acted like he was in charge of the most impressive force in the entire galaxy.

Hewn found himself wondering whether Tara Oakley was still hiding on Cradle or whether her parents had sent her to some distant system. Hedmun was seemingly very fond of her, despite the number of men she had iced, and was quite protective about all of his family. The whole Oakley dynamic seemed fucked up.

Hewn couldn't help thinking of Rae. She may have been his wife but she was also a member of Echo and the only way she would ever have agreed to stay apart from him for so long was to have an important task to focus on.

Looking after the brewery on Warren was perfect. Not only did it give her the responsibility of ensuring Echo earned good money from their product, it also kept her and Wes safe. He yearned to visit them; to hold them again and tell his son how much he had grown.

'Jaffren?'

Hewn gave Fischer a wry smile. 'Getting old. Keep drifting off.'

'Just say the word and I'm ready to take over.'

'Fuck off.'

'What do we do next?'

Hewn pointed his second towards the door. 'Move the *Glaive* to Miller. I don't want to be sat in one place too long.' As Fischer made to leave, Hewn called out. 'And make sure the fucking *Erudite* leaves the Expanse.'

Minerva
Berg system

Hayes was cold, as though the chill of deep space had seeped into the entire colony.

Mitchell's breath hung in the air as he waited for the elevator to arrive. He hoped it would be warmer in the sub-levels.

'Haven't they heard of heaters out here?' It was clear O'Brien was shaking from his wavering voice.

Mitchell looked over his shoulder at the three officers. 'Would you rather still be locked in a cell?'

'No, sir,' O'Brien replied quickly. 'Although I can't speak for these two.'

'You usually do,' snapped Byrne. 'I'd rather be anywhere than in that cell.'

'I quite like the cold,' Ishlan remarked. 'Keeps the senses sharp.'

Mitchell gave a curt nod before turning back to the elevator. All three would still have been rotting in that prison on Galt had he not integrated them into his crew. They had been awaiting trial for the crimes they had committed while following Santa Cruz, and getting them out had been troublesome to say the least. Still, the only other member of the board who knew what he had done was Lenaghan and Sapphire Nova had done him a favour getting rid of that useless piece of shit.

It was a pity that Fernandes and Thomadakis had both died. Having all five of the officers who had been close to Santa Cruz would have been preferable. They had been loyal to that twisted madman and Mitchell just hoped they showed as much dedication to the man who had spared them from certain court martial and possibly execution. Of course, they all had to be demoted and the ships they once commanded had already been reassigned. So, here they were acting as his personal advisory officers, about to embark on another classified mission.

He wouldn't make the same mistakes Santa Cruz made.

When the elevator arrived and the doors slid open, the only occupant was a woman dressed in a clean grey uniform, the sword and stars standing out starkly on her shirt.

'Welcome to Hayes, general. I'm Lynn White, senior research officer to Doctor Li. Please.' She stepped aside, beckoning them in.

As the elevator began its descent, O'Brien couldn't seem to help himself.

'So, do we call you Doctor White or just Lynn?'

She gave him a coy smile. 'Doctor.'

O'Brien looked disappointed. 'Well, I guess you can call me Lieutenant then.'

'The upper colony is looking rather run-down,' Mitchell said, intentionally interrupting O'Brien's clumsy attempt at flirting. 'I hope the labs aren't in the same state.'

'No, sir.' White's body language showed that she didn't want to be stuck in a lift with them. 'We've been waiting for maintenance teams from Taurus for some time now. Most of us prefer staying below the surface. We don't feel quite so exposed down there.'

Mitchell chose to ignore her sharp tone. He had heard that the people living on Minerva were as cold as the system they inhabited. Reports from various sources noted that humans living so far out would inevitably become distant and lose any people skills they might have once had. He had also read that they were prone to losing their sanity too.

'I'm sure we can arrange for engineers from the shipyard to come down here and help,' Ishlan assured the tall doctor.

'Hayes will soon become a temporary home to a number of explorer crews,' added Mitchell. 'It's imperative that the colony becomes a much warmer place to live. Temperature and attitude.'

White smiled again, more to herself this time. 'Understood, general.'

When the descent slowed and the elevator jolted to a halt, she led them out into the sub-level. Mitchell was genuinely impressed as they followed the brisk woman down long hallways and interconnecting corridors, passing a number of different rooms filled with all manner of tech he couldn't even begin to understand.

'If you have any app implants, you may find them disrupted for a time while you are down here.' White waved a hand at one of many devices installed on the walls. 'We don't allow the use of apps unless they are on the Hayes secure network.'

Mitchell also noticed the way in which everyone they passed kept their eyes down, staring at HDUs or the floor. It was disconcerting, as though the Hayes colonists had forgotten how to interact with one another.

Eventually, they arrived at a door marked *Level One Access Only*. White spun on her heel. 'General, I'm afraid I can only permit yourself entry.'

Mitchell nodded. 'Is there somewhere my officers can wait?'

'Next door along.'

O'Brien and Ishlan exchanged frustrated glances but took their leave.

Byrne leant closer to Mitchell.

'Sir, we've all seen the *Grail*,' he said, his voice low. 'Santa Cruz kept us out of the loop until things started heating up. That was a mistake. If we know what we're dealing with from the start, we can be of better use to you.'

Mitchell looked him in the eye. 'You have my word that I will brief you fully once we head back up to the *Victory*.'

Byrne grimaced. 'Understood.'

As the hulking officer trudged away, Mitchell turned to White with a rare smile. 'After you, doctor.'

He had read the confidential reports and examined the numerous data files, but the sight beyond that door still caught him by surprise. The expansive chamber was lined on either side with labs, all segregated by strengthened glass walls. Members of the research team were active in each, their protective suits illuminated by a variety of colours emanating from the app interfaces surrounding the centre of their focus.

Mitchell counted sixteen labs, each containing one of the alien artefacts uncovered by Taurus Galahad. No two looked the same. One was cube-shaped but covered in jagged ridges, another oval with distinct markings etched across it. Most were a shade of black or dark green. All displayed an almost neon blue light gleaming brilliantly from orifices of varying dimensions.

'Where are the rest?' he asked, finding it hard to look away from the strange devices.

'In secure units nearby,' White replied. She waved a finger towards the labs. 'These ones have not been dormant for some time and have been kicking out data at an unbelievable rate. Even our apps can't keep up with them.'

They passed into another chamber, where the left-hand wall curved to give the room a crescent shape. Consoles were lined up on the right and five scientists studied displays intently. One of them looked up and whispered something to his colleagues before stepping forward.

'General, it's been a long time.'

'Doctor Li.' Mitchell was trying to recall the last time they had met. 'Apologies it has taken so long to get out here.'

Li pushed the spectacles back up his nose. 'Well, it's not like we were going anywhere. I imagine you have had your hands full with Nova.'

'Let's just say you're lucky to be this far out. The inner systems are utter chaos.'

'I wouldn't exactly describe us as *lucky*,' White said in the same sharp tone.

'Okay, Lynn.' Li gave her a scathing look before pointing towards a door at the opposite end of the chamber. 'Let's talk in my office, general.'

As he followed them, Mitchell noticed the locking clamps in the middle of the curved wall. 'How are the infusion tests going?'

Li gave an abrupt laugh that sounded forced. 'Ah, straight down to business I see. The patient is still in a dormant state but we are monitoring the way in which the antecedent technology seems to be interacting with human organs and tissue.'

'Will he wake up?'

'Not until we want him to. It is uncertain quite how his brain will react if he does though.'

'I'd like to see the latest test reports before I leave Minerva.' Mitchell's eyes lingered on the clamps. 'You certainly have him locked up tight.'

'Indeed.' Li stepped inside his office. 'I'll open the containment unit up once we're done so you can take a look at him.'

The office was kitted out just as sparsely as the labs and, while Li picked up a HDU and began tapping furiously at the screen, White poured a glass of cloudy water, offering it to the general.

'Sorry.' There was no sincerity in her apology. 'Water processing needs fixing too.'

As Mitchell accepted the dubious-looking drink, Li swiped an image from his HDU onto a larger screen built into the wall.

'I'm assuming your key reason for coming here was to see the latest developments first-hand,' began the lead scientist. 'What you are seeing here is new data being emitted by most of the artefacts.'

Mitchell sipped the water, trying not to grimace at the metallic taste. 'I'm afraid you'll have to break it down for me.'

Li smiled. 'Of course. Several months ago, during the incident with the *Grail*, this new data began appearing. Much of this has been hard to decipher as it is not like anything we have seen previously.'

Mitchell studied Li's face for a moment, noting the signs of fatigue. His thinning hair was beginning to turn grey and his skin was taut, making him look seventy instead of fifty. He still found time to shave though.

Realising the general was waiting on him, Li continued. 'We have managed to determine however that there are coordinates embedded in the data. Since we started unearthing these artefacts, there have been various coordinates to certain points in space, both in known systems and the unexplored regions. The biggest revelation was naturally finding the coordinates of the *Grail*.'

'It was also the biggest mistake,' White added bitterly.

Mitchell's gaze swung to the research officer, who was tying back her long dark hair to expose the narrow, attractive face. 'There were many regrets regards the *Grail*, doctor. Had we known Santa Cruz's plan, many lives could've been saved and Taurus Galahad wouldn't have been blamed for what happened.'

'I take it you lost a lot of people trying to stop him?' Her expression was one of anger, but there was a sadness in her eyes.

'By the time we knew what he was doing, there was no way for us to get to Flint quickly enough. We had been distracted by Nova attacks unfortunately.' He recognised the look on her face. 'Who did you lose?'

'My father was serving on the *Tucana*. By the time I received his final message, the ship had already been destroyed.'

'Santa Cruz tore many lives apart,' said Li, jumping in. 'We must look to the future though, to ensure nothing like that happens again.'

Mitchell's eyes lingered on White before turning back to the screen. 'Please continue.'

Li nodded. 'The new coordinates within the data are for a location in Coldrig, 13,000 light years from here.'

'Your thoughts?'

'Another antecedent site.' Li shrugged. 'Whatever is there must be important for all artefacts to show the same data.'

Mitchell struggled with the term the scientist used. Everybody else referred to the artefacts as *alien*. Li had coined the use of *antecedent*, which he saw as an apt description of the dead race and the tech they had left behind.

'I would've recommended we send some of the explorers in orbit out there,' the general said, thinking aloud. '13,000 light years is too far without a jump point though.'

'Then perhaps you'll be interested in the other important discovery we have made.' Li sounded almost excited. 'We've been studying one very specific set of symbols and codes we found repeated in the data. Take a look.'

A new image was swept onto the screen and Mitchell squinted at the strange scrolling shapes. As he watched, the symbols came to a halt and a map of the Milky Way descended over them.

'They represent the systems.' Mitchell moved closer to examine the map. 'Every single one that's owned by a corporation.'

'No, they represent the jump points,' corrected Li, smiling weakly as the general's jaw dropped. 'This means that the antecedents used to use them too. Centuries or even millennia before the human race finally crawled off Earth and discovered the first jump point, this race was active across the entire Milky Way. The fact we discovered the artefacts on worlds we colonised leads me to believe that they once lived in the same places.'

'We don't know that for certain though,' White remarked. 'If they had, where are the ruins of their civilisation?'

Li scowled. 'There is much to speculate over. It could be that the antecedents actually created the jump points. The *Grail* used a technology that could open a temporary gateway in space so it makes sense that they could also build stable wormholes and use them for swifter travel.'

'So why build one on the outer edge of Sol?' Mitchell's question seemed to catch the two by surprise. 'Earth would have been a suitable world to colonise, right?'

'Perhaps,' pondered Li. 'Perhaps not. We only know the perfect conditions for some classifications of life to flourish. Oxygen, liquid water, a food chain evolved over thousands of years. What if Earth didn't have the conditions for the antecedents to thrive there? Maybe the answers lie at the Coldrig coordinates.'

Mitchell watched as Li stepped up to the screen and placed a finger on one of the symbols. He couldn't help but smile.

'As you can see, general, there appears to be jump points within Coldrig too.' Li was clearly proud of this discovery. 'Give us some more time and we will have coordinates that the explorers can use to jump to new systems across that sector. They will be able to use these as stepping stones to whatever lies 13,000 light years away.'

Mitchell shook his head in wonder. 'This is excellent work, doctor. In one fell swoop, we will have access to Coldrig and be able to expand Taurus' reach even further. I'll brief the command crews of the explorers and explain that this will be their priority mission, no matter how long it takes.'

White gently cleared her throat. 'We need to be careful. We don't want another incident. I mean, what if there is another *Grail* out there?'

'I do agree with Lynn, general.' Li tapped a bony finger on the Coldrig sector. 'We need to know more before heading into unknown space. There is information yet to be gleaned from the artefacts. The antecedents have more to tell us. For example, I believe that each is a power unit of sorts and could hold highly volatile energy. Why would they create individual devices like these just to contain data? They had some other use, I am certain.'

'We also need to examine the fact they are still active so long after their creators died out,' commented White. 'Whatever their power source is, it must be immense.'

Mitchell held up one hand, which seemed the best way to silence the two excitable scientists. 'You make valid points, both of you. On one hand, we don't want to go blindly into the darkness without all the facts. On the other hand, Sapphire Nova are pushing their exploration plans into Krondahar while Libra Centauri are edging closer to Farrin. With the pressure being placed on us from all of the other corps and Nova assassinating our people, we can't afford to delay too long.

Taurus Galahad will be the first to harness the alien...antecedent technology and there is every reason to believe that going into Coldrig will help us do this. While your teams continue the research here though, there is another way for us to speed the process up.'

Li shared a bemused glance with his colleague. 'Do tell, general.'

Mitchell approached the screen and placed a hand over the Flint system. 'I need a science team to go with us.'

White gave a bizarre laugh. 'That's suicide. Nova have it locked down.'

'The trouble with living so far out, doctor, is that you don't often know what's happening back home. We recently received confirmation that Straunia has been officially labelled as a quaran and that Nova have vacated Flint altogether to gather their forces elsewhere.

You have been studying this data longer than anyone so who best to help us gain entry to the *Grail*.'

Li pushed his spectacles up again. 'As much as we would love to get our hands on it, we can't spare anyone. I am sure there is a breakthrough coming here.'

Mitchell was silent for a moment as he tried to gauge their true thoughts on the matter. 'I'm afraid this is not a request but an order. You will put together a team who will accompany us to Straunia. This team needs to be led by an expert on the antecedents.'

'General, I must protest...'

Mitchell decided to cut Li off quickly. 'Understood. My order stands though. Now, while you transfer these most recent findings to the *Victory*, I'd like to take that look at the infusion patient.'

Galt
Lincoln system

Hayward stared up at the central spire, marvelling at the way the sleek structure seemed to be reaching for the low cloud cover that often blocked out the Galt sky. Since she had arrived at the impressive Kingston colony, she frequently found her eyes drawn to the spire . She planned to ascend to the upper platform at least once before she went back to Earth. If nothing else, it offered amazing views of the whole colony. The landscape certainly wouldn't be awe-inspiring.

The only similarity between Galt and Earth was the breathable air, and even that had a strange smell to it outside of Kingston. The flora that grew in abundance did not have the same bright colours as those back home, instead tending to be varying shades of brown, green or, on occasions, grey. Thanks to a startlingly different evolution, the insects of Galt were not drawn to vivid displays, as most were blind. The eyesight of the indigenous animals was poor, leading scientists to the conclusion that the fauna located food via sound and an astounding sense of smell alone.

Hayward couldn't possibly fathom what caused the evolution to be so different on this world 23,000 light years from Earth. One thing she did know was that humans would always bring a piece of their homeworld to another planet, no matter how far away. The beautiful blooms established throughout the main plaza of Kingston were testament to that.

As she made her way across to the eastern district, the scent of the flowers gave her reason to smile. Despite the Revenant threat, she still missed Earth.

After she passed through the security checkpoint, Kingston became a little less impressive. No colourful flowers or views of the great spire. Just throngs of people heading to and from their daily jobs through metal hallways. Even the windows offered little in the way of distraction and most of the workers passed them with nary a glance.

Following the signs to ensure she didn't get as lost as she had the day she arrived, Hayward found her way to the meeting rooms nestled near to the landing pads, noticing the increased military presence the closer she got. Taurus soldiers monitored all new arrivals at the colony and had been on high alert since Nova's hostile activities first began. That was a long time to remain focused and she had heard rumours of many soldiers using newly implanted boost apps. That worried her, as so many other matters did.

The man she was meeting had seemingly arrived much earlier and was waiting patiently in a quiet room looking out over two of the landing pads.

'Sorry if I'm late. Don't really know my way around here yet.'

Akeman offered a smile. 'You're not the only one, Miss Hayward. I only got off the transport from Carson thirty minutes ago.'

She tried not to look at his facial scars. 'Well thank you for coming here on such short notice.'

'You're welcome.' He held out a glass half-filled with cloudy orange liquid. 'Whisky?'

'A little early for me,' she declined, taking a seat. 'Besides, I've never much had a taste for it.'

Akeman sipped the drink as he sat opposite her at the long table. 'I move around so much that I tend to forget time. As for the whisky, it's the last of a batch I once bought from Temple. Commander Santa Cruz was partial to it.'

At the mention of that name, Hayward raised an eyebrow. 'You and he drink together often?'

'Only when he wanted something,' Akeman replied. 'Is this why you called for me? Am I to be reprimanded for my dealings with a traitor?'

'If that were the case, you'd have been locked up a long time ago,' she told the spy, giving him a wry look. 'No, the reason I wanted to meet with you was much more selfish. Having looked through all of the agents in the employ of Taurus Galahad, I realised that you were the one best equipped to help me.'

Akeman gave a throaty chuckle. 'Probably 'cause I'm one of the only ones still alive.'

'What is your current brief?' Her question was direct and abrupt.

'To monitor the comings and goings on Carson Freight Station,' came his equally direct response. 'To ensure there are no unwanteds arriving there and also to keep an ear out for reports from mercenary and pirate organisations.'

Hayward sat back, regarding him with a look bordering on suspicious. 'You have a lot of contacts in those organisations. Santa Cruz used to pay you to move regularly between systems, gleaning intel on the latest activities of the Knights Templar, Jericho's Bold and the like.'

'And all of the corps, yes.'

'Not all.' She watched him intently as she asked her next question. 'Do you have an allegiance to any of these other organisations?'

Akeman downed his whisky. 'I'm sure you have picked your way through my file, Miss Hayward. I'm a Taurus Galahad agent who is good at his job because the people I deal with don't know I'm a Taurus Galahad agent. I don't work for the highest bidder, like some.'

'And yet you worked for Jorelian Santa Cruz, who paid you with disguised transfers.'

'I did, and he did. He was a Taurus officer after all, and one very high up the ladder. I never knew he was planning mass genocide.'

'If you had?'

'I wouldn't have agreed to work for him.' Akeman's rough voice had a tinge of regret.

'So now your orders come from Junior Exec Billings, is that right?'

Akeman made to reach for the bottle of whisky then decided against it. 'Correct.'

Hayward fell silent for a moment, weighing up the man before her. His eyes never left her own and his responses were confident. Still, there were dubious instances throughout his service record that gave her reason to doubt his sincerity. He had the most useful contacts of anyone she knew though, so trusting him would be a double-edged sword.

The other niggling thought in the back of her mind was that Billings was one of the execs she was due to investigate. He had worked for Lenaghan until recent events and had been given more responsibility by senior board members. Billings was also working over in the western district so there was time for her to pay him a visit during her stay on Galt.

'From this moment on, you work for me,' she told the agent, noting the lack of surprise on his face. 'You will close your existing account that Billings pays into and open a new one, accepting transfers only from myself. Is that understood?'

'It is, Miss Hayward.' Akeman scratched at the scar over his left eye. 'What would you like me to do?'

'Firstly, you will relocate here.' There would be no turning back once she issued his orders. 'Whilst on Galt, you will watch every member of the board and report their movements or conversations to me and me only.'

'Also understood. Should I be looking for anything in particular?' He didn't seem fazed by the reassignment. 'Listening in on conversations would require the use of hacking apps.'

'Monitor all of their comms activity. Long range, short range, localised...everything. Shadow them too. Tell me who they meet with, where they are going and why.'

'If they go off-world?'

She thought for a moment. 'Tell me beforehand and I will let you know whether or not to leave Galt.'

Akeman tapped at the surface of the table. 'What about General Mitchell? He is the most senior member now.'

'*Every* member,' she reiterated. 'That goes for both the general and Colonel Garrett.'

'Right, that's the easy part of the assignment,' grinned Akeman. 'What's the hard part?'

Hayward allowed herself to smile at his nonchalance. 'I want you to keep a close eye on the Knights Templar. Their presence in this system unnerves me greatly, even more so since they allowed Lenaghan to be murdered. Their agreement with Taurus is going to come to an end and they will move Temple on. Until then, you'll watch them and tell me if anything seems out of place.'

'Of course.'

'Finally, I need you to get me in touch with some of your contacts.'

At this, Akeman's head tilted slightly. 'Can I ask why, Miss Hayward?'

She glanced out at the landing pads as a small planethopper swooped into view, turning in mid-air before starting its descent to Kingston.

'Because Taurus Galahad needs allies.'

Echo flagship Glaive
Miller system

Kurcher couldn't take his eyes off Drake's backside as they made their way into the command room of the *Glaive*.

No point lusting after her, said Frost. *You know her type.*

Aggressive, violent, deadly, listed Ercko. *You fuck when she wants and feelings don't ever get in the way. Turned on by adrenaline, not to mention bloodshed. Perfect.*

He smiled. If Drake wanted to use him for sex whenever they blew someone away, he was all up for that. He was always attracted to the dangerous ones.

So true, Trin whispered.

The room was busier than he had ever seen it. In addition to the usual command crew at their posts, there were a number of Hewn's most trusted pirates gathered around the star map. Next to the Echo leader himself was Fischer, who shot Kurcher a venomous glance as he entered before his eyes were drawn to Drake.

Guess she has more than one admirer, noted Frost.

Among the throng, Kurcher spotted a familiar brooding face and gave Broekow a nod which was not returned. The man standing alongside the sniper was the pilot charged with taking Broekow from one dull task to the next.

You got the better fucking deal when it came to pilot allocation, laughed Ercko.

'Stay alert, all of you,' boomed Hewn, coming to the end of some speech that Kurcher was glad to have missed. 'We don't want anyone sneaking into the Expanse via the back door while eyes are fixed elsewhere.'

When none of the pirates moved, Fischer flailed an arm. 'Well, you have your orders. Get to it.'

Once the room had emptied, Kurcher and Drake approached the map. Hewn was wearing a fixed scowl that didn't disappear as he regarded them both.

'Did you have to kill Keening?'

Drake bristled as expected. 'The cowardly fucker tried running. We weren't prepared to let him go back and tell his clients Echo were onto them.'

'You're a law unto yourself, Shannon,' smiled Fischer.

'I don't find it fucking funny,' Hewn snapped. 'Fortitude are up to something, allying themselves with Sigma Royal and buying stock from this *Luminary* bastard, plus swaggering around Tidewell City like they own the place.'

Kurcher tried to catch Broekow's eye. 'That must make Impramed nervous.'

'It's probably down to you.' Masami stepped in when Broekow remained silent. 'The shoot-out you had with Nova left permanent scars. The blood stains can still be seen in that plaza.'

Kurcher shrugged. 'Maybe it gave them the wake-up call they needed.'

'I'd recommend you read the report.' Hewn gave him a knowing look. 'And steer clear of Fortitude.'

As Drake made her way to a vacant seat, Kurcher looked down at the map. He instantly recognised Flint at the centre.

'What the fuck's going on?'

Hewn tapped the display, bringing up lines of coded data beneath the map. 'We monitor as many comms as possible and getting an ear on Flint after what happened was...difficult.'

'That's an understatement,' muttered Fischer.

Hewn turned to his second. 'Haven't you got somewhere to be, Vance?'

Fischer seemed startled by the unsubtle hint. 'I...uh...guess I do. Shannon, care to come with?'

Drake was leaning back on the chair, both feet up on a nearby console. 'Not really.'

Looking thoroughly dejected, Fischer strode from the room, not even willing to give Kurcher another of his scathing glances.

I'd watch that one, said D'Larro.

Pirates can't be trusted, enlister, added Santa Cruz.

'As I was saying, we've been listening in to corp comms for some time now.' Hewn waved his hand at the data. 'With all the shit going on elsewhere though, this latest intel is cause for concern.'

Kurcher wanted to tell him to get to the point. Why some people had to draw out conversations was beyond him.

Hewn continued. 'Each corp uses varying levels of frequency depending on the nature of the message being sent. They all have a coded band only to be used for the most confidential reports or broadcasts, and we've been trying to crack that code for years without much success.'

'Fascinating.' Kurcher hadn't meant to utter that.

'While you and Broekow were making your way back here, a message was sent from somewhere near Flint using Taurus Galahad's coded signal. Then another was sent using Sigma Royal's, and then Libra Centauri's.'

So the corps are whispering about Nova systems, big fucking deal.

Angard's words made Kurcher smile. 'I'm guessing you're about to tell us something we don't want to hear.'

Before Hewn could respond, Masami stepped forward. 'It's showing Straunia.'

At this, Kurcher noticed a slight twitch from Broekow, whose eyes finally lifted to stare at the map.

'It is,' Hewn said, watching the others intently. 'While we can't decipher most of the code, we worked out that all three mentioned Straunia and showed jump point activity. This set us to take a closer look at Nova's movements and their ships have vacated Flint completely, as far as we can tell.'

'Why would they remain there?' Broekow decided to join the conversation. 'Their home world was poisoned, their defense ships either destroyed or left dead in space, and there are no other suitable planets in the system they can colonise.'

'There is a very good reason for them to stay there,' Kurcher shot back. 'Have you forgotten that fucking *Grail* stranded on the surface?'

Broekow ignored him, instead turning to Hewn. 'Why the concern then?'

'Kurcher's right,' the pirate replied. 'They wouldn't abandon it. Nova hold all the cards when it comes to the *Grail*. Everyone else wants to get their hands on it and they know that. You wouldn't just give up alien technology like that.'

I don't like that glint in Hewn's eye, Frost said.

You brought that fucking Grail here, Angard growled.

'I don't need reminding.' Kurcher's outburst drew confused reactions from the others, including Drake. 'I mean, I know just how *important* that thing is lying on Straunia. We all do. It isn't going anywhere though so there's no point debating what Taurus, Libra or any of the other corps are going to do.'

'I like to know what they're up to.' Hewn was still looking at him strangely. 'You should too, especially as you're wanted by Devlin, Hengeveld and now Morton Hurst it seems.'

'I was a wanted man long before all this shit happened,' Kurcher cried, struggling to hold his temper. 'Sigma Royal are still after me for killing their people on Kismet. For all I know, Impramed are paying Fortitude to find me so they can interrogate me, just like Devlin wants to do.'

'Hengeveld wants me to hand you over to answer for the death of his brother.'

Kurcher didn't like them all staring at him. 'Fuck him.'

'That's your answer to everything and everyone,' snapped Broekow suddenly. 'As long as Davian fucking Kurcher survives, nothing else matters.'

The angry retort caught him by surprise, considering how quiet the sniper had been. It gave Hewn the chance to step in.

'I want both of you to go into hiding for a while, until the people looking for you start getting bored and focus their attention elsewhere. Having Libra putting pressure on me isn't good for business and I have other matters that need dealing with, like trying not to get shanked in the back by Jericho's Bold.'

'Hiding?' Kurcher wanted to laugh. 'We're in the Echo Expanse, where corps fear to tread. I'll just stay here on the *Glaive*. Broekow too.'

'I can speak for myself.'

'Maybe I should send you down to Seko with Vance,' suggested Hewn. 'You can help the Cobb Resistance settle in.'

'No.' Kurcher's refusal was swift. They may have been on a different planet now but he had no intention of spending more time with them. It had been hard enough stepping back onto that dying world when Rane took him there, knowing that some of those people could have been related to the ones he massacred. That all seemed so long ago now.

It was a different life back then, Frost assured him.

Once a killer, came Ercko's mocking voice.

'Fine, both of you will remain here for the time being.' Hewn couldn't be bothered arguing. 'Go get drunk or something. Just steer clear of trouble. Some of the crew would love to take their frustrations out on a Taurus enlister or an ex-corp soldier.'

'I could introduce you to a few if you like,' smirked Drake.

Hewn shook his head at her. 'You and Tariq will keep them both out of trouble, or I'll consider reassigning you to maintenance duty in sewage processing.'

Drake's blue lips pouted as she rose from the seat. 'Whatever. Come on then, fuckers, let's go.'

Kurcher waited as Broekow staggered past, looking like he was about to crumple to the floor any minute. Masami gave a nod to Hewn as he fell in behind.

'You're not telling us the full story.' Kurcher tried to read the Echo leader but always found it difficult. 'I don't want to wake up one day with a gun in my face, be it Hengeveld, Devlin or one of your people.'

'What would be the point?' asked Hewn, lowering his voice. 'You're dealing with matters I haven't got time to look into, even if the outcome isn't exactly what I hoped.

I once thought you to be a lying piece of shit corporate lapdog but you do have your uses.'

'So do you.'

As Kurcher left the command room, his mind was reeling. All of the corporations were up to something. Strange alliances were being made, bizarre coded messages were being whispered across the depths of space and the people he had fallen in with were holding something back. He didn't like not knowing.

Santa Cruz's fucking voice still swirled round his head. *Pirates can't be trusted.*

Cobb
Kalbrec system

'This is taking too long.'

Fuller didn't look up as he manhandled one of the heavy containers onto the waiting cart. He had heard that statement over and over during the last couple of months, to the point where he couldn't be bothered to give the same reply any longer. Instead, he wiped the sweat from his brow and shook his head as he moved to the next container.

'Cal, you'll give yourself a heart attack,' came Cho's voice, her tone always pleasing to his ears.

'Well, if you lot didn't stand around complaining so much and actually helped, we'd get done much quicker and I won't need a defib.' This time, he dared a glance back at the team and noticed an unsurprising absentee. 'Where the hell's Cretin?'

'Said he was going to help Vasily's guys in the hangar,' replied Cho, as she moved to the containers. 'Apparently his *skills* were best used over there.'

Fuller cursed under his breath. Most of the team dismantling the old Resistance base had volunteered to remain on Cobb while their friends and families followed Marie to the new home on Seko. Rettin had been ordered to stay behind and was proving more difficult to manage than usual.

'He needs to stop moping around,' grumbled Monk, a burly engineer who had been on Fuller's ship during the battle in Flint. 'Or he needs his head banging against the wall.'

As the others began moving the rest of the supply crates, Fuller found himself wishing things had been different. Sure, they were set to move to a world with greenery and water in abundance, but the cost of doing so had nearly destroyed everything he and Marie had worked towards.

They had lost so many people during the fight against the rogue fleet that he wondered whether it had all been worth it. Jennaut had been one of the first to die, his ship imploding after being stung by a wasp. Fuller missed the pessimist, just as he missed the rest who gave their lives. He didn't blame Jennaut's son for leaving once he found out what had happened. The lad simply boarded one of the transports Echo had provided and vanished, like so many others.

The tension upon their return had been unbearable at times. Opinions were divided as to whether he should have agreed to the alliance with the pirates. The benefit was the call of a new home, where they could thrive in a relatively safe region of space. Echo had upheld their promise, but the alliance would only have happened if they helped fight against the rogue Taurus fleet and the chances of them making it out alive were slim. He was slammed by many of his comrades for leading their loved ones to their deaths, yet now the remnants of the Resistance had a future and allies. No matter how he looked at it, Cobb would have eventually stopped giving up any hidden supply caches and their plans to raid Taurus depots would have resulted in them being hunted down and eradicated.

Then, of course, there was the emotional fallout. Marie and Rettin argued over her leading the Resistance to Seko, with the engineer understandably anxious about their unborn child. Not one to suffer fools lightly, Marie grew weary of his incessant nagging and ended their relationship, ordering him to stay behind and help with the dismantling operation like he was just some random grunt.

Fuller smiled as he remembered his last conversation with her, via the comms system on one of the Oakley's vessels. She had given birth to a healthy boy and wanted to name him Cal. She never even asked about Rettin.

'Which ship is this stuff going on?'

Cho's question brought him back to the moment. 'Whichever has the room.'

'This is the last load though, right?' Monk asked.

Fuller noticed all nine pairs of eyes turn to him. 'For you guys, yeah. It's going to take us a while longer to get the last of the materials up from the lower level so I'll be staying behind with a handful of volunteers to sort them, then lock up.'

'How much longer we talking?' Monk's eyes had narrowed.

'Month, maybe a bit longer.'

The big engineer thought for a moment, glancing around his colleagues. 'Count me in as a volunteer then.'

'Me too,' smiled Cho. 'Plus I'm sure Leeson is up for staying around here for a bit. Maybe some of Vasily's team too.'

Monk gave a rumbling laugh. 'And Butler would volunteer for Cretin to stay, I guess.'

'He could stay here permanently.' Cho was grinning as she activated one of the full carts and hopped onto the edge to avoid walking. 'He always thought he could run the place better than you, Cal.'

Fuller appreciated them volunteering. It saved him having to ask later. Most of the clean-up team would head off to Seko shortly and he had worked out he only needed seven or so to help with the remaining materials in deep storage. He was glad to have Monk and Cho stay. Vasily was an abrasive bastard at times but a hard worker, and Cho knew Leeson would hang around if she was, such was their relationship. He had already decided Rettin would be among them too.

The team guided the carts through the quiet hallways of the bunker and could hear the echoing voices from the hangar ahead long before they got anywhere near. It still seemed odd to walk into that vast chamber and not see many ships. The only five present were at the other end, bathed in daylight from the open access hatch above.

Fuller eyed his own ship with regret. The hull was two thirds scorched from close calls with the wasps, but it had held together. Once they reached Seko, it would be dismantled for parts.

The other four weren't exactly pristine. The one belonging to Vasily reflected the pilot's personality well: rough round the edges, yet solid and reliable. Another had been flown by Jennaut's son for a time but he had left that behind too.

'I'd like to get this shit to the surface some time before nightfall.' Vasily was yelling at the men around him, most of whom were members of his personal maintenance and engineering team. 'Ah, our esteemed leader honours us with his presence.'

Fuller always hated sarcasm. 'We on track?'

'Yes, sir.' Vasily poked a thumb at a group of men loading one of the ships. 'Despite having Cretin helping us.'

Everyone else used the nickname behind his back. Vasily knew Rettin wouldn't dare challenge him. The glare from the latter though before he disappeared into the ship didn't go unnoticed.

'Cho, make sure all those crates are kept together up there,' Fuller called, as the carts were wheeled onto the lift.

She smiled and waved as the old machinery spluttered to life. As he watched the team ascend to the surface and the hangar was plunged back into artificial light, Fuller led Vasily to one side.

'We're taking too long getting this penultimate load away. The longer we delay, the higher the risk of receiving a *visit* from your old friends.'

Vasily grimaced as he leant forward. 'Nobody from Taurus is my friend.'

Fuller wanted to take a step back. Having the ugly face so close was unnerving enough but he knew Vasily was not one to upset.

'Poor choice of words. Look, we need to get those ships up top and ready for launch.'

'Understood. I'll crack the whip harder.'

'Have you managed to sort those devices we spoke about?'

Vasily gave a slow nod. 'I'll place them myself once the others are above ground, you have my word.'

'And they'll do the job?' Fuller tried not to sound desperate.

'They will. Nobody will be able to access the lower levels again once they go off.'

Fuller gave him a thankful pat on the shoulder and, as Vasily wandered away barking his orders once more, the leader of the Cobb Resistance headed back out of the hangar. He didn't like putting all his trust in Vasily, especially considering the man had once been a Taurus Galahad goon, but he was the only one left with experience setting explosives. There was no way he was about to let Taurus or anyone else descend on the abandoned base and unearth what they were leaving below.

As he made his way through the base, peering into darkened chambers, he arrived in the meeting room. The metal table and surrounding seats were still present. They would have new furniture for the senior members of the Resistance to meet around soon, not the cold grey shit that was the best Cobb could offer.

He ran his finger along the table surface as he passed, finding a thick layer of dust had gathered since it was last used. It struck him as madness that he was looking forward to arriving on Seko to start a new life, but that at the same time a part of him would miss the uninviting bunker.

'Reminiscing?'

Fuller's heart damned near stopped but he managed to smile as he turned to face Hedmun Oakley. 'Always. What can I help you with, captain?'

'Please, no need to be so formal.'

Fuller knew the man wouldn't have been saying that had some of the others been present. He watched as the officer paced around the opposite end of the table, shooting amused glances at the bland furnishings and dull walls. In a room of browns and greys, Oakley's blue and green uniform seemed very out of place. However his hair was nearly the same colour as the table.

'I admire you, Cal, I really do.'

Fuller didn't like the condescending tone. 'Why's that?'

'You could've just laid down and died after the war. You never gave up though, despite the fact Cobb was finished.'

'Many did,' Fuller reminded him. 'Their bodies are still out there on the surface buried under the dust and debris.'

'I can't imagine what it must have been like.' Oakley placed his hands on the back of one of the chairs. 'Cobb was supposed to be a great success story.'

Fuller allowed himself a wry smile. 'It was, for many years. Jefferson was an outstanding colony. As with most corp-owned worlds though, there is always something to spark the conflict.'

'True. Civil war is rife on many planets unfortunately. Cradle has been in danger of descending into chaos too for years thanks to disagreements between families.'

'I don't know why what happened here is referred to as a *civil* war,' said Fuller, feeling a need to correct him. 'There were supply incidents between colonies and they got out of hand. It wasn't a war until Taurus got involved.'

'Forgive me, I didn't mean to stir up bad memories.'

Of course he did. 'It was a long time ago, Hedmun, and my people have suffered enough for it. It's time for a new chapter.'

Oakley straightened, nodding in agreement. 'This alliance will only help us moving forward. We both lost a lot in that battle and need time to regroup.'

Fuller approached the officer. 'We appreciate your help in moving the remaining goods to Seko. If we can help the Oakley fleet in any way, you need just ask.'

'If you have any ideas on how we can keep Taurus Galahad out of the Oralia system or how I can protect my own family from those on Cradle who would usurp us, I'm all ears.'

Fuller saw a change in Oakley's demeanour then; concern behind those intelligent eyes. No matter how arrogant or patronising he was, the officer was clearly loyal to the loved ones on Cradle. A part of Fuller wanted to ask how such a stoic family could protect a cold-blooded killer like Oakley's niece, Tara, but he would keep his knowledge of her quiet for now, along with the source of that information.

'Most of my people will be ready to leave soon.' He decided to redirect the conversation. 'Then it will just be myself and several others left here to lock it all up.'

'As mentioned before, Cal, I'll remain on Cobb with you, then see you safely to Seko. I did promise your feisty head of ops I would.'

Fuller chuckled. 'And you don't want to get on her bad side.'

Oakley gave him a quick look up and down. 'You need some rest. When was the last time you slept?'

‘Oh, I think it was about eighteen years ago.’ Fuller shrugged. ‘I’m sixty-two years old, Hedmun. I always look like I need rest.’

At this, Oakley gave a strange cackle. ‘Only five years older than me.’

As the two shared a rare moment of mirth, a figure shuffled into the room.

‘So, we’ve got a problem with the lift,’ Rettin announced. ‘Won’t come back down.’

Fuller’s smile faded as he regarded the engineer with obvious contempt. Cretin’s arrival always had that effect on him.

‘Sorry, Hedmun. No peace for the wicked.’

Straunia
Flint system

The shuttle jolted for the sixth time and Mitchell tried to give a reassuring smile to the only passenger who was noticeably affected by the turbulence.

'It will pass in a moment, doctor.'

Li looked up at him, his face pale but eyes burning angrily. 'Straunia has undergone many changes, including unusual activity throughout both the lower and upper atmosphere. To my reckoning, we shouldn't be experiencing any problems like this.'

Mitchell scanned the rest of the faces around them. 'Do they look worried?'

'*They* have probably been dropped onto more planets they care to remember. This is new to me.'

The general noticed a couple of his men exchanging smirks and let it slide. The doctor was indeed the odd one out among the twenty soldiers on board the shuttle. They were all hand-picked personally by Mitchell; experienced men and women who were proven in battle. They were reliable and handy to have in case they ran into trouble. The same went for the additional forty soldiers descending to the surface in the other two shuttles. One squad was led by Byrne, the other by O'Brien. Ishlan had been left in command of the *Victory* in orbit, watching for any signs of activity from the other corps.

'Sir, ten minutes,' came the pilot's voice through his comms app.

'Get us as close to the *Grail* as possible,' Mitchell responded.

'Afraid it will have to be a landing just south of Brandt, sir. The ground is too unstable around the *Grail* itself.'

'Fine.' Mitchell meant to sound pissed off. 'Can you patch a feed in here so I can see what we're heading down into?'

A moment later, two screens built into the cabin walls flickered to life and they all turned to take in the scene below.

'Christ.' Mitchell watched as the fallen *Grail* appeared.

They could only see half of it, such was the immense size, but could make out the lower section. In the bottom right corner of the screen sat the remnants of Brandt, the colony just tiny dark squares against a grey surface. A rotating circle of light showed exactly where the shuttle would be setting down.

'Look there, general.' Li's discomfort had evaporated upon seeing the *Grail* in all its glory. 'The main body of the structure isn't even broken. It didn't tear or shred either, which is quite frankly amazing considering it fell onto a planet.'

'Glad you came now, doctor?'

Li didn't take his eyes off the screen. 'Indeed. It feels somewhat surreal though, don't you think? Here we are heading down onto a world that was bustling with life several months ago. Three Taurus shuttles descending to the Nova homeworld.'

'I didn't think I would ever set foot on Straunia,' Mitchell admitted. 'We can't pass up the opportunity though.'

'I find it hard to believe Nova vacated Flint completely.' Li's eyes were still firmly fixed on the *Grail*. 'Are you not worried they will come back here? They must know Taurus would send people.'

Mitchell saw some of the soldiers glance his way, keen to hear the answer to that particular question. 'Their fleet is a long way away, doctor. When we received word that Straunia was officially branded a quaran and that Nova had upped and left, I was suspicious of course. However, that same coded report contained tracking signatures for most of their fleet, showing that they were spread across systems like Valen, Armstrong and, more importantly, Ixxis. The Nova ships in Ixxis checked out. I'm not surprised either, as Ixxis is the closest of their systems to Berg and Coldrig.'

'But the research...' blurted Li, finally looking at the general.

'Don't panic. Nova wouldn't dare go to Berg with the number of ships we have there. The guardians alone are deterrant enough.

Anyway, Ishlan is monitoring the other signatures for their fleet from orbit. If they decided to return to Flint, we'd be long gone.'

Li seemed satisfied with the reply as his gaze once more went to the screen, a finger tapping nervously at his lip.

'General?' The pilot's voice had an urgency to it.

'Go ahead.'

'Sir, we're seeing a ship down there. Scans didn't pick it up for some reason but it's near the centre of Brandt.'

'Can you tell what it is?'

The pilot was silent for a moment. 'Looks like a small explorer-class vessel. Probably Nova. I'll highlight it on the screen for you.'

Mitchell saw a new circle appear. The pilot certainly had keen eyes. To him, it looked like just another small structure. Sure enough though, he saw the shape of the wings and the hull as they got closer. He recognised it then as a Nova design.

The screens suddenly both flickered with static then went dark. At the same time, the shuttle pitched violently to the side, making even the hardened soldiers grip the arms of their seats. Li vomited.

'Report,' cried Mitchell, linking to the pilot's comms.

'Sorry, sir. We just lost local navigation so I've taken back full manual control. My apps have been affected too. Quite a few systems just went offline.'

'Just get us down.' Mitchell looked around the cabin. 'Apps still alive?'

His sharpshooters shook their heads, then one of the medics followed suit after checking his HDU. As a few others gave negative responses, Mitchell cursed and tried to link his comms to the other shuttles.

'Byrne, O'Brien, can you hear me?'

There was only static for a few seconds, then a gruff voice boomed into his ear. 'This is Byrne, sir. Everything okay?'

'Tech is being temperamental here.'

'Same here.' This time, it was O'Brien's jovial tone that came through. 'We need new app manufacturers, general.'

'When we land, I want Byrne's squad with me. O'Brien, you'll take your men to the centre of Brandt and investigate that Nova ship before joining us at the *Grail*. Understood?'

Both men did.

'This disruption could be something to do with the *Grail*,' Li remarked, wiping his mouth with a shaking hand. 'Some of our technology in the labs struggled as we delved deeper into the artefacts, occasionally going offline or giving one of the team an unfortunate shock.'

Mitchell's brow furrowed. 'You didn't tell me that, doctor.'

'The amount of information we were gleaning was immense, general. Some things just became an everyday occurrence that we didn't think much of.'

'If we plunge suddenly from the sky, we'll know who to blame then.'

Li slouched back in his seat, looking distinctly green. Mitchell tried to peer out of one of the small windows nearby but could only see grey. He looked down at the assault rifle on his lap. That was tech he could trust, but there wouldn't be much need for it on a dead world.

~

'Don't take your eyes off that screen.'

The comms officer was only too keen to oblige. 'Yes, lieutenant.'

Despite being back in the big seat, Ishlan was uncomfortable. The *Victory* wasn't her ship. Her beloved *Ravenedge* was somewhere in Galt, under the command of a man destined to take Mitchell's place once the general stood down. Here *she* was in orbit of Straunia, of all places.

Ishlan checked the HDU, studying the various Nova signatures dotted around the galaxy. Her eyes were drawn to the main screen. Alongside the *Victory* sat the two other assault ships the general had chosen to accompany them on the mission. Both were smaller than the flagship, yet packed quite a punch. She had seen the *Austin* on many occasions, as it often followed Mitchell wherever he went. The *Riordan* though was a relatively new ship, built for protection not speed.

If it had been her call, she would have brought half the fleet with them. She had advised the general and he had chosen to ignore her. Perhaps that was why she was sat in orbit and the others were down on the surface. Mitchell didn't like being told what to do, especially by a strong woman. She could only imagine his wife must have been a meek creature.

The more she thought about it though, the happier she was to be sat on the command deck of the *Victory*. She had seen the *Grail* in action and didn't want to lay eyes on it again any time soon, despite the fact it was so vast it could be seen easily from orbit, like some odd-shaped mountain range.

Ishlan sat in silent contemplation for some time, listening to the chatter among the anxious crew. This was not how her life should have turned out. Everything had been progressing so well until the day Santa Cruz assigned her to his personal fleet; the rogue fleet, as it had come to be known. There was simply no turning back once he had unleashed the alien weapon on unsuspecting Meta. Watching that sickly aura spread across the Sigma homeworld had left a permanent scar in her mind. She had wanted to take the *Ravenedge* and run, but career was always the priority for her. Looking back, her common sense must have completely abandoned her, to have thought that Taurus Galahad would actually reward them for what had happened. She had played a part in the escalation in the violence between the corps since that time. Perhaps she should have stayed in the cell.

'Lieutenant?'

She hated being reminded of her demotion too. 'What is it?'

A bead of sweat had formed on the comms officer's forehead. 'Two Sigma Royal assault ships approaching Straunia.'

Ishlan nearly launched herself from the command chair. 'How the hell didn't we detect them sooner?'

'They must have conflector tech,' offered another of the officers.

Sigma had always shunned conflectors, claiming it was used only by cowards. They preferred the direct approach.

'So how come we're detecting them now?' she asked, angrily. 'And why didn't we pick up the jump point activating?'

There was no answer to that, just perplexed faces.

'Bring all weapons online.' Ishlan took up a position next to the tactical console. 'I don't want them firing first, if it comes to that.'

She was surprised to see Sigma ships anywhere outside their own systems. They had, relatively speaking, kept to themselves since the attack on Meta. She just hoped they weren't out for revenge and had come to Flint for the same reason Taurus had, although it raised the question as to how they found out.

'There's something different about their ships,' the comms officer said. 'Reinforced hull plating by the looks of it.'

Ishlan swore quietly. 'Send word to the general, then tell the *Austin* and *Riordan* to take up intercept positions.' She drew in a deep breath. 'I want to speak to the Sigma commanders as soon as they are in range.'

~

Mitchell's breath was loud in his ears as the *Grail* grew ever closer. The ground had risen significantly when the structure crashed onto the surface, meaning an awkward climb. Splinters of rock protruded up like small peaks all around the *Grail*, making their approach less direct than he had wanted.

Behind him, Li had been joined by the other four scientists who landed with O'Brien's squad. Mitchell could see their awestruck expressions through the masks as they gazed up at the behemoth before them.

He glanced back at Brandt. The colony had made a chill run the length of his spine when they first left the shuttle. No sounds, no movement, no bodies. The people had disappeared completely, as had all of the animal life that would have been rampant on Straunia. The *Grail* had wiped every last speck of life from the planet and then made sure there wouldn't even be any breathable air. He had seen worlds torn apart by war, leaving death and destruction everywhere. But it was more unnerving to walk on a planet that seemed so peaceful in its demise.

Mitchell heard Byrne shout an order to some of the soldiers up ahead but the sound was muffled somewhat by the mask. He hated wearing them but there was no alternative. Byrne was on point with his squad spread out either side, the brutish officer quick to ensure there was ample protection ahead of the general and science team.

'There is a strange feeling here,' Li stated, his voice clear via comms app. 'Like there is a charge in the air and the gravity shifts with every step.'

'It feels like the closer we get, the harder it is to walk,' Mitchell added.

The *Grail* may have been blocking the entire horizon but it was still some distance away.

Li and his colleagues began tapping furiously at their HDUs, trying to understand what might be causing the bizarre sensations.

'General, O'Brien here.' The lieutenant's voice crackled with static. 'We've arrived at the ship and doesn't seem to be anyone home. Designation is *Cognis*. Haven't been able to check our intel on it as comms to the *Victory* are shit.'

'Can you gain access to it?'

'If our apps were working properly, perhaps.'

Mitchell looked up at the *Grail*. 'The crew must be here somewhere. Run a quick sweep of the ruins then catch us up.'

'Understood. Sir...hearing...coming from...not...' After cutting in and out, O'Brien's voice faded into static.

Byrne looked at Mitchell and shrugged, showing he was having the same problem. Then came a single shot, echoing loudly off the surrounding rocks. Mitchell initially thought it had come from Brandt until he saw the head of one of his men up front snap back, a spray of red billowing into the air.

'Take cover,' yelled Byrne, as several figures rose from hiding places among the stone splinters and opened fire with assault rifles.

Mitchell swung his own rifle up, sending a burst in the direction of the ambushers before grabbing Li and shoving him towards the nearest jagged boulder. The other scientists scuttled after them, one dropping his HDU in the panic.

As there was an exchange of gunfire and the sound of bullets bouncing off the terrain, Mitchell dared a glance out and saw three Taurus soldiers already down, with Byrne pinned fifteen or so metres ahead. The officer was angrily tapping the side of his helmet, clearly unable to get his apps functioning.

He glimpsed one of his sharpshooters flit between cover opposite, then another single shot rang out and a fourth Taurus soldier crumpled to the ground, his mask shattered where the bullet passed through.

'Who are they?' Li asked, clearly on the brink of panicking himself.

Mitchell knew his apps weren't exactly working properly. If they were, he would've been alerted to the presence of non-Taurus personnel. He tried to activate his sense link anyway. When he scanned the vicinity, there were a couple of lifesign pings and three of his own soldiers showed up on thermal. Then a lone figure several metres above them was highlighted, only to vanish five seconds later. It was enough time for him to get a read.

'Fucking Libra Centauri,' he snarled, more to any soldiers nearby than to Li. He opened Taurus-wide comms. 'Anyone who can hear me, these cowardly bastards are Libra. Their sniper is six point six metres west of my current position, up top. Take him out.'

As the exchange continued, only increasing in ferocity, two of Mitchell's squad sent grenades up into the rocks where the Libra sniper was lurking. The explosions sent stone fragments in all directions, some pelting the general and the frightened scientists. When Mitchell glanced out again, he spotted the sniper darting for new cover, green armour clear against the terrain. Before he could utter another command though, the Taurus sharpshooter he had seen briefly moments ago swung into view and sent two shots at the moving target. The first missed by inches. The second struck the sniper in the side, spinning the man into the air and off his perch.

The sharpshooter waited too long to move though, and a burst of rifle fire cut him down, his body falling clumsily into a gap between two boulders.

More Libra soldiers were appearing and it was clear they had a significant force. It was also clear to Mitchell that they had at least one assault ship hiding in orbit somewhere. He wouldn't have expected Libra to shoot first and ask questions later. Then again, this was a unique situation they found themselves in and nobody was willing to share the *Grail*.

Two Libra soldiers broke from cover, rushing towards the trapped Byrne. Mitchell stepped out behind them and gunned both down.

'Everyone regroup near my position,' he ordered.

The desperate battle raged for another ten minutes as thirty Taurus soldiers made their way to the rocks surrounding their general. Two had been wounded and were being supported by medics. Byrne was the last to make a run for it, covered by the combined Taurus gunfire which made the Libra force think twice about moving into the open.

'O'Brien,' called Mitchell. 'We need your squad here now.'

He knew that the other twenty soldiers would swing the battle in their favour, unless Libra had even more waiting in the wings. For now, they had to hunker down and hold position, hopefully giving O'Brien enough time.

As the dust settled and a deafening silence fell on the area, Mitchell noticed Byrne's arm was bleeding and pointed it out to one of the medics.

The lieutenant simply grimaced as he was examined and a painkill shot administered.

'How the fuck did they get here before us?' Byrne asked. 'They must've been lurking near Flint, waiting for an opportunity.'

'Libra have spies everywhere,' replied Mitchell. 'Small wonder they picked up on Nova leaving.'

'Well they're certainly not in the mood to talk.' Byrne checked his rifle. 'I say we kill every last one of them while Ishlan hunts down their ship.'

'We need the equipment on the shuttle to contact orbit. Apps are damned near useless.'

Li tapped Mitchell's shoulder. 'General, I think we should return to the shuttles for now then. The *Grail* isn't going anywhere. Besides, I'm growing concerned with the fact our mobility is being affected by this charged atmosphere. You must all be feeling it too.'

Mitchell nodded. 'Just lifting a rifle is making me sweat. Those Libra soldiers will be experiencing it too though.'

'Do you not think this is exactly what Sapphire Nova wanted?' Li asked, causing a few uneasy glances among the nearby men and women. 'Bringing us here at the same time as Libra Centauri would only ever result in bloodshed.'

'Of course it's what they wanted.' Mitchell didn't want to admit that he may have walked them into a trap. 'Then again, Libra and Nova could be working together here. There are stranger alliances out there.'

Byrne pushed the medic away and hefted his rifle. 'Let's just kill them and then work out what they were doing here. Not really the time for chatter.'

Mitchell wanted to order Li and his scientists back to the shuttles but anyone stepping out into the open was dead. This was not a good situation for any of them and he had to find a way out of it quickly.

Rifle fire was heard in the direction of the *Grail*, which was odd. O'Brien wouldn't have been able to find a way to flank the Libra force yet, and the gunfire was too distant to be aimed at them, unless one of the missing Taurus soldiers had managed to get lost in the rocks.

'Sir, they're coming,' said one woman, her armour covered in dust and scratched by the jagged terrain.

Mitchell tried to activate his sense app again. He had to suffer an irritating tickle behind the eyes before he saw at least twenty thermal forms moving towards them. There was no time to wait for O'Brien's reinforcements.

'This is it.' He raised his rifle. 'Kill them all.'

Byrne was the first to step out, his rifle instantly bursting into life. This gave the other Taurus soldiers the courage to move up alongside him, including Mitchell.

As the Libra force began returning fire, once again trying to dive for cover, the sound of a shuttle could be heard above the clamour. Within seconds, a vessel soared overhead, coming to an abrupt halt directly above the battle. The emblem emblazoned on the red and black hull was unmistakeable.

As both sides ceased fire to stare up at it, the underneath of the Sigma Royal shuttle opened and two large shapes were dropped. The assault mechs landed with such force that Mitchell felt the ground shake and, when their pale blue visual sensors blinked on, the general knew the situation had just sunk further into the shit.

'Move,' was all he could yell.

The four shrikes mounted on both mechs buzzed briefly before unleashing a terrifying barrage into the Taurus ranks. Mitchell and Byrne barely managed to avoid being torn apart, flinging themselves to the ground at the feet of the scientists. A number of the soldiers were not so lucky and ended up lying several metres from where they had been standing, some with limbs even further afield.

Just as Mitchell tried to fathom an alliance between Libra and Sigma, one of the mechs turned and opened fire on the ambushers, moving like a mechanical insect on its four legs. There was something much more fluid about their motions though when compared to other mechs he had seen in action.

Beside him, Byrne fired up at the hovering shuttle and it slowly moved off. The chances of a bullet actually piercing the reinforced hull plating was slim, yet Mitchell had seen a lone gunman bring a shuttle down before with one lucky strike.

The red and black mechs began another attack. The one focusing on Taurus began moving forward, closing on the position where the survivors were huddled against the rocks. The constant hum of the shrikes filled the air while debris flew in all directions, causing clouds of dust to engulf the scene.

Mitchell saw an opportunity as visibility became vastly reduced among the chaos. 'Retreat,' he yelled, hoping his people could hear him above the clamour. 'Get back to the shuttles.'

Li and his scientists didn't need to be told twice, sprinting away from the general. Through his mask, Mitchell tried to see where the rest of the soldiers were. His app was unresponsive, making it even harder to pinpoint who was where.

Byrne suddenly lurched into view. 'Get back, sir. We'll cover you best we can.'

Through the dust cloud, Mitchell could make out the glow of the mech's sensors. He turned and ran, Brandt appearing through the gloom. Li was a good ten metres or so ahead but one of the scientists had fallen, a rogue bullet having driven into his back. Behind him, Mitchell heard assault rifles firing and frantic shouts from both Taurus and Libra personnel alike. The sound of the shrikes was relentless, buzzing in his brain.

A stream of bullets fizzed past him, inches from his shoulder. Another scientist stumbled and fell, her body lifeless before it hit the ground.

Mitchell needed to gauge what was happening behind him so slid to a halt, crouched and spun, rifle ready to open fire on anyone other than a Taurus soldier bearing down on him. The dust cloud had shifted to reveal the true carnage. Bodies were sprawled across the terrain, both Taurus and Libra, and many of the rocks they had taken cover behind were broken or spattered with blood. One of the mechs had gone after the Libra force, the echo of its shrikes still resounding off the jagged landscape. The other was engaged in a battle with Byrne and eight soldiers who had managed to survive the onslaught and were trying their best to outflank the mech. Mitchell wanted to tell them it was futile, especially as the construct could simply swivel three-sixty to engage opponents. The mech was also managing to track all the soldiers, which struck him again as strange considering it seemed to know their position even when they were hidden.

Mitchell looked up at the Sigma shuttle, which was still lurking nearby. Somehow, the men on board must have been relaying tactical information to the mech.

The *Grail* formed a sinister backdrop to the firefight, casting a monstrous shadow across the entire region as the Flint sun began to move behind it.

It was then Mitchell noticed several figures standing high up among the rocks, much nearer to the *Grail*. He was too far away to make out uniforms or colours, so could only assume it was perhaps the Libra officers watching the mechs ruin their ambush plans. It could of course have been Sigma Royal, hoping to witness a bloodbath when their ship dropped the mechs.

As the pained cry of one of the Taurus soldiers pulled his attention back to the battle, Mitchell's eye was drawn to movement just behind the mech. At first, he thought that one of the two fighting corps had managed to manoeuvre men into the robot's blindspot, but it became clear that the people emerging from the rocks were not wearing armour. They were not even wearing helmets or masks.

'What the fuck?' was all he could utter as he watched more and more forms walk calmly into the open, their hands devoid of weapons.

His own soldiers ceased fire as they too saw the newcomers, Byrne glancing back at him no doubt with a similarly confused look. Even the mech's shrikes whirred to a sudden halt. As silence descended once more and the unprotected men and women quietly approached, Mitchell felt a need to run for the shuttles. He stood and turned, startled to see that more had appeared from the terrain alongside him, but promptly froze to the spot as he looked into the writhing silver sockets where their eyes had once been.

~

'Prepare to fire,' ordered Ishlan. 'We give them the five minutes to leave orbit.'

Her talks with the commanding officers of the two Sigma assault ships couldn't have gone any worse. Realising that they were just buying time for that shuttle to enter the Straunia atmosphere had really pissed her off though. There must have been something important on it. She had never seen a shuttle fitted with short range conflector tech before.

'I don't think they will back off,' said the comms officer, stating the obvious.

'More fool them,' she snapped. 'Have you managed to break through the static yet?'

The officer looked exasperated. 'No, lieutenant. There is so much interference coming up from the planet. I've never seen anything like it.'

'Keep trying. The general needs to know what's happening up here and we need to know what the hell is going on down there.'

Ishlan looked at the screen. The two Sigma vessels had definitely taken up an aggressive stance. At least the *Austin* and *Riordan* were ready to pounce should the need arise.

She grabbed her HDU, checking in on the Nova signatures again. None of them had moved. Inspecting the position of the Nova fleet was becoming an obsession.

She found it difficult to comprehend what it must have been like, having so many people snuffed out in the blink of an eye. Had Nova felt guilty afterwards for not being able to protect their citizens? Had it been that guilt that drove them to retaliate against the other corps in such a strange way, assassinating key officers and members of the board? Of course, it wasn't common knowledge among Taurus citizens that they had killed some of the Sigma and Libra hierarchy too. Not even those two corps were aware Taurus knew, but Mitchell had made good use of an expansive spy network.

'Lieutenant Ishlan?' The comms officer sounded nervous.

She strode to his console, taking note of the fact he was gripping the side of his screen tightly, his knuckles white. 'More bad news?'

'Ten ships have just jumped into Flint. All carry Sapphire Nova signatures.'

'Not possible,' she frowned, glancing between the screen and her HDU. 'All their ships are elsewhere.'

The officer checked his systems again, via console and app. 'It's confirmed. We have a fleet of ten Nova assault vessels heading for Straunia.' He looked up at her with fearful eyes. 'Led by the *Harbinger*.'

Ishlan needed to think fast. If the comms data was correct, they were now trapped in Flint. She scanned over the signatures on her HDU again. Taurus had been given false intel, yet it had come through a secure coded channel unique to their organisation. The only way it could have happened was if someone was working with Nova to supply those codes.

'The Sigma ships are breaking orbit,' came a shout behind her.

Sure enough, the red and black assault vessels were moving away. Ishlan didn't know where they could go apart from deeper into the system, to try hiding close to the Flint sun. Perhaps they would head for the asteroid belt on the edge of the system and hope to somehow reach the jump point by circling around behind the Nova fleet.

'What are your orders, lieutenant?' asked the comms officer.

She couldn't leave Mitchell, Byrne, O'Brien and their squads behind, plus there was still time before the Nova ships arrived at the planet. There really was only one course of action befitting the flagship of the Taurus Galahad fleet.

'We hold our ground.'

~

There was no waking up from this nightmare.

Mitchell's lungs were burning as he ran and the shuttles didn't seem to be getting any closer. The strange air surrounding him was making it hard to move, although those *things* didn't seem to have the same problem.

Li had managed to stay several paces ahead, although only one other scientist remained now. The others had been grabbed by those eyeless abominations, just as so many of the surviving soldiers had been. Behind him, Byrne was trying to keep up but the lieutenant was struggling with a leg wound he had sustained while trying to escape. Mitchell didn't see how he had been injured. It was clear he wouldn't reach the shuttle before the crowd of maskless men and women caught up.

The crack in Mitchell's mask was making it difficult to see clearly and he focused on Li, making sure he followed the scientist as best he could. All he could hear was Li's muffled voice saying over and over that he wished he had never joined the expedition.

He daren't look back, afraid of what was pursuing them. It hadn't taken him much time to realise that they were colonists. Some were still wearing clothing marked with the Sapphire Nova logo. It was the child he saw that had horrified him the most though, a badge pinned to the lad's dirty shirt that read *Brandt School.*

Questions had reeled through Mitchell's mind when he first saw them all. What had the *Grail* done to these poor people? How were they alive? What had happened to their eyes?

The silver he had seen in their sockets was a strange type of tech, like metal strands constantly moving and flowing across one another. Beneath their exposed skin, the occasional glimpse of silver or occasionally light blue could be seen, as though their very veins were filled with the same tech.

Every single man, woman and child was the same, walking calmly towards him silently and without expression. The answer to one of his questions was that they weren't alive, at least not in the human sense of the word.

Mitchell had seen Byrne open fire on them. The bullets tore holes in the skin, but no blood poured from the wounds, just shards of silver. One shot had hit a man square in the skull, blowing part of it away and exposing a grey brain riddled with tech, like tiny metal maggots infesting the tissue. None of the colonists had fallen to Byrne's rifle, so the officer had thrown an explosive into their midst. Bodies were flung in all directions, scorched and broken, yet still they rose and began the unnervingly calm walk again, albeit staggering on twisted legs.

Mitchell heard a roar above and saw the Sigma shuttle vanishing into the sky, keen to flee the planet. He wished he was on board, even if that meant at gunpoint. He hadn't seen the two mechs for some time and wondered why they had stopped firing.

'Sir.' Byrne's voice came through hoarse. 'I'll buy you time to get to the shuttle. My leg's fucked so no point flogging a dead horse.'

This time, Mitchell did look back. His lieutenant had come to a halt and was removing the heavier equipment slung around his body. Behind and to the side of him, the colonists were closing. He gave the general one quick salute, then turned his rifle on the approaching mass.

'Good luck, Byrne.'

Behind the crowd, Mitchell spotted one of the mechs lurch into view. Its movement seemed less fluid now, he noticed, and the visual sensors had changed colour from blue to silver. Fear knotted his stomach yet again as it began moving forwards.

Mitchell, Li and the last scientist found energy from somewhere, driving for the shuttles. The general heard Byrne's gunfire abruptly cease and it was O'Brien's voice that suddenly rang in his ears.

'General, we have to get the fuck out of here.'

Mitchell was about to ask his position when the officer came sprinting into view on the other side of the shuttles, near Brandt. He was hoping to see more soldiers following the lieutenant. Instead, a second crowd of colonists meandered from the ruins, streaming from the alleys and streets.

O'Brien leapt into one of the shuttles, its engines slowly coming to life, then appeared in the doorway beckoning frantically to the three survivors.

A familiar hum filled the air, followed by a fresh barrage of shrike fire which flew over Mitchell's head and struck the shuttle. O'Brien threw himself back inside as the mech's bullet stream hammered the hull, moving quickly down towards the engines. The sheer impact of the combined shrike attack broke through the plating around the engine ports and the rear of the shuttle exploded, flipping the rest of the small ship into the air.

Li and his scientist were thrown onto their backs by the blast. Mitchell instinctively dived to the ground as debris rained on them.

'Doctor, are you okay?' he called.

Li groaned and propped himself up on one elbow, his spectacles nowhere to be seen. The look on the man's face was one of defeat.

As Mitchell began pushing himself up, grabbing his rifle, the mech broke through the approaching wave of colonists, shrikes still smoking. Something dark was attached to the construct's chassis; something moving. Mitchell rubbed at his eyes to make sure he wasn't seeing things, then watched as whatever it was unfurled, revealing slivers of silver and pale blue across a long body. Bizarre tendril-like appendages appeared from it, four of them black and jagged, the other two gleaming with the same silvery tech.

There was something oddly familiar about the creature and Mitchell's gaze momentarily shifted to the fallen leviathan lying across the horizon, shafts of the fading sun striking out from behind it. There was a distinct similarity between the two; same ridged, almost chitinous body, same dark hue and same alien design.

The creature moved up to perch alongside the head of the mech, showing Mitchell that it was much larger than he had first thought. Six narrow limbs each clung to the chassis near its abdomen, if that was what he could call it, and it seemed to be watching him, despite the fact he couldn't see any eyes in the darkness.

'Sir...help...'

Mitchell glanced back at the smouldering remnants of the shuttle and saw O'Brien crawling from the broken cabin. The colonists that were following the lieutenant appeared around the edge of the ship and Mitchell could only watch as another of the creatures clambered over the shuttle to stand directly above the stricken officer. Two of the dark tendrils reached out, wrapping around O'Brien's torso before lifting him effortlessly into the air. In an instant, one of the silver-flecked appendages lashed out and embedded into the back of his neck. A moment later, his body spasmed then went limp, the creature lowering him back to the ground surprisingly gently.

The silver-eyed colonists were surrounding them and Mitchell looked over at the two scientists, who were struck either by awe or fear, possibly both.

'I'm sorry,' he told them, before aiming his weapon at the creature poised on top of the mech.

'General, stop,' Li cried, slowly getting to his feet. 'Perhaps there is another course of action instead of violence.'

Mitchell pressed the butt of the rifle hard against his shoulder. The creature moved slightly and the mech's silver sensors focused solely on the general.

'You should listen to the doctor, sir.'

The voice caused him to hesitate and he watched in utter disbelief as Byrne stepped from the crowd. The Taurus officer's mask had gone and he was wearing a broad smile as he slowly approached the general.

'That's close enough,' Mitchell growled, his rifle still trained on the dark form watching from the safety of the mech. 'What the fuck is going on?'

Byrne held both hands aloft, showing he had no weapon. 'Please put down the gun, sir. We don't want this to end badly for you. We would rather you joined us.'

'Us?' Mitchell looked around at the abominations. 'A few moments ago, you were trying to kill these people.'

'True.' Byrne shrugged. 'That was before I understood.'

'Doctor Li,' called Mitchell. 'What's happening here?'

When his question was met only with silence, the general glanced back and all hope drained from him. Li and the last scientist were in the sinister embrace of the creature that had attacked O'Brien, their bodies lifeless.

‘You see, you’re the last one now,’ Byrne said, taking another step towards him. ‘Join us and you’ll understand everything.’

Mitchell’s rifle swung to aim at the officer. ‘You’re not one of them.’

Byrne gave a strange laugh. ‘I have eyes, if that’s what you mean. Only dead eyes need to be replaced.’

From behind the lieutenant, several soldiers emerged to stand by his side, some Taurus and others Libra. They too had faces now exposed to the hostile air, their eyes still human.

‘Sir, there really is nothing to worry about.’

Mitchell’s body began to tremble as he heard O’Brien clearly. The fallen officer was standing near the wreck of the shuttle, the familiar stupid fucking smile on his bruised and singed face. The wounds to his body were still obvious, yet he showed no sign of discomfort. The general also noticed movement from Li as the scientist brushed himself down, looking unaffected by the ordeal.

‘If there is nothing to worry about, then what the fuck are those things?’ Mitchell jabbed a finger at the mech’s passenger.

Li ventured towards him. ‘The only word I could use that you might understand in this current situation is *antecedent*.’

Mitchell realised that Byrne had closed the gap between them significantly, close enough for him to see every scar and blemish that made the ugly lieutenant who he was. However, the tiny silver specks in the irises of Byrne’s eyes were wholly inhuman.

Gritting his teeth, the general pulled the trigger, and the mech opened fire.

~

It was time for her to make the decision. There had been no word from Mitchell or the rest of the Taurus force, and the Nova fleet were bearing down on them. The Sigma assault ships were long gone and, in their desperation to get away from the planet, had left behind their shuttle. She had felt sorry for the crew of the tiny vessel as they rose from Straunia to find themselves alone. If Byrne had been left in charge of the *Victory*, he would have blasted the shuttle as soon as it appeared. She just watched as it broke orbit and scampered off into the darkness.

Around her, the command crew were focused on their stations. She could see the fear in their eyes though and knew she had to keep their minds sharp.

‘Any luck?’ she asked the comms officer.

He gave a brief shake of the head. ‘I can’t get a signal out on LDC, lieutenant. The codes are being blocked every time. Short range is the same.'

'Keep working on long distance. We have to get word out to Taurus HQ and to the rest of our ships.' She turned her attention to the weapons officer. 'Double check all fusion and missile systems. We have to be ready, just in case Nova don't want to talk.'

'We're still remaining in orbit?' asked the navigator incredulously.

Ishlan gave him a scathing look for his outburst. 'For now. If I give the word though, I want you ready to move us away from Straunia without hesitation.'

She looked up at the other two Taurus vessels in orbit ahead of them, then scanned the planet beyond. Straunia was stubbornly refusing to give them anything, and yet there was hardly any cloud cover. Comms should have been able to reach the surface without a hitch. Perhaps she should break from corporation policy and take the *Victory* into the upper atmosphere, to get a better view of what was happening. The *Grail* was visible, but there was no way to tell where her colleagues were.

She thought back to her previous foray into Flint, when the system was buzzing with activity. The *Grail* had wiped out the crews of those ships left to defend Straunia, leaving ghost ships in orbit. The rest of the Nova ships they encountered were destroyed by the rogue fleet. She didn't want the *Victory* to join the long list of ships lost in the system.

'How are the other ships faring?'-

The comms officer brought up new data on his screen. 'Same as us. Perhaps we could send one of them out to the edge of Flint. LDC might function better out there.'

'No, we need them here. Together, the *Victory*, *Riordan* and *Austin* are a formidable force and even Nova would think twice about taking us on.'

The wait was excruciating, as engineering teams tried their best to help the comms officer access long and short distance systems, to no avail. The point of no return came and went. Ishlan made sure her hair was tied back and her jacket straightened, lifting her chin to show confidence.

Before she could issue orders, the comms officer called out. 'Lieutenant, we are receiving a message from the *Harbinger*.'

Ishlan couldn't help the quizzical expression on her face. 'My bet is we'd be able to respond to them, despite other comms being down.'

'You think Nova are blocking us?'

'I do.' She waved a hand. 'Let me hear it.'

To all Taurus Galahad ships in orbit of Straunia, this is Tomas Klein, commander of the Harbinger. You will remain where you are and await our imminent arrival, or we will take offensive action against you.

Ishlan knew what fate awaited the Sigma Royal ships then. She would expect nothing more from Nova.

'Make sure all three of our ships are in formation when they arrive,' she ordered the command crew. 'Everyone remain calm and focused.'

As they awaited the approaching fleet, Ishlan read up on Klein. She had known of the man for many years due to his military record, and hadn't been surprised to find he had taken control of the corporation after the death of their board. His profile didn't describe an aggressive man. He was intelligent, tactically adept and not afraid to speak his mind. She was sure he would be doing so shortly.

The Nova fleet emerged boldly from the darkness, lighting on the assault ships announcing their approach long before they settled into orbit. Nine were standard assault vessels, similar in design and shape to the *Austin*, if not slightly larger. The *Harbinger* stood apart from them, a veritable dreadnought. While the other ships proudly displayed the colours of Sapphire Nova, their flagship was a darker shade of blue with the corp emblem painted on both port and starboard sides in yellow. Even the *Victory* paled in comparison.

Ishlan watched as the ships took up positions equal distances apart from one another. Enough room to safely open fire, she realised.

'Lieutenant, they are requesting to speak with General Mitchell on the private channel.'

Ishlan saw all eyes turn towards her. 'Understood. Await my orders.'

She headed into the general's office just off the bridge, where she drew in a deep breath before activating the screen.

'Commander Klein, this is Lieutenant Neri Ishlan. I am in command of the *Victory*.'

Klein's face appeared, one eyebrow raised inquisitively. 'This is quite the surprise. I arrive expecting to speak with the general and come face-to-face with one of Santa Cruz's subordinates instead. Quite how you are still wearing that uniform is a mystery to me.'

She had to keep her resolve. 'The events that happened in this system those eight months ago, commander, will haunt me for the rest of my life. We were all betrayed by Santa Cruz and I wish...'

'Wishing won't get us anywhere now, will it?' Klein regarded her coldly through the screen. 'It's clear to me that General Mitchell reinstated you solely on the basis that you were among those who survived that terrible ordeal. You're useful to him. A simple demotion was punishment; a smack on the wrist.'

‘We have much to discuss, commander,’ she said, trying to redirect the focus of the conversation away from herself. ‘We find ourselves in quite the embarrassing situation, but we were not about to flee like the Sigma ships.’

‘Or the Libra ship.’ He gauged her reaction. ‘Oh, you weren't aware of that naturally. They’re experts at lurking in the shadows.’

‘You wanted to see who would seize the opportunity to come here. You were hoping the other corps would race to Straunia. Were you also hoping we would fight over the *Grail*?’

Klein smiled. ‘We thought that Sigma and Libra would take the bait. There was a part of me though that thought Taurus would see through the ruse, but the pull of such a dangerous weapon just lying there on a dead planet was obviously too great.’

‘So what happens now?’ she asked.

‘First, you will tell me where General Mitchell is.’

‘With all due respect, I think you know the answer to that, commander.’

‘He is...*was* a rash man. I do hope he didn’t take many with him to the surface.’

A creeping sense of dread started clambering up her spine. ‘Why? What’s down there?’

‘I think that’s enough questions,’ said Klein, glancing to his left at something. ‘What this comes down to is the fact Taurus were prepared to trespass in Nova space, to the very world our organisation called home. You had no qualms going down onto a planet that had allegedly been classed as a quaran; no fears for what might be waiting for you there. Taurus are reckless, greedy and still looking for the slightest advantage against us, even if that means trying to steal something that is ours by right.’

Ishlan could argue the fact that it was Taurus who found the *Grail*, but that would only antagonise the situation. ‘I’d like to know what happened to the general. If we can get him back up here, then you and he can talk.’

‘Nobody who goes down there comes back,’ Klein stated.

She realised that he wasn’t going to tell her anything more about Straunia. ‘What now then, commander? You fabricated data to make us think your fleet was light years from Flint, drawing us into your trap. There must have been a reason for it other than just to see who showed up.’

Klein was silent for several seconds, purposefully making her wait. ‘Sapphire Nova nearly crumbled when Santa Cruz destroyed our foundation. Contrary to the official reports Taurus issued denying all responsibility for what that evil bastard did, I have reason to believe your board knew. Your good general certainly did, which is why he was stupid enough to bring the

Victory here on such short notice.'

Ishlan knew the truth of course. 'Even I didn't know what Santa Cruz was planning until it was too late. He was not acting on orders from the board.'

Klein's eyes narrowed slightly. 'And you promptly left his side to help the rest of the Taurus fleet stop such an insane plan.' He gave a derisive snort. 'Mitchell watched events unfold, hoping Santa Cruz would succeed in landing a blow against us that split the corporation asunder. Even Libra Centauri joined the battle alongside pirates, mercenaries and a handful of angry colonists. Against you, no less.'

Ishlan was starting to grow more uneasy by the second. It was time to be bold. 'So you aim to kill us then? Send another message to Taurus Galahad, like you did with Fraser Lenaghan and other senior officers in the hierarchy?'

'I would be within my rights to destroy your ships,' he said, matter-of-factly. 'You've trespassed into Nova space uninvited with three assault ships. Last time I checked the news reports, our corps were in a state of war.'

'Nova are at war with everyone,' she muttered.

He gave a weak smile. 'Not everyone.'

'If you were aiming to destroy us, you wouldn't be engaging me in conversation.'

'Indeed, so here is what happens next. I wanted Mitchell to come with us but, as he is likely already dead, I will settle for you. Actually, you're *better* than the general. You were alongside Santa Cruz for a long time, joining him for meetings no doubt and discussing confidential matters, including details on both the *Grail* and those who were sent outside the Milky Way to retrieve it.'

Ishlan understood now. 'You haven't been able to search the *Grail* yourselves. Your people never came back. It must be frustrating to have it lying right there on Straunia, yet you're unable to unlock its secrets.'

'Careful, lieutenant,' he warned. 'I'm more than happy to use force to get what we need. It would be easier if you surrendered yourself to us now though.'

Ishlan knew what awaited her on the *Harbinger*. They were sure to have their own Santa Cruz readying an interrogation chamber where she would be guest of honour. Then again, the reality was the Nova fleet could obliterate them if she refused and she would be responsible for the death of all three crews. She didn't want more guilt on her conscience.

'See our ships safely through the jump point, commander, and I will remain behind with you, as you wish.'

Klein thought for a moment. 'Taking the flagship of the entire Taurus fleet would certainly be advantageous, along with prisoners to use as bartering tools. However, letting them all go would send a message that Sapphire Nova are not without mercy.'

Ishlan forced a smile. 'It would.'

'Unfortunately, that's not the message we aim to send.'

Ishlan's smile vanished in an instant as the *Victory* shuddered. She sprinted back onto the bridge, staring in horror at the main screen. The Nova fleet had all fired on the *Austin*, fusion beams slicing into the assault ship or punching holes through the hull. When the *Harbinger* unleashed the full fury of its powerful fusion generators, the *Austin* broke in two, one of the pieces exploding violently and peppered the *Riordan* with thousands of hull fragments and tens of bodies.

'Your orders?'

Ishlan heard the shout but couldn't recognise the voice. Her eyes were locked to the blood stains dotted along the *Riordan*'s starboard side.

'Lieutenant.'

No more talking, she thought, turning to face the command crew. 'Return fire.'

~

'You are playing a dangerous game.'

Klein managed to pull his gaze away from the destruction raging on the screen, turning to Rist with a genuinely amused expression. 'During war, all games are dangerous. You should know that.'

Rist cast an emotionless eye to the *Victory*'s desperate defense, the remnants of the *Riordan* reeling away in the background. 'Those ships could have been useful to you. If not salvage then additions to the Nova fleet. It is a waste destroying them.'

'I will agree with you there.' Klein shrugged. 'However, it strikes a blow against the arrogance of Taurus, who think they own the galaxy. Besides, I don't intend on destroying the *Victory*, I just aim to batter her into submission.'

Instinct nearly drove Rist to shake his head. Had Nova learnt nothing during the last few years? When the opportunity arose for them to gain an advantage over the other corps, they still took the most aggressive route possible, and look how that particular strategy had worked for them in the past.

'Your plan comes with a high risk level,' he stated. 'Taurus still have more ships in their fleet than Nova, and plentiful resources to support a quick retaliation.'

Klein looked decidedly unimpressed. 'By the time they do retaliate, the next stage of the plan will be in effect and that's when they find out what it's like to have their foundation knocked from beneath them.'

'What is my role to be during this *next stage* then?'

'As always, you'll be key to our success,' replied Klein quickly. 'Had you not secured the LDCR codes required to draw them all here, we wouldn't have the satsfaction of sending out a report to Taurus telling them that General Mitchell is dead, or that their flagship is being dragged back to one of our shipyards.'

'You don't know the general is dead for certain, just as it is unknown where your exploration teams are.'

'Nobody has returned, Mikan. No comms received or detected. There is no life on Straunia. Ships that scan the surface from the lower atmosphere run into technical problems, but none of them ever reported movement below.'

Rist hated being addressed by that name. It meant nothing now. 'Yet it is not clear what is causing the people to disappear or the tech to fail.'

A flash of impatience passed across Klein's face. 'It's the *Grail*. There's no other possibility. When it crashed onto Straunia, the poison it used had to have seeped out and infected the very air across the planet. It's a worldkiller, for god's sake.'

'I'm afraid it is still heresay, commander.'

'And yet it still did the job,' cried Klein, pointing at the screen. 'As for your next task, all will become clear when we meet shortly with Bavelli and Fletcher.'

An explosion from the *Riordan* lit up the *Harbinger*'s bridge and Rist watched as it burnt, trapped in orbit. Somewhere deep within his memory, flames began to rise. That smell of the burning brambles was everywhere suddenly, mixed with the pungent scent of charred flesh. His lungs were filling with sickly sweet poisonous smoke.

'You should be proud, Mikan.' Klein's voice broke through the all-too vivid reminder. 'You're the catalyst for the downfall of Taurus Galahad.'

Rist gave the commander a disdainful look. 'Just a shame so many of your own had to die in order to get what you wanted.'

Sullivan's Rest
Vega system

Coyle paced like a caged animal during their ascension to the main hub. His six guards tried to engage each other in small talk for the extent of the journey, desperate to avoid getting their heads bitten off.

They had searched every nook and cranny of arm K, managing to discover two illegal gambling dens, a pusher selling some homemade drug to the undesirables and a plan by a group of disgruntled storage workers to send stolen goods off-station by falsifying cargo data. At any other time, that wouldn't have been a bad haul. Unfortunately, they had been down there in search of Coyle's latest missing patrol, of which there was no sign.

He had until Hurst returned from his trip to Summit to get answers and now the pressure was beginning to weigh heavy. More Fortitude guards had gone missing in the last six months than over the previous six years combined, which was a worrying statistic to say the least. In the past, those who disappeared nearly always turned up, most of them dead. The lower levels of many arms were dangerous places to go, even for armed mercs, and the murders could be associated with debts, guard interference or them simply being in the wrong place at the wrong time. A small percentage of those who vanished were found in other systems, spending money stolen from Fortitude or just wanting to get away from such a shit life. Either way, Hurst always made a point to locate them and bring them back to Sullivan's Rest, to be made an example of.

Now though, whole patrols were disappearing each month and the latest had been working arm K. Coyle could no longer leave the investigation to others. If he failed to get results by the time Hurst got back to the station, his job would be forfeit.

He had wondered whether Jericho's Bold were behind it, as they had grown more aggressive lately. He wanted to ban them from the station completely, considering the amount of fights they picked every week. Doing that would just make the situation worse though. He kept hearing the name *Harz* muttered among the Bold too; some new pretender to their dirty throne. Those pirates only ever talked about the most dangerous individuals in their organisation so he would need to keep one ear out.

The other big concern for Fortitude was the rise in illegal apps being sold and distributed on Sullivan's Rest. The tech was questionable, showing that most were being created by amateurs in some shithole back room somewhere. One batch of sight apps had even malfunctioned, killing several users by blowing their eyes from their sockets and reducing part of their brains to mush. There was no way he and his men could stop this trade but they might be able to slow it down.

'You seeing this?' asked one of the guards, interrupting Coyle's troubled thoughts.

On one of the screens in the lift, news reports were scrolling slowly. The main headline was particularly eye-catching.

Taurus Galahad officer and board member Mitchell dead. Sapphire Nova claim responsibility.

'Fuck.' Coyle rubbed at his beard as he read the text beneath. 'They're going to wipe each other out at this rate.'

'There's going to be a shitstorm now,' mumbled another merc.

'We have our own problems to worry about,' snapped Coyle, turning from the screen.

Although he wouldn't admit it, the news bugged him. With members of all the corps passing through Sullivan's Rest at one time or another, he didn't want to have to deal with fights breaking out between them on top of their current concerns. His guards were spread thinly enough as it was.

The lift finally reached the hub and the sound of the market in full swing seeped in when the doors retracted. It was a sound Coyle had come to depend on. A silent market was a big problem.

'We're going to go over the movements of the missing patrol again,' he told his men as they stepped out into the crowd. 'On our way across to command though, I want to rattle a few cages.'

Both pedlars and customers stepped aside as the Fortitude squad made their way into the heart of the hub. Many people avoided Coyle's glare and he noticed some quickly shifting goods out of sight. Right at that moment, he couldn't be bothered to challenge them.

The first trader they visited offered nothing of interest, explaining how he didn't pay much attention to the comings and goings of Fortitude. Coyle knew that was bullshit, yet let the man get back to business. There were others in the market who would know more; those who sold information on a daily basis beneath the guise of their more mundane wares.

In one section of the market, they were attacked by the pungent odours of the meat trade. Most of the animal carcasses on show were recognisable.

Coyle turned his nose up at one stall that seemed to favour the more exotic. The combined smell of Valandran river eels and giant grubs from Aridis burnt his nostrils. He never understood how certain creatures smelt so bad and yet tasted so good when cooked.

The second potential informant could only offer him intel on more missing equipment from various arms of the station. There was a growing concern among many of those bringing in electronic and metal wares that their goods were being targeted by some robber band. Coyle would rather the culprits be simple thieves than the alternative.

There had been whispers for months that members of The Kindred had descended on Sullivan's Rest, with their odd symbols rumoured to have been painted in various spots around the station. Strangely, said spots had always been cleaned by the time he had gone to look into it. To him, it seemed someone was trying to spread panic by making people think the terrorists were active on the station. Why anyone would want to pretend to be one of those lunatics was beyond him.

There was an exchange of wary glances as the Fortitude squad passed a group of Jericho's Bold. The tattooed pirates were unusually deep inside the market, making Coyle suspicious, and the fact they were drinking just added to his fears. A sober member of the Bold was difficult enough to handle. The drunk ones tended to remind him of the berserkers from norse mythology. Not that anyone from the Bold would know much about Earth history. They were barely human.

They were nearing one of the great metal support pillars when the first explosion rocked the station. For a few seconds, the market fell quiet as the thousands of people all looked around at one another blankly. Then came the second explosion as one of the security towers on the perimeter vanished among flames and smoke.

With the silence giving way to terrified screams and panic-stricken voices, Coyle pulled his pistol, his other hand retrieving the HDU. Alerts were pulsing on the screen and the map of the hub appeared, two sec towers flashing red.

He linked his comms app to the command tower. 'Someone tell me what the fuck is going on.'

Behind him, the six guards were staring up at the distant smoke rising to blot out some of the lights. Alarms began sounding all across the hub, only adding to the panic.

'We need support...' The voice sounded disjointed but Coyle knew it was coming from his base of operations. 'We have multiple...'

The link was severed abruptly as a third explosion erupted and the command tower itself went up in flames, sending a fresh wave of terror and panic across the market.

Coyle turned to his men. 'We need to get across there now. Move it.'

They fought against the mass of bodies rushing in the opposite direction. Coyle led them towards another of the supports, aware that there was also smoke rising from several points across the inner market. There had been smaller explosions set off too but the boom of the larger infernos had drowned them out.

As they approached the support, Coyle noticed a lone figure trying to attach something to the metal structure. It soon became very clear what it was.

'Stop or we'll open fire,' Coyle yelled as seven Fortitude rifles were aimed at the man.

Realising his warning had no effect whatsoever, Coyle fired a single shot that struck the target just below his buttock. Despite the leg buckling slightly, he remained standing and continued to attach the makeshift device to the base of the support.

'Motherfucker,' spat Coyle. 'Take him down.'

The rifles burst into life and the dishevelled-looking man slumped forward, his device hanging from a single clamp he had managed to lock into place. There was no apparent display; no lights of any kind. Coyle hoped that meant he hadn't had time to activate it.

'Stay away until we can get someone in to disarm it,' he told his guards.

'What the fuck?' blurted out one of the mercs.

When Coyle turned, he saw two more dirt-streaked men calmly approaching, having emerged from the market stalls nearby. When he saw their emotionless expressions and blank stares, he knew just who they were dealing with.

'Don't let them...'

Both terrorists threw themselves forward, then exploded. Coyle was thrown backwards by the blasts, landing near the body of the one they had shot.

He did not know how long he lay there for. All he could hear was the ringing in his ears and his vision was blurry. There was a burning pain across one side of his face and his chest. The smell of charred flesh reached him and there was only the taste of blood in his mouth.

Eventually, his vision began to clear. His other senses were shot. What was left of his team of guards smouldered nearby. There was no sign of the bombers themselves; no doubt they had been obliterated by their homemade cocktails. The market stalls around them had also vanished, blown to pieces by the blasts.

Coyle looked around for his rifle. If another member of The Kindred was spotted, he would need to pick them off at distance. As he tried to push himself up, pain surged through his left arm and he crumpled back to the floor. A strange noise escaped his lips when he saw his hand was missing.

'Fucking bastards.' His voice was barely recognisable through the constant ringing echoing in his head.

He checked his other hand, relieved to see it was intact, complete with all digits. Looking around, he couldn't see his absent hand. There was however a smoking torso, the lower half of a leg and several bloody smears within reach. He went to try rising again then hesitated. The boot on that severed leg was his.

With the hub of Sullivan's Rest in disarray and three security towers burning brightly on the perimeter, Coyle collapsed in shock and could only stare up at the drifting smoke overhead as the alarms rang somewhere in the distance.

Echo flagship Glaive
Miller system

The galaxy was going to shit.

Kurcher rubbed at the scar on his wrist as he wandered along the narrow corridor, his mind threatening to overload on the various news reports that had been coming in from all corners of known space.

He wasn't surprised to hear that The Kindred had finally upped their terror attacks, and it showed that there was an underestimated intellect beneath the emotionless visage they all wore. Bombs had gone off on major stations across numerous systems at the same time. There was no focus on one or two corporations. All five had facilities hit by the terrorists. Kurcher couldn't help thinking that the outcome should have been much worse though. The attack on Sullivan's Rest had killed many, although most were Fortitude men and women: but it had been centred around the main hub. Had the bombs gone off among the pylons, it could have destroyed ships and exposed the interior of the station to space.

Titan Station was hit just outside several of the medical labs, Carson suffered an attack focused on one of their busier cargo bays and Libra's Grade Station had a firebomb detonate inside their wiring ducts, wiping out their power and bringing the whole place to an abrupt standstill.

Kurcher felt that The Kindred had perhaps chosen those specific targets to prove a point. Rather than plant explosives in a simple location, they were showing that they could infiltrate deep into the heart of well-protected structures. If they had wanted to, they could have turned the stations into burning beacons, so it raised the question as to why didn't they.

Two Echo men passed him. He could feel their glares but couldn't be bothered to look up at them. A few pirates disliking his presence seemed petty when compared to warring corps, terror attacks and dead soldiers on a dead planet.

What the fuck had happened to Mitchell though? The question wouldn't go away. Nova had been quick to claim responsibility for the general's death, and for the capture of the *Victory*, stating that he had trespassed on Straunia. Surely Mitchell wouldn't have risked going after the *Grail* during such severe hostilities between Taurus and Nova. Then again, Hewn believed that the latter had laid a very clever ambush, in order to get rid of such a key figure in the Taurus hierarchy.

Of course they did, Santa Cruz stated. *The greatest prize in human history is lying stricken on their late homeworld. What a sweet temptation.*

Kurcher stepped inside the large rec room and looked around for any familiar face. It was more like some seedy bar on the lower levels of Sullivan's Rest, but he kind of liked it. It helped him forget he was on Echo's flagship.

She'll be busy humping someone else, chuckled Ercko.

He was telling himself he hadn't gone there to find Drake. If he just happened to bump into her then so be it.

As he pushed his way through the men and women crammed into the room, Kurcher noted the number of dilated pupils on show and the intoxicated smiles worn by some. He couldn't work out why Hewn would allow his crew to use drugs and drink so openly. Sure, they were off duty, but he tried to imagine what might happen were they to be called suddenly back to their posts in the event of an attack from say Jericho's Bold.

These people aren't corp personnel, don't forget, said Frost. *Hewn has to keep them happy somehow.*

He could smell the drugs in the air and that old craving began to tap at the back of his brain. He needed a fucking drink.

You've got to stay clean, D'larro told him.

As Kurcher found his way to the bar, he found Broekow already there, sitting with his back to the rest of the room.

'Thought you would've given up the drink for a while after getting your ass handed to you on Summit.'

Broekow chose not to reply, instead downing the dregs of his drink and beckoning the man behind the bar for another.

Kurcher watched him for a moment, trying to gauge what exactly was going on behind the bloodshot eyes. 'You been given a new assignment yet?'

Broekow remained silent.

You don't do small talk, Frost reminded him.

'Listen, you moping motherfucker, it's not my fault you got jumped by Hurst's thugs.'

Much better.

'Nothing's ever your fault.' That had certainly fuelled Broekow's anger. 'You walk around as though the last few months never even happened, making your stupid fucking quips at other people.'

Kurcher sighed, realising there was a lot the sniper was about to get off his chest. He spied a bottle of Echo's honey mead and beckoned to the dour-faced pirate behind the bar. He found he had developed quite a taste for it.

'Do you actually realise that you're responsible for everything going on out there right now?'

At this, Kurcher gave Broekow a sideways glance. 'I'm responsible for the corps all fucking each other over, am I? Responsible for The Kindred bombing the shit out of everyone?'

'The *Grail* was brought here by you. All those deaths on Straunia and Meta were down to you. Angard, D'Larro, Rees.' Broekow finally turned to look at him with drunk, mournful eyes. 'Frost.'

Kurcher waited for his beer and took a long swig before replying. 'I could drink myself into a stupor like you every night. I could feel sorry for myself like you. I know what I did and I have to live with it. I'm alive and they're dead, so what's the point dwelling on that?'

Hearing their voices and their screams every day is punishment enough, whispered Frost.

'I made a mistake out there in that rogue system,' he continued. 'I can't go back and change that.'

Broekow snorted and shook his head. 'A mistake? You're a selfish prick and I should've put a bullet in your head when I had the chance.'

'I didn't kill Justyne,' growled Kurcher, biting back his rising temper. 'It wasn't my decision to go to Cerberus.'

Broekow suddenly straightened and spun to point a finger into Kurcher's face. 'Don't blame Hewn. He was just trying to get us away from Santa Cruz.'

Kurcher noticed the nearby pirates shooting the two a few quizzical looks. 'Why don't you calm the fuck down?'

'You act like she meant nothing to you,' Broekow yelled. 'She saved your life over and over again, but you failed her. You let her die.'

'Go on then.' Kurcher pulled his revolver and held it out to the trembling drunk. 'Shoot me in the fucking head. Put me out of my misery. She'll still be dead.'

Most of the people around them had stopped their conversations and were watching the exchange.

'Fuck you,' muttered Broekow.

'No, go on.' Kurcher forced the gun into his hand. 'You'd be doing me a favour. You could even try claiming the bounty on my head.'

Broekow glanced at the revolver. 'I...I don't...'

Having an audience just made Kurcher angrier. 'You ungrateful piece of shit. I saved your miserable fucking life.'

At this, Broekow's eyes seemed to clear momentarily. 'I never asked you to.'

Dropping the revolver, the sniper lunged forward, throwing a clumsy punch that Kurcher easily swayed back from. Broekow toppled and hit the floor instead.

There were several chuckles from those around them as whispered comments were made.

Kurcher couldn't bring himself to look down at the struggling man, instead scooping up his weapon and turning back to the bar. For a moment, the image of the *Kaladin*e plummeting to the surface of Cerberus hung in his mind.

You can't block it out forever, said Frost.

If you don't block it out, you'll end up like Broekow, D'Larro pointed out.

'So you just going to leave him down there then?'

Kurcher glanced across at Masami, hiding his surprise that Drake was standing alongside Broekow's pilot. One of the potent-smelling cigarettes hung from her mouth and her skin was glistening with sweat.

'Might as well,' he shrugged. 'He's no good to anyone right now.'

Masami gave the slightest shake of his head as he helped the drunk back to his feet and half-carried him away from the bar.

Drake stepped close enough for Kurcher to inhale her arousing scent. 'Hewn's got new assignments for us.'

'I only just got here. Why don't you join me for a drink before we go see him?'

'You sure it's just a drink you want?' she asked, blowing smoke into his face.

Kurcher breathed it in, feeling slightly light-headed for a second. 'A drink, one of your cigarettes and then back to my quarters.'

Drake pulled the cigarette from between her lips and held it out. 'You really want to smoke this shit? Want to get high again and feel that buzz?'

'Yeah. Better than getting back on the Parinax.'

She offered the half-finished one, her eyes staring intensely into his. Kurcher tried to give her his most wicked smile as he reached out to take it.

'Fuck off.' She pulled her hand back and stubbed the cigarette out on the bar. 'No drugs for the ex-addict. Hewn's orders. Now let's go.'

Kurcher couldn't help but bite. 'He's a fucking hypocrite. Echo are responsible for one of the most potent drugs in the galaxy being created and distributed to tens of thousands of people, just to fund his cause. Then again, it isn't even a cause when his ambition is to sit in the Expanse and hide like a bunch of cowards.'

Drake tilted her head to one side, sighed then punched him square in the face. 'If you want to be thrown out of an airlock then by all means keep talking. I suggest you shut the fuck up though and follow me to see Hewn.'

Kurcher could feel blood running from one nostril and his cheek would likely swell up nicely over the coming days. All he could hope was that inflicting pain on him would turn her on.

When they entered the command room, Broekow was nowhere to be seen. Masami arrived on his own a moment later.

'Three out of four then.' Hewn was in his usual position next to the map. 'Perhaps I shouldn't send him on this one.'

Masami stepped up to the console. 'I'll sober him up in time. He needs to get off the *Glaive* for a while.'

'I thought we were being kept here for safety reasons,' Kurcher said as he looked down at the map, recognising the whole of the Expanse.

'Something's come up.' Hewn's eyes lifted from the screen and narrowed when they saw the enlister's face. 'Been making friends I see.'

'I'm more popular than you know. So what's going on?'

'Two things have happened that we just can't ignore. The most recent convoy coming here from Cobb was intercepted by Taurus ships. Three got through and made it to Seko, but the rest were captured. The route they took was carefully plotted to avoid any corp activity, so someone on Cobb sold them out.'

'What makes you so certain of that?' Kurcher asked. 'Maybe Taurus picked up on comms or just got lucky.'

'No. They knew the manifest. One of the Resistance pilots who made it to Seko told us the Taurus officers referred to the different types of cargo being carried when they ordered them to surrender.'

'Best tell the Resistance then and let them deal with it.'

'I'm sending you and Drake to help them do just that.' Hewn's gaze was intense. 'You'll go to Cobb, help them find this informant and get rid of them before Fuller leads the final convoy here.'

'No fucking way.' Kurcher could hear the distant screams threatening to return. 'That's the last place I want to be. Send Broekow and Masami.'

'This isn't open for negotiation,' snapped Hewn, clearly anticipating the reaction. 'Your take-no-shit attitude will be required in sorting this out. At the same time, you can ensure that the Resistance leave Cobb for good, then nobody will ever have to go back there.'

'You think they'd leave people there?' Masami frowned. 'Can't see that they would.'

'They've built quite the facility since the war and I wouldn't be surprised if Fuller planned on leaving a skeleton crew to keep it running, just in case things on Seko went south.'

'Cobb is in Taurus space,' Kurcher stated angrily. 'You'd send me there knowing that they're looking for me? I'd be a sitting fucking duck.'

'They'd never know we were there.' Drake decided to add to the conversation. 'And if we arrive and find Taurus all over the place, we leave. I've got confidence in my skills as a pilot, even if you don't.'

'I never said that.' Kurcher shook his head at Hewn. 'Why not send Fischer or someone else in Echo? How do I know you haven't sold me out to Hengeveld and he'll be waiting for me?'

Hewn waved a metal finger at him. 'You just have to trust me on this. Besides, Fischer is down on Seko questioning Marie Butler and you are a member of my organisation, whether you like it or not.'

When did you start being a pirate's lapdog? taunted Ercko.

Hewn hasn't fucked you over once since you joined Echo, Frost told him.

Seeing the turmoil behind Kurcher's eyes, Hewn continued. 'You know Cobb and you know these people. Consider this a step towards redemption.'

Kurcher expected to hear Maric's voice chime in. 'I'm not taking any chances. I'll choose our approach route to the Kalbrec system.'

'*We'll* choose it,' corrected Drake.

He had come to trust her much more than anyone else in Echo, Hewn included. Something was telling him not to take her for granted though.

'So what's our assignment?' Masami asked.

Hewn looked back down at the map. 'A Libra transport named the *Magnussen* was attacked and destroyed on the edge of the Galen system. As it was just inside the Expanse, naturally Libra assumed we had something to do with it. To show them we didn't, and to try salvaging what's left of our alliance, I've agreed that we'll find out who did it.'

Masami gave him a puzzled look. 'How are we supposed to do that?'

'The distress call from the *Magnussen* stated that their attacker was hiding in orbit of Vir, one of the moons belonging to the only gas giant in the system. From what we can gather, no ship has left Galen since then, although readings from the jump point there are sketchy at best.'

'And if we find the culprit?'

'Try to determine who the fuck they are and why they are attacking corp ships in one of our systems. It was an extremely bold move, so watch your back.'

Masami peered at the map, tapping a finger over the highlighted Galen. 'Why were Libra there in the first place?'

Hewn shrugged. 'Still trying to find that out too.'

'If you ask me,' began Kurcher, fully aware that nobody had. 'I'd say Libra are studying the systems on the border of the Expanse and someone didn't like them snooping round. Wouldn't be surprised if your next meeting with these corp pricks ends up with them demanding colonisation rights to Galen and other systems like it. Could be they are looking for resource-rich planets.'

'There may be some truth in that,' Hewn agreed. 'Question is who might already have crept into Galen without us knowing.'

'We'll find out,' Masami said, his eyes still fixed on the map. 'We need to get some surveillance buoys out to these systems.'

Hewn gave a curt nod. 'Load some onto the *Crius* before you head out. I'll give you intel so you can drop them off once you're done.'

Masami gave a wry smile. 'Guess I just talked myself into more work.'

'I don't like what's going on out there,' Hewn told them. 'Kindred blowing the shit out of corp and merc facilities alike, intel being leaked and jeopardising our plans, corp ships being destroyed in our own territory. It's time to get involved.'

Kurcher turned to Drake only to find her already heading for the door.

'No time like the present, dickhead,' she called back. 'Grab your gear and let's get the fuck out of here.'

He caught sight of Hewn and Masami exchanging amused glances, saluted them with his middle finger and followed her.

Going back to Cobb is a big mistake, warned Frost.

If Fuller and the others find out what you did when you were in the military, they'll put a bullet in your head, said D'Larro.

Kurcher knew the chances of them discovering his past were slim to none, but he was more concerned that returning to the dead planet would awaken his demons.

Grow some fucking balls, growled Angard.

As he followed Drake out of the command room, he wondered whether he could persuade her to just disappear with him once they had finished on Cobb. Why should he continue to put his neck on the line for Hewn and his so-called *business*?

Suggest that to her and she's more likely to break your neck with her thighs, pointed out Frost.

Kurcher couldn't help but grin. What a way to go.

Sapphire Nova Assault Ship Harbinger
Haskell system

Fusion beams stood out stark against the darkness of the void as the Nova fleet continued their exchange with the Taurus ships.

Klein studied the battle intently on the screen, looking for any gaps where they could punch through to the station beyond the defenders. He had to give the Taurus commanders credit. They were quick to react to the attack and had, so far, held their lines despite being outnumbered. Then again, he had held the *Harbinger* back.

By the number of ships Taurus had in Haskell, they were clearly not expecting such a bold move on their primary fusion supply. Behind its meagre defense fleet, the station hung in space like a gigantic dead spider, eight supply pylons arching over the main hub, which was releasing numerous emissions from the generators.

Klein had batted the idea around for weeks as to whether or not they should try to capture the station and harness the huge amounts of energy it was kicking out, but Taurus would make it a priority to retake the station. It was more prudent to destroy it, although the thought of turning it into a trap and taking out more Taurus ships in the explosion was tempting.

There was a brief flash of light from one of the defense vessels as combined attacks sliced off a section of the hull, and Klein was entranced momentarily by the pattern formed by crisscrossing beams.

'Continue to hold,' he told the command crew, seeing their expectant faces turning to him.

The battle was unfolding at a slow pace. He would ramp up the pressure soon enough. He checked his personal console, looking for any new reports, but all was quiet. He knew that he should have had complete faith in Bavelli and Fletcher, yet the lack of communication was making him nervous. Maybe he should have taken on one of the other two tasks instead of leading the attack on Haskell.

By now, Bavelli and his smaller fleet would have arrived in Wagner and engaged any defenses of the outer fuel depots. Klein hoped that the hot-headed officer stuck to the plan they had agreed on, and had not ventured too far into the system in an attempt to take out some of the larger depots.

They could easily be flanked and trapped if Taurus had a high number of assault ships available.

Fletcher wouldn't have reached Kalbrec yet. There may well be a significant welcoming committee waiting for him when he arrived though. Cobb was still of great importance to Taurus it seemed, despite them deciding to kill off the planet when the colonists revolted. There was a reason, of course, and the intel they had received unexpectedly from the surface laid this bare. The Resistance had found a way off Cobb, after joining forces with Echo, and the last members of this tiny faction were due to leave for good shortly. The materials they were leaving behind would be worth acquiring, but Klein had made the decision they needed to capture the leader of the Resistance too. Cal Fuller would prove useful to Nova, not just as a bargaining chip.

He cast his eyes over the report stating that a large percentage of the Taurus fleet had descended on the Lincoln system, as their board converged to discuss everything that happened on Straunia. This meant that the other systems were possibly vulnerable and he had entertained the idea of heading to Earth. It had always left a bad taste in his mouth that Nova was the only corporation not to have a presence on the original homeworld. Then again, his predecessors had caused that with their impatience and greed. The last thing he wanted to do was lay siege to Earth. Despite everything that was happening on the surface of the beautiful planet, there was still a strange respect for it.

'Sir, looks like we're making headway.'

Klein realised he had been lost in thought as he first glanced at the navigation officer, then the main screen. Two Taurus vessels were listing away from the fight, their hulls showing severe damage in several places. This had opened a gap in the defensive line, which another enemy ship was trying to plug.

'Time to punch through,' he announced loudly.

The *Harbinger* opened fire on the smaller assault ship moving to close the breach. High concentration beams struck it just below the bridge and tore a raw hole deep into its interior. A second later, the bridge of the doomed ship was consumed by explosions and it began to drift lifelessly away.

At the same time, the rest of the Nova fleet focused their combined attacks on two of the other Taurus vessels, creating a wide gap in their defenses, and Klein issued the order to destroy the fusion station.

However, he was not expecting the sudden burst of weapon fire that came from the station itself, striking the first Nova ship through the breach and cutting the bow apart with rapid fusion attacks from mounted cannons all over the main hub.

Watching one of his ships take such a barrage opened the way for doubt to creep back in and Klein reacted aggressively, leaping from his seat then bounding to the tactical console.

'Target the station. Let them have everything we've got.'

The longer range fusion beams at the *Harbinger*'s disposal whipped through the breach, almost brushing the hull of the Nova vessel being peppered by the cannons. Time and time again, they slammed into the reinforced hull plating of the station, trying to find a way through to the softer metal behind. Missiles joined the fray, their detonations erupting in a firey pattern that would have wiped out most regular ships. Still, the fusion station held together, pock-marked and blackened.

Around the Nova flagship, the rest of the fleet were tearing apart the remaining Taurus vessels. Klein smiled as others joined the *Harbinger* against the station. Cannons spat their bursts in defiance but fizzled out before they could even scorch the sleek assault ship.

There was a moment of elation followed by apprehension as the combined attacks finally broke through. One of the supply pylons spun away with a sickly green flash and exploded violently seconds later, searing the section still attached to the main body. This seemed to cause a chain reaction and bursts of green flame began belching out from various locations across the station. The Nova fleet had backed off by the time the fusion generators imploded, obliterating the gigantic spider in an awe-inducing ball of light.

'Head back to the jump point,' ordered Klein, returning to his seat.

'Sir, we could push further into Haskell,' said a particularly bold officer. 'Destroy more fusion stations.'

Klein eyed the dissipating green haze. 'We've completed our mission. No reason to put the fleet in jeopardy by staying in the system any longer than we have to. Now carry out my orders.'

As the Nova ships followed the *Harbinger*, Klein checked the position of any remaining Taurus assault vessels and was pleased to see they were retreating deeper into Haskell, like dogs with their tails tucked firmly between their legs.

Some of his fleet had sustained damage yet their engines were still operational. Even the ship that caught the brunt of the opening volley from the station cannons was limping along behind, ugly scars gouged across her bow.

There was still no word from Bavelli or Fletcher. He shrugged off the doubts, positive that they would both carry out their respective tasks to the letter. With Taurus turning their attentions to the Haskell, Kalbrec and Wagner systems, it would open the way for Rist to carry out the next part of the plan, delivering a hammer blow to their foundations that would topple the once-mighty corporation and allow Sapphire Nova to finally snuff out the Galahad Suns once and for all.

Galt
Lincoln system

The meeting had spiralled out of control quickly. Hayward had expected it to, of course, just not so soon after they had all sat down.

At one end of the long oval table sat the newly promoted General Garrett, arms folded as he watched the fiery exchange between other members of the board. Known for being much more patient than his late predecessor, even he was starting to show the telltale signs of a temper pushed too far.

Hayward was sitting exactly halfway along the table and was in the midst of the rowing executives, although she was yet to make her voice heard.

'We have lost too many ships in the last year,' yelled Pavleachenko for the third time. 'If we go out there to engage Nova in these systems, we run the risk of the whole fleet falling apart. I mean, the *Victory* is in their hands for Christ's sake.'

'And you would have us just sit here while our key depots and stations are obliterated?' Kort asked incredulously. 'When you took over from Lenaghan, I thought you might show more courage than he ever did.'

Hayward watched the two executives closely. Pavleachenko was standing directly opposite her, both palms planted firmly on the table's varnished surface and an almost wild look on his face.

He had been one of the team Lenaghan had requested move with him from Earth and, at that time, had been a charismatic charmer with a slight Russian accent. With recent events clearly taking a toll, he was now twitchy and there was no sign of that accent.

Kort was sat between Pavleachenko and Garrett. He was an abrasive, arrogant prick and yet Hayward couldn't fault the man's loyalty to Taurus. There seemed to be no skeletons in his closet, which she found unusual considering he had been running Kingston with Tench for nearly thirty years.

'Oh, I'm sorry for being a little on edge,' bit Pavleachenko sarcastically. 'Having two of your best friends murdered tends to play on your mind.'

Kort gave him a sideways glance. 'Come off it. Lenaghan was nobody's friend and you hadn't seen Culman for months.'

Pavleachenko went to reply, then saw the look on Garrett's face and instead slumped back in his chair like a sulking child.

'You all seem to think I'm asking for your permission,' said the general, his voice slow and steady. 'I'm not. Part of the fleet is already on its way to Kalbrec, with reinforcements heading to Haskell too. At the conclusion of this meeting, I will be leaving on the *Ravenedge* to try tracking down those who attacked us.'

'Is that wise though, sir?' piped up Chaldevert from his seat to Hayward's left. 'I have already put the exploration fleet on alert and told them to watch for Nova activity across the galaxy.'

'I am not Mitchell,' stated Garrett calmly. 'I'm not about to go blundering into Nova space. Your explorers will feed their scan reports to the *Ravenedge* and we will start to put together an idea of where these warmongers are.'

'I suppose you're okay with this?' Kort directed the question at Tench, who had been sitting in silence at the other end of table.

Galt Operations Officer Tench gave a nod and a smile. 'Of course. We can run things here while the general works on protecting Taurus from any more surprise attacks. He knows full well that we can't afford to lose more ships and their crews. The man's got double the amount of brains Mitchell ever had.'

'He can also speak for himself, thanks.' Garrett rose from his seat. 'While I am away from Galt, I have assignments for all of you which you will prioritise above your normal workload.'

As he reached for the paper folders in front of him, Hayward couldn't help but admire the general's retro approach. He didn't believe in top secret data being kept solely in Taurus tech and preferred writing it out by hand before delivering it in person. His view was that data was likely to be hacked. Given the increase in illegal apps designed for just that purpose, she had to agree.

Her eyes flicked around the table to the other six execs in turn, trying to read their body language and expressions. Her gut feeling was that at least two of them were corrupt at some level and it was down to Akeman to determine the how or why.

Kort was clean, she was certain. Pavleachenko had worked closely with Lenaghan before his untimely demise on Temple, or off Temple depending on how one looked at it. She didn't really trust any of the team the fat idiot had picked to transfer to Galt.

Billings had sat quietly during the meeting so far, with a fixed smile etched on his youthful face. Hayward was sure the junior board exec was hiding something and her chat with him over potential leaked intel had solidified this belief. He had not liked the way she took Akeman off him and the agent had already divulged some of the activities Billings had assigned him previously. It was all highly suspicious and she just needed some solid evidence against him before she could act.

Tench was a Galt man through-and-through who seemed a solid individual. She hadn't ruled him out completely but he seemed to be just as clean as Kort. He was ex-military and was in charge of the operations of all Galt colonies so she certainly hoped he was as loyal as he looked.

The financial officer, Marris, had not uttered a word either throughout the meeting. She tended to speak only when asked a question direct and many saw her as meek. But Hayward had read her file, and she was a ruthless individual when it came to corporation revenue and spenditure. She had volunteered to move from Earth long before Lenaghan and his cohorts did, doing so to get her family away from the danger of the Revenants. She was of course just one of many finance execs in Taurus, yet had made enough of a mark to wind up on the board.

Chaldevert was perhaps the one board member she couldn't put her finger on. Born on Galt, he had one of the highest IQs of any Taurus officer and yet had decided to take on the responsibility of managing the exploration teams. He was an explorer himself at heart, often taking trips out onto the planet surface to study the animals and search previously uncharted regions. Did he have it in him though to betray Taurus?

Garrett handed Kort the first file. 'Kingston security is your priority. Sec team duties and patrols, plus checks of all ships arriving at or departing from the colony. You also need to keep an eye on incoming and outgoing traffic at the other colonies.'

'Consider it done.'

Garrett moved on to Pavleachenko. 'I want you to start the backing up of all our data here, to protect ourselves from cyberterrorism. Other factions may want to take advantage of the situation.'

Hayward had to smile at the use of such an old word. Nobody referred to them as cyberterrorists anymore. Yet another retro aspect of the general that appealed to her.

'Is that it?' Pavleachenko asked boldly.

'Read your file,' Garrett replied gruffly, continuing round the table. 'I want you to do some research on our comms facilities too.'

Hayward would have preferred someone else to focus on the Taurus Galahad communications. Pavleachenko looked a bit too pleased with that particular duty.

Her eyes turned sharply to Billings as the general handed him his folder.

'You've covered a lot of duties over the last few months,' Garrett told the beaming junior exec. 'I know we asked a lot of you following Lenaghan's death and the support you gave the board was invaluable. Now is the time for change though. You will prep to leave Galt and return to Earth, where you are to assist Miss Hayward.'

Billings grin vanished in an instant. 'I...I don't understand.'

Hayward caught the glance from the general. She liked that he had paid attention when she made her recommendations prior to the meeting.

'What don't you understand?' Garrett asked. 'You will leave with her and continue your excellent support back on Earth.'

'But...' Billings looked at Hayward and frowned. 'I was hoping to move up from a junior position to...well, to...um...'

'Become a permanent board member?' Garrett gave the briefest of shrugs. 'Perhaps one day.'

'Your position was temporary,' added Tench. 'We did make that clear.'

Hayward liked the fact that someone else was backing the general's decision up. 'Come now. Working with me won't be that bad, will it?'

Billings blinked in disbelief and sank into his own thoughts.

'Commander Tench.' Garrett had moved on. 'For you, supplies review and analysis of the trade routes between colonies here on Galt. Also, look at the scheduled trade due to visit the Lincoln system over the coming months. Then, you can help Kort with his long list of tasks.'

'Understood, sir.' Tench gave him a smile and a weak salute. 'Just as long as you stop calling me commander, eh? I think the joke has run thin now.'

'Not much of a joke,' sniffed Kort.

Garrett handed Marris her file. 'This is very important and you'll need help, so I'll let you choose your own team. It has come to my attention that there are a number of Taurus accounts in the corporation's databank which may need investigating. I want you to begin a full review of these accounts and ensure there is nothing untoward going on.'

Hayward cast another glance across at Billings and saw the exec's worried expression briefly before he hid it behind his false smile.

'I'll do my best, sir,' Marris said softly, her eyes widening when she looked at the list just on the first page alone. 'A couple of these people are deceased though.'

'Indeed they are.' Garrett loomed behind Hayward. 'Make those your priority.'

Marris took out her HDU and began tapping at the screen, a puzzled look etched on her usually stoic face.

'Miss Hayward, your folder.' The general placed it carefully in front of her then jabbed a finger at it. 'You have permission to hire the enlisters you need. We can't afford to let the crims out there think they've got away. Liaise with Marris on the financial aspects and Billings here will help you get this underway.'

'Thank you, general.' Inside, she was overjoyed that he had taken everything on board, but she couldn't let the others see that. They would think she had manipulated him or, even worse, seduced him to get what she wanted.

'And the other matters you requested be signed off? All the paperwork is right there.'

Hayward might have fallen in love with Garrett somewhat at that moment.

'That just leaves Monsieur Chaldevert.' The general slid the final folder onto the table and returned to his seat. 'Keep doing what you're doing with the exploration teams. It's very important they continue to look like they are...well, exploring.'

The stereotypically smart-looking Chaldevert gave the slightest of smiles, choosing to remain silent and not to follow suit by opening his file.

Garrett addressed them all. 'Do not be under any illusion. The situation with Sapphire Nova is at a critical stage. We are most definitely at war. Keep your staff calm and their minds focused.'

'These are surreal times,' muttered Tench. 'Alien discoveries, insane suicide bombers and rogue officers. All I hear people talking about is that damned *Grail*.'

'I'm going to be away from Galt for a while,' continued the general. 'Taurus needs to be seen out there, to show the other corps we aren't afraid of them. I'm trusting you all to steady the ship both here and on Earth.'

The meeting continued for another half an hour as more mundane topics arose and were briefly discussed, mostly problems that had surfaced in Kingston itself. Once Garrett thanked them all and dismissed the board, such as it was, Hayward made sure she had a few minutes alone with him as they headed for the elevator.

'I'm sure I don't have to remind you that your name will be at the top of Nova's hit list now.'

'You don't, but thank you for the warning.' Garrett smiled, yet his eyes betrayed the concerns stacking up in his mind. 'I take it you have everything you need now?'

'I do. I expect Billings to make a mistake now that we've rattled him, contacting whoever he has been leaking the intel to. When he does, Akeman will be ready and waiting.'

‘I’m still wary of this spy you’ve been using. He was close to Santa Cruz after all.’

‘True, but he isn’t corrupt. He simply works for the highest bidder.’

Garrett scowled. ‘Just keep an eye on him. It’s a risk using him to unearth all of these traitors. How long do you reckon it will take to get them all?’

‘From what I’ve gathered, Lenaghan was the key figure,’ Hayward explained. ‘His team consisted of Billings, Pavleachenko, Kulman and a handful of other junior execs. The thing is Lenaghan was just out to make money from his dealings and he kept away from the likes of Nova or Libra. Billings is clearly out to make money from delivering information to the corps instead.’

‘And Pavleachenko?’

Hayward shrugged, which she quickly realised wouldn’t look particularly positive. ‘I have a feeling his panic is legitimately regarding Kulman’s murder. Guess we’ll find out soon enough though.’

Garrett called the elevator and turned to face her. ‘You still don’t think this corrupt group were working with Santa Cruz and Mitchell?’

‘I read the reports from Rees. Lenaghan had no idea what Santa Cruz was up to and had even openly berated him several times for his actions. Mitchell fooled everyone into thinking he was just as much in the dark.’

‘I went over Mitchell’s official logs and there were a number of gaps. No deleted files. He just didn’t make any reports at certain times.’

Hayward frowned, pushing a rogue hair strand from before her eyes. ‘You’re aware both he and Santa Cruz visited Minerva on more than one occasion?’

Garrett’s expression told her he was. ‘I’m going to head out there as soon as I can. It’s obvious Santa Cruz had spent a long time tracking down that *Grail*, and Mitchell was just letting him do so while feigning ignorance to the rest of the board. There are too many other questions unanswered though.’

‘There are some out there who could help us get those answers,’ she smiled. ‘So thank you again for giving me clearance to do what it takes to find them.’

Garrett returned the smile and turned as the lift doors opened. ‘Keep me in the loop.’

‘We’ll keep an eye out for Saul Winter’s stalker too,’ she added, stepping into the lift alongside him.

‘Good.’ There was a lengthy silence as they descended. ‘It may well be on Cerberus, but the reports given to Mitchell by the crew under Santa Cruz were sketchy at best. As the *Requiem* was sent to Berg by our late general before anyone else could get their hands on it, I think it's worth a look when I visit Minerva.'

Garrett left her alone in the lift, heading to gather his belongings before making his way to the *Ravenedge*. Hayward found herself disappointed to no longer be sharing such a small space with the charismatic officer.

Kingston was beginning to quieten as the day drew to a close, lighting flickering on overhead to illuminate her route back to the smaller meeting room near the landing pads.

'I trust it was a productive meeting,' said Akeman as she entered.

Hayward spotted the agent's usual tipple and was tempted. 'This time, I can actually say yes it was. Got anything else to drink other than that dirty booze you seem to like?'

Akeman chuckled and fetched two other bottles, holding them up for her to see. 'It's either water, vodka or my *dirty booze*.'

She found herself liking the man more each time they met. Sure, he had a dubious past and was as ugly as sin, but he got things done quickly and quietly. He also knew exactly which brand of vodka she preferred.

'Billings nearly cried when he was told he was going back with me.' She waited for Akeman to pour her a generous shot of vodka. 'Now we just wait for him to take the bait.'

'It's clear from his confidential files that he sends an unusually high number of messages to locations outside Taurus space. I'm certain we'll have the evidence shortly that he is leaking intel.'

Hayward enjoyed the burn of the alcohol. 'You're tracking the others too?'

'Yes.' Akeman sipped his own drink, his eyes regarding her carefully over the rim of the glass. 'You have more than one corrupt official here, Miss Hayward.'

She closed her eyes and drew in a deep breath. 'I need to get to them before they can sell Taurus up the river.'

'And you will.'

'Any other news?'

'Yes.' Akeman handed over his HDU with a wry smile. 'The pirates are willing to meet with you.'

Echo vessel Falcata
Kalbrec system

We shouldn't be here.

Kurcher had to agree with Frost yet again. 'No shit.'

'You talk to yourself a lot,' noted Drake.

He could only just make her out through the smoke. 'Just thinking aloud.'

She glanced back, her cold yet strangely enticing eyes staring into his soul. 'You can stop fucking lying. You hear them right? People you lost.'

Kurcher was taken aback. 'Sometimes. I don't mean to speak to them though. Makes me sound like a schizo I once knew.'

Drake turned back to the screen. 'Maric. Yeah, Hewn told me about him. Bit ironic, don't you think? Hearing the voice of a schizophrenic inside your own head.'

She knew more about him than he realised. 'I don't hear that fucker's voice. Either of them.'

'Why not?'

'I didn't see him die.' Kurcher thought back to the manic firefight on the *Huntress*. 'We left him behind on a doomed assault ship with no way back. I don't give a shit what happened to him after that.'

Drake gave a slight smirk. 'You really are damaged goods.'

'Aren't we all?'

'Not like that. You're fucking mental.'

Kurcher wanted to laugh but held his resolve. 'Smells like one of Hewn's drug factories in here.'

'Good.' Drake tapped at the console to her right. 'Masks the stink of alcohol and sweat emanating from you.'

As the *Falcata* travelled deeper into Kalbrec, heading for the dustball that was Cobb, Kurcher could feel his stomach beginning to knot. The last time he had been there, he had barely been able to bring himself to look any of the survivors in the eye. Even the ruins of Jefferson had reminded him of the innocent blood he spilled there. The fact he had arrived with Rane had only made the Resistance more suspicious of his presence. To them, he was just another criminal and he didn't blame them for treating him as such.

He had given a lot of thought to the task that lay ahead. *If* they managed to get to Cobb undetected, he still had to find the one who gave Taurus the convoy. For all he knew, it could be someone else on the surface who had been watching the Resistance; a corp spy. He had no idea how to determine who this person was, or where to start. Cal Fuller would be the man to ask, but he would need to get to know the Resistance leader better if he hoped to work with him. Hewn had said he chose to send Kurcher as he knew the people. Meeting someone once didn't really qualify as *knowing* them.

There's bound to be one person left on Cobb whose family you murdered, Santa Cruz said.

If that's the case and they recognise you, guess you'll die there too, added Ercko.

Just do the job and get back to the Expanse quickly, Frost ordered.

'We've got corp assault ships in the system,' Drake announced suddenly in a calm tone.

He sat forward, craning his neck to try seeing her console data. 'Fuck. Taurus?'

'And Nova.' She gave an amused snort. 'They're really hammering the shit out of each other by the looks of it.'

Kurcher moved quickly from his seat and peered over her shoulder, being careful not to lean on her beloved chair. 'They're fighting?'

'That's generally what *hammering the shit out of each other* means. Picked them up just now. Looks like both sides have significant fleets here.'

'How far out from Cobb are they?'

Drake checked her displays. 'The bad news is that they are blocking our direct approach. The good news is that we can take a longer route around the battle, sneaking onto Cobb through the back door. There are no guardians in orbit and all of the assault ships are too preoccupied with each other to notice us.'

Kurcher shook his head. 'I don't like this. Taurus and Nova are both looking for me. Cobb's not worth getting caught.'

'Don't be such a pussy,' snapped Drake. 'We've come this far and I'm not turning back now. I do this for a fucking living, you know.'

'Why are Nova here though? Doesn't make sense to just openly attack Taurus in this system. Must be here for a reason.'

'You think?' Drake turned the *Falcata* away from their direct approach route. 'Maybe whoever betrayed the Resistance contacted more than one corp.'

Or maybe Hewn betrayed you and sent you right into a shitstorm, remarked Ercko.

Cobb remains an important world even now, stated Santa Cruz.

'Just get us there in one piece,' Kurcher muttered, returning to his seat. 'If I need to, I'll just shoot every remaining member of the Resistance so we can fuck off home.'

Drake laughed, the sound easing his tension slightly. 'And where is home exactly?'

It was a fair question and one he didn't know the answer to.

Shard
Lincoln system

The air smelt stale and tasted bitter inside the confines of the research base. Flynn had expected it to be much like breathing in the processed oxygen of Temple. Then again, perhaps his body had become accustomed to life on the station and he should spread his wings more often.

'Where the fuck is he?' came the nervous question from behind him. 'He knows we haven't got time to dick around.'

'Just keep calm, Suren.' Flynn glanced back. 'He's not just going to lead them all out shackled together like some chain gang. Takes time to shift that many without drawing too much attention.'

Suren pulled at the ill-fitting uniform he had been forced to wear, raising smirks from some of the other Templars standing alongside him. 'Can't wait to get back in my armour. Dressing like some sec goon isn't my idea of fun.'

'Stop complaining,' Flynn growled quietly. 'There are still Taurus military in the base and we don't want them asking questions.'

'Just shoot the assholes,' grinned Suren. 'Save us a job later.'

Flynn returned to gazing at the airlock opposite them. It was a risky move coming to Shard, but the rewards would be great. Besides, with the Taurus fleet leaving Lincoln, it was the perfect moment to execute their plan.

The heavy clunk of the door told him to put his thoughts to one side for the time being and he offered a smile to the science team who were pushing several cumbersome units into the chamber. He noticed that Gotzer was the last person in, quickly sealing the airlock behind them before ushering the others forward.

'I know this isn't what we agreed,' began the sweating scientist. 'You'll be able to move them much more easily like this though.'

Flynn stepped up to one of the units. Through the ice-encrusted panel, he could only just make out a broad face, scarred and glinting with metal plates.

'How long do they need to fully thaw?' he asked, examining the life readings flickering across the lid of the cryo pod.

'Few hours would be best,' Gotzer replied, moving from one pod to the next and tapping his HDU after each check. 'I wouldn't stand next to them as they're waking up either.'

Flynn eyed the science team. 'We can take them from here.'

They looked to Gotzer, who simply nodded his head at the airlock then waited for them to leave before speaking again. 'These seven were due to be destroyed but I've marked them as donors. If you get stopped on your way back to Temple, simply refer to their identity implants. You're just transporting them to a medical facility to be harvested for transplants.'

'Harvested?' snorted Suren. 'You really don't give a shit about them, do you?'

'And you do, I suppose,' snapped Gotzer. 'Making them fight each other to the death in your arena is so much better.'

'Really not the time.' Flynn's tone made both men think twice about speaking again. 'Get them on board, Suren.'

The brooding merc beckoned the others forward and Flynn watched as they took the sleeping biomechs through to the ship.

'Wasn't easy,' came Gotzer's voice. 'Managed to get the clearance to use them as donors, but Weir asked a lot of questions. She always does.'

'You've come through for us as always,' Flynn reassured him. 'I understand the risk you take by helping us out and we always give you the VIP treatment on Temple.'

Gotzer cleared his throat. 'Appreciated, of course. However, I'm going to need something more for this. Call it danger money. A Taurus scientist helping a merc outfit populate their gambling arena with lethal biomechs? I need enough to disappear for a while.'

Flynn made sure his stare was suitably unnerving. 'I can't hide you on Temple, if that's what you're asking.'

'No. I have contacts on Athena so need to get there. If you could take me with you now and get me into the Barclay system, plus pay me for getting you the fighting stock, I'll be safe.'

'You'd defect to Libra Centauri?'

Gotzer shushed the towering merc. 'Can you do it or not? If so, I'll send Weir a message once we're away telling her I needed to go to monitor the cryo units.'

Flynn made a show of thinking for a few seconds, then shrugged. 'It's your funeral.'

The two made their way swiftly onto the Templar ship, with Gotzer nodding to a shocked-looking Suren as they passed him in one of the cargo bays. Flynn led the scientist to an unused section of the deck, showing him a tight cabin.

'Make yourself comfortable,' the leader of the Knights Templar said, pointing to a basic pallet bed in one corner. 'Best you stay in here until we are some distance from Shard.'

Before Gotzer could say anything else, Flynn slammed the door shut and locked it. He then accessed his comms app and gave his pilot the order to get them off Shard and back to Temple.

He sought out Suren once more, who was securing one of the cryo pods.

'We have a passenger,' stated Flynn. 'Wants us to get him to Athena.'

Suren laughed. 'Like fuck. Does he know we're moving to a Nova system yet, or that we're planning on using his biomechs against Shard when the rest of the shit hits the fan?'

Flynn shook his head. 'Do me a favour, will you? Make sure we don't have a passenger by the time we reach Temple.'

Echo vessel Crius
Galen system

The gas giant nearly filled the entire screen. Vivid red and orange swirled with mundane brown, making it seem as though they were flying into some psychedelic cloud.

Broekow eventually had to avert his eyes from the colourful display, for fear he might suddenly go blind. The alcohol would probably destroy his vision before anything else, of course.

'She's certainly a monster,' said Masami softly, gazing into Aven's hypnotic vortex. 'No wonder there aren't any other planets here.'

Broekow watched the pilot for a moment. Nothing ever seemed to phase him and he had a strange fascination with everything he encountered in the wilds of space. There was something innocent about Masami at times, yet Broekow knew the man had a significant amount of blood on his hands. Come to think of it, they all did.

'Don't the moons count?'

Masami shot him a wry smile. 'That's why they call them moons. I'm just surprised Aven doesn't have more, such is her pull.'

'I read up on Vir,' Broekow told him. 'Reports say it is similar to Europa, which I remember passing once as a child. These cold worlds have always intrigued me.'

'How so?'

'They're harsh environments and yet often beautiful. Life evolves very differently too and the whole place just feels...' Broekow couldn't find the right word.

'Pure,' finished Masami.

The *Crius* turned towards a pinprick of white slowly orbiting the looming Aven.

'You really think the *Magnussen* was a transport?' Broekow asked the pilot.

'It may have been once. No reason for a Libra transport to be in this system though.'

'And your theories on who destroyed it?'

Masami made sure that Vir was directly in the centre of his screen before answering. 'Probably Jericho's Bold or Schaeffer's Nine. I expect both have been skulking around the outer systems of the Expanse for some time. The Bold will be looking for any opportunity to gain an offensive upper hand on us, while the Nine will use the alliance with us as a smokescreen to make moves on our territory.

I reckon the *Magnussen* encountered whoever it was while they were both doing recon, but clearly were slower to react. The attack on them was ruthless, which tells me it is one of the pirate organisations.'

Broekow stroked his beard as he pondered this. 'Everyone's ruthless, even Echo.'

He tried to focus on what might be waiting for them near the frozen moon, his brain conjuring up all manner of outcomes. The one that made him more uncomfortable was the idea that Sapphire Nova was lying in wait and that he was being unwittingly delivered into their hands. There was no point trying to read Masami, although he had come to regard the pilot as a friend over the last few months and doubted he would be quite so emotionless were he about to betray him.

Broekow's mind inevitably reminded him of the beautiful face that haunted his dreams most nights, unless he had passed out from the drink. It was crazy to think that she had come to mean so much to him considering he had only spent a very short amount of time with Frost. Then again, it was more the *what if* that kept plucking at his sanity. Had she not been in the cockpit of the *Kaladine* at the moment they were attacked, she would have made it down to the surface of Cerberus with them. Had Hewn not suggested they go to his supply cache on that fucking quaran, she would still be alive. Broekow could have taken her far away from Kurcher and the death that surrounded the enlister.

He flinched as the burning sensation flashed briefly through his chest and back. He had meant what he said to Kurcher back on the *Glaive*. He wished that the enlister had left him to die rather than suddenly growing a conscience and dragging him off the *Grail.*

'Got a weak signal,' announced Masami as Vir grew ever larger on the screen. 'Looks like we've got a ship on the surface, although...'

When he trailed off, Broekow looked across to see the pilot busily consulting his various app displays. 'What's wrong?'

'Old distress code, but the *Crius* barely picked it up as it is badly degraded. Can't be the ship we're looking for.'

'Can we take a look?'

Masami pursed his lips and frowned. 'I'll take us into orbit. Don't really want to enter the atmosphere if I can help it though. It all seems a little odd.'

'Understatement.' Broekow's eyes scanned the rest of the image before them, trying to make out anything unusual against the violent swirls of Aven or the more peaceful white of the moon. 'Anything else out there?'

'The *Crius* says no. I say yes.'

Masami wasn't often wrong and the hairs on the back of Broekow's neck stood up as he began to get the feeling they were being watched.

Cobb
Kalbrec system

Kurcher was having a hard time shutting out the voices of the dead. He had wanted to close his eyes as the *Falcata* landed and to try to ignore the ruins of Jefferson. The faces of those he had killed watched him from every broken window or door.

Despite knowing a great deal about his recent exploits, Drake wouldn't have a clue of what he had done on Cobb during his military service. Even she might have been shocked. Then again, she might have just told him to stop being such a pussy and man up. She was nothing if not unorthodox, which was why he had insisted she remain on the ship.

'I find it hard to believe anyone here would give up their colleagues; their friends.' Fuller scratched at his greying beard. 'They've all been a part of the Resistance for years and helped us survive.'

Kurcher glanced around the dusty room. 'And yet someone did betray you. Someone with their own agenda or perhaps a corp spy who infiltrated your operation a long time ago. Doesn't change the fact it's happened and that you need to get the fuck off this planet now.'

Fuller nodded slowly. 'We're almost ready. Tell me why you're here again?'

'To find whoever is feeding intel to Taurus and to put the boot up your ass. You've lingered here too long and now you've got two corp fleets fighting it out up there. Whoever wins will arrive here and that could be any minute, so you need to pack up and get your people to Seko.'

'What do you need?' asked Fuller, giving him a wary look.

'A list of everyone still here, and access to your whole bunker.' Kurcher knew it could have been more than one person he was looking for, or it could be none of them. He just wanted them to get moving.

The Resistance leader continued to give Kurcher a suspicious eye. 'The lower levels are empty now so everyone will be up here, either prepping in the hangar or gathering the last of their belongings.'

'We'll see.' Kurcher forced a smile. 'Time is short though so let's get moving.'

Fuller moved to grab a HDU from the nearby desk. 'Give me a second and

I'll get the list for you. Thanks for your help by the way. Good to know Echo give a shit.'

Kurcher's smile vanished. 'Don't ever thank me for returning to this place.'

Careful, warned Frost.

Fuller didn't query the sharp response, instead handing the HDU over. 'Hedmun Oakley is also still here with his crew.'

Kurcher knew that of course. He had seen the Oakley ship when they arrived and their presence just meant more work for him. Perhaps it was one of Hedmun's crew who gave up the Resistance or maybe it was the old man himself. It might explain why they were so keen to remain on Cobb and help; to delay Fuller's departure.

This could still be a trap designed to fuck you and the Resistance, Ercko remarked.

Giving up both to Taurus or Nova would be a fantastic deal sweetener if Hewn wanted to forge a new alliance, explained Santa Cruz.

Kurcher stared down at the list of names as an exhausted-looking Fuller hurried from the room. He vaguely recalled one or two of them from his previous visit, although the whole Resistance was still on Cobb at that time so there were more faces in the dirty halls.

If I were Fuller, I'd want to rip Taurus apart to help his people who were captured, snarled Angard.

He knows there's nothing he can do for them, said Frost.

Kurcher knew he had to get moving. If he could uncover anything before they launched, it would make matters easier. The problem would be fleeing the system before whichever corp came after them. Perhaps it was worth trusting Hedmun Oakley and arranging for everyone left in the base to leave on his ship. It was faster than the shitheaps the Resistance used. Others could leave in the *Falcata*, although Drake may have something to say about that.

As he headed for the door, he put a hand down to his revolver. As an enlister, he had no qualms hurting innocent people to get the job done, so why was he hesitating now?

Being responsible for the deaths of entire worlds will do that to a person, Santa Cruz answered.

'Shut up.'

Your old methods were what got all those people killed, laughed Ercko.

'Fuck off.'

As long as Davian Kurcher survived, everyone else was expendable, added Santa Cruz.

Kurcher let out an anguished roar that echoed along the corridors of the bunker. ‘Get the fuck out of my head.’

You knew the consequences of coming back here, said the voices of the dead simultaneously.

Vir
Galen system

'I don't see it.' Broekow squinted at the display.

Masami accessed his app and a shape became highlighted against the surface ice. 'There you go. Definitely an old ship, but no designation.'

'No way that destroyed the *Magnussen*.' That was obvious. 'Although it may hold data that we could find useful.'

'I'm not landing,' Masami told him bluntly. 'It feels like bait.'

Broekow had to agree with the pilot. He looked up at the main screen, seeing only a grey sky. 'Vir has a breathable atmosphere, right?'

'Yeah, but hard on the lungs. I just said I'm not landing.'

'I heard you.' The familiar dryness in Broekow's mouth was returning and the fact Masami had refused to bring any alcohol with them was playing on his mind. 'I just wondered whether anyone could've survived down there.'

Masami shrugged. 'Not for long without food or shelter. Someone could conceivably build a base of some kind on the surface. The ice is thick enough to hold considerable weight.'

'So what's our next move?'

'Head back into orbit, run some more scans and then venture round to the opposite side of Aven to make sure nobody is hiding out there.' The nose of the *Crius* tilted upwards at Masami's command. 'I think whoever destroyed the *Magnussen* is still in the system. I suggest we drop one of the surveillance buoys as we're leaving and see what it captures.'

Broekow shivered, even though the cockpit was relatively warm. 'Sounds good to me.'

As the *Crius* ascended through the upper atmosphere, Masami seemed to relax slightly. 'You feeling okay?' he asked.

'Not bad,' lied Broekow. 'I imagine I might feel worse in a few hours as withdrawal kicks in properly. Those meds you gave me have kept it at bay for the time being.'

'You're of more use to Echo sober.' Masami gave him a meaningful look. 'You don't want Hewn deciding you're not worth the hassle.'

Broekow knew that the pilot was doing his best to protect him, but even Masami would have his limits. 'I'm sorry for the shit I've put you through,

Tariq. On Summit, you put your life at risk taking on Morton Hurst's men when you could easily have walked away.'

'Listen, my friend, you've been through enough shit to last you a lifetime and you've seen things that most of us can't even begin to comprehend. It has a lasting effect, but you are strong enough to come through such a difficult time as long as you steer clear of the drink. You once told me that you judged Kurcher for his drug addiction. People judged you for becoming an alcoholic. Both of you can and will be better people.'

Broekow smiled. 'You're the most optimistic person I know, to think Davian Kurcher will ever be a good person.'

'I said *better*, not necessarily good.'

'Still quite a long shot for...'

The *Crius* suddenly jolted violently and a horrendous metallic screech threatened to deafen both men. A moment later, the ship began to lose altitude and it was clear that Masami was wrestling for control.

'What's happening?' yelled Broekow above the continuing noise.

'Hang on,' came the reply. 'We're under attack.'

As if to back this up, there was a flash of green ahead of them as two narrow fusion beams cut through the grey and slammed into their hull. Alerts began to fill the cockpit with their shrill cries as Masami purposefully pitched the *Crius* downwards. For a split second, Broekow caught sight of a ship looming ahead of them before the surface of Vir filled the screen.

Another fusion beam cut through the air, barely missing them, and Masami turned the *Crius* sharply, trying to see their pursuer more clearly. They saw it for a moment before it swooped beneath them and back out of view.

'Who are they?' asked Broekow, not recognising the w-shaped ship design.

Masami grimaced. 'Don't know. Highly manoeuvrable though.'

Once again, the *Crius* made for the upper atmosphere, pitching and turning every now and then to make them a difficult target. The screeching sound had stopped but the alarms continued to issue their warnings.

Broekow could hear the engines straining, pushing them upwards as quickly as they could to escape Vir. Masami was willing his ship to get them to safety through gritted teeth. Then everything began to spin.

One of the *Crius*' engines was struck by a fusion beam, knocking it out and sending the ship veering away from its trajectory before it began plummeting towards the surface once more. This time, all Masami could do was fight to keep the nose as level as possible.

'I'm sorry, my friend,' he uttered, before the *Crius* struck the surface.

Cobb
Kalbrec system

Kurcher watched the remaining men and women of the Cobb Resistance from the shadows, as they made final preparations to leave the planet that had been their home. A handful of ships that seemed more likely to disintegrate than make the long journey to Seko sat waiting for their passengers. Above them, the hangar doors were open and small specks of dust floated down from the surface, where Hedmun Oakley's ship, the *Cradle's Reach*, was ready to launch, along with the *Falcata*.

Occasionally, Kurcher glanced down at the data unit Fuller had given him. He had met most of the people in the hangar in passing; had engaged with some in idle conversation to gauge how nervous they were when speaking with a member of Echo who had risked his life getting to them.

He saw Cho cast a scathing look his way then mutter something to the man next to her. She was feisty alright. Then again, all the members of the Resistance had an edge to them that only came with surviving on such a barren world. Cho seemed to hold Fuller in high regard though, and was fiercely loyal to their cause. Still, that didn't rule her out completely.

He had to check on the name of her companion. Leeson was her on and off fuck buddy apparently, although he wouldn't describe their relationship that way. Kurcher saw the man as someone in the grip of a sickness, which made him follow Cho around like a lovesick pup. Kurcher had been somewhat surprised when Leeson turned out to be a strong character. It must have been her that made him weak.

People often lose their identity when they're in love, noted Frost.

Or lust, added Trin.

Kurcher shifted uncomfortably, moving his gaze to other members of Fuller's depleted team. There really weren't many of them left now. He had expected them all to want to get off Cobb and start their new life in the Expanse, joining the rest of the survivors, and yet they seemed to be reluctant to leave.

He saw the engineer, Monk, walk through the square of daylight beaming through the hatch. He was pushing one of the rickety carts laden with various metal crates and the sweat was glistening off his forehead. The man had spoken up for Fuller, telling Kurcher that many of the Resistance had wanted to turn on their leader after the alliance with Echo. Marie Butler had calmed most of them and opted to take the potential troublemakers with her to set up on Seko, leaving behind only those loyal to Fuller. Monk had also told him though that some may have been harbouring resentment and were just very good at hiding it.

Kurcher scrolled through the list of personnel again, his eyes lingering on one individual. It was also Monk who had mentioned Vasily's past to him, which raised more than just an eyebrow. If Fuller's decision had angered so many people, it must've been likely for someone to believe they would be better off with Taurus. Who better than a man once employed by the corp and who apparently took great effort in mentioning how much he hated them during most conversations. Vasily had been a member of a Taurus demolitions team who also got his hands dirty as security from time to time. Kurcher found it interesting that the man had apparently spent recent days in the lower levels of the bunker when he was usually in the hangar. It was Vasily he needed to speak to.

Too obvious, said Santa Cruz.

Perhaps Monk is trying to push the heat away from himself, remarked D'Larro.

Kurcher left the hangar and made for the nearest stairwell. As he traversed the barely illuminated tunnels, he continued to study the data Fuller had given him. He went over and over the names, eventually starting to say them out loud in an attempt to remember who was who.

'Fuller, Vasily, Monk, Cho, Leeson, Rettin, Oakley...'

'A name you know all too well.'

He hadn't seen the man approach. The uniform gave his identity away.

'I don't believe we've actually met before.' Kurcher held the HDU up, using the light from the screen to make out the weathered face. 'Hedmun Oakley, right?'

'You know who I am, just as I know exactly who you are,' smiled the self-appointed officer. 'I never thought to see Davian Kurcher here on Cobb.'

Be careful of this one, warned Frost.

Kurcher dropped the false ignorance. 'So what the fuck do you want?'

'I know what you did here during your military service,' Oakley began, pushing the HDU light away gently. 'It couldn't have been easy coming back here, and I'm assuming nobody here is aware of your past crimes.'

Kill the fucker before he talks, snarled Ercko.

'I'll ask again then. What the fuck do you want?'

The elderly officer stepped closer. 'Echo sent you here for a reason and, knowing your portfolio, I doubt it's to help move these people. I've seen you watching them; talking to them. That means you aren't here to kill them though. You don't exactly hang around when it comes to executions.'

There was a strange look in Oakley's eyes and Kurcher took a step back instinctively. 'I'm not an assassin. Are you aiming to blackmail me or something?'

'Of course not. It's just that you're considered a very dangerous man. Wanted by Sapphire Nova, Taurus and even Sigma Royal, I believe. Your presence here could get these people killed, mine included. Many tend to die when you're around, just like on Cradle when you came for my niece.'

'I was doing my job,' snapped Kurcher, trying to keep his voice low.

'Yes, working for a sadistic madman, as I recall.' Oakley held his hands up, almost defensively. 'However, despite the fact you stole into our compound and took Tara on a fateful jaunt that resulted in the deaths of millions, as well as getting her shot in the process, you did allow her to return home when you could've executed her.'

'She was injured, traumatised and lost one of her only friends,' Kurcher stated. 'A bullet might have been mercy.'

Take the lifeline, you idiot, tutted Frost.

'Perhaps.' Oakley dropped his hands, one of them grazing the edge of the pistol at his side. 'I know she was damaged a long time ago. Doesn't mean she isn't a part of our family and that I love her.'

A fucked up family, noted D'Larro.

'Just keep her on Cradle,' Kurcher advised him. 'There's a lot of men out here for her to prey on.'

'I won't tell Fuller or the others who you really are.' Oakley straightened his jacket and his air of arrogance quickly began to grow. 'You have my word.'

As the officer brushed past and began heading away, Kurcher called after him. 'How loyal is the Oakley fleet to the Cobb Resistance and Echo?'

Without stopping, the response came back almost rehearsed. 'People like us have to help each other survive at such a dark time.'

As Kurcher set off again for the stairwell, he passed an open doorway. Inside, several lamps showed it to be a room used as quarters. He saw three beds, each with their own footlocker, plus other pieces of makeshift furniture to give the drab chamber some sense of home. He spotted a small data unit lying on one of the unmade beds.

With a glance along the corridor, he stepped into the quarters and began searching. He wasn't sure what for exactly but anything out of the ordinary would be useful at that moment in time.

Doubt there's much left behind by now, Frost said.

He swiped the HDU from the bed, the motion waking it from slumber. He read the message on the screen, quickly realising it was from Leeson. The sordid contents made it obvious the device belonged to Cho, so he quickly accessed any other files kept in the memory. Nothing leapt out at him, although an internal note sent several months previous by Butler to all personnel piqued his curiosity. It told them to hand over their data units to two electronics specialists, for them to customise, and to ensure that no signals could be picked up and amplified outwards by the satellites in orbit of Cobb.

Satellites used for long range communications to Taurus perhaps, mentioned Santa Cruz.

One of those specialists is still here, said Frost.

Kurcher hurried from the quarters, realising as he headed back to the hangar that he was still clutching Cho's HDU. He hid it as he approached Monk, especially as the engineer happened to be in conversation with Cho herself.

'You need something else?' Monk asked him with a groan.

'Yeah. Where can I find Dale Rettin?'

Vir
Galen system

Flames licked from the torn walls of the *Crius*, bringing with them a pungent smoke that quickly filled the interior of the stricken ship.

Broekow was still reeling from the crash landing, his legs feeling weak and a numbing sickness eating at his guts. The scene was reminding him of how the cockpit of the *Kaladine* had looked moments before she plunged to her death on Cerberus.

A blast of cold hit him in the face, which was a bizarre sensation when the fire was threatening to burn him alive. It was blowing in through the tear in the hull from frozen Vir. A battle of the elements.

A spread of bullets ricocheted off the wall behind him and Broekow dived for cover behind the rec room table. He had almost forgotten they were under siege.

'Tariq?' he called into the smoke.

For a moment, there was no reply and he feared the worst. Then Masami stumbled into view and crouched down next to him, pistol in hand.

'You okay?' the pilot asked him.

Broekow noticed the raw skin on Masami's arm where he had been caught by the flames. 'Better than you.' They heard gruff voices somewhere ahead. 'Any ideas?'

'We can't stay in here much longer,' Masami stated. 'And they know that. If we can reach storage, I've got a few tricks up my sleeve there for them.'

'Who are *they*?'

'Guess we're about to find out.' Masami raised his pistol. 'You with me?'

Broekow checked his own weapon and grimaced. What he wouldn't give to be holding his old rifle. 'Yeah.'

They darted from cover, keeping low as they moved swiftly across the rec room. The exit leading to the rear of the *Crius* was open, the metal door having clearly malfunctioned. As they stood either side and peered into the gloom, a gun barrel flashed. One bullet narrowly missed Broekow's head, cutting a groove in the wall.

He recognised the sound of the weapon. Heavy duty automatic rifle that had been customised. One of those bullets would likely shred through skin and bone.

Masami let off two quick shots along the corridor, crouched and fired twice more. This time, two rifles replied.

'You go high, I'll go low,' the pilot told him.

Broekow gripped his pistol tightly as he realised just how long it had been since he had fired a weapon. He hadn't even been able to pull the trigger when the barrel was in his mouth several weeks back. Masami swung round the corner of the doorway and opened fire. A split second later, Broekow did the same. It was a strange sensation as he felt the old familiar recoil up his arm.

There was a pained grunt from somewhere ahead and Masami boldly pressed the advantage. Broekow staggered after him and the smoke cleared slightly the further they moved down the corridor. At the far end lay a body, slumped against a wall still clutching one of the rifles. For a moment, Broekow couldn't make out the corpse as Masami darted from one side of the corridor to the other, his pistol trained on the junction. Then he saw exactly who was trying to kill them.

The man was dressed in thick dark grey clothing to protect against the chill of Vir and was wearing a mask that covered all but his eyes, which had glazed in a death stare. The skin between the eyes showed part of a blue tattoo. When Broekow noticed the serrated knife attached to the barrel of the dead man's rifle like a crude bayonet, it just confirmed that they were dealing with Jericho's Bold.

He exchanged the briefest of concerned looks with Masami. The Bold were considered savages compared to Echo or Schaeffer's Nine, usually killing those they attacked or raided. It seemed this encounter would be no different.

As Masami opened his mouth to whisper something, a voice called out, deep and venomous. 'Time for you to surrender. No point drawing out the inevitable.'

Broekow edged to the junction and peered around to the left. Cold wind nipped at his exposed skin as he saw just how large the rip in the *Crius* was. The ship had struck ridges of ice jutting up from the surface and had nearly been snapped in half. The bright grey light of Vir shone in along the port side. As Broekow's vision adjusted to the sudden light, he saw a number of dark figures standing just outside the tear.

'So are we just going to fight our way out?' he asked Masami. 'There's a lot of them.'

'The Bold aren't exactly known for their mercy in these sorts of situations.' The pilot thought for a few seconds. 'We need to keep them busy while I get to storage.'

'Your ship is likely to explode any minute,' came the same voice. 'Time for you both to come with us.'

Masami looked like someone had just slapped him across the face. 'How the hell does he know there are two of us?'

Broekow's mind began to race. Perhaps Hewn or one of his cohorts had arranged the whole thing, and the Bold were just waiting for them...for him. Surely they wouldn't want to lose the *Crius* or someone as talented as Masami though. That didn't make sense.

'Fuck this,' he said suddenly. 'I'll die on my own terms, not on some frozen moon at the hands of a painted pirate.'

Handing his pistol to Masami, he scooped up the dead man's rifle, quickly getting used to its weight as he clasped it in both hands. With a nod to his friend, Broekow stepped out and opened fire, sending a barrage through the open wound in the side of the *Crius*.

The pirates seemed shocked by the attack and, whilst some dived for cover, others slowly raised their own weapons to retaliate. Two of them were blown backwards immediately, their broken bodies sprawling onto the ice. As two more returned fire, Masami stepped alongside Broekow, both pistols blazing into life. Both the attacking pirates shuddered as bullets struck them and, in his death throes, one spun whilst still firing, almost blowing his comrade in two.

Broekow didn't let up and jogged to the tear, unleashing a wide spread among the scrabbling Bold who were trying to escape the onslaught. Behind him, Masami was reloading when a hidden figure emerged from the ship, having been waiting for the right moment to pounce. The pilot noticed him just before the vicious knife stabbed into his side, spinning away from the thrust and bringing the handle of one pistol round in an arc, striking the man across the face. The pirate was resilient and quickly lashed out, his blade catching Masami lightly across the forearm and drawing blood.

The rifle in Broekow's hands ran dry and he threw the heavy weapon down. It wouldn't take the pirates long to regroup and he didn't fancy heading out into the exposed air. When he turned and saw Masami struggling to best his opponent, Broekow ran to his aid and caught the pirate's wrist as he tried again to skewer him. Masami didn't waste the opportunity, slamming a boot into the man's groin before taking his legs out from under him. Before the pirate could recover, Masami had reloaded one of the pistols and put a bullet through his skull.

As both men tried to catch their breath in the oppressive atmosphere of Vir, that familiar menacing voice called out again. 'I'd heard you were too drunk most of the time to aim a gun properly. That was more like the old Sieren Broekow.'

Broekow spun at the sound of his name, watching as another group of Bold pirates began to approach the *Crius* warily. The man leading them was dressed the same and yet his jacket was adorned with all manner of metal trinkets, no doubt taken from his past victims. He also had his mask pulled down to reveal a broad bearded face heavily tattooed down one side. His lips were painted blue.

'Time to come with us,' grinned the pirate.

Broekow tried searching his memory for the face, but he didn't recognise it. 'You here for the bounty on my head?'

Masami aimed his pistol at the approaching pirates. 'Time you walked away. Take another step and I'll kneecap the lot of you then leave you all here to freeze.'

The Bold pirate pointed a thick gloved finger at the pilot. 'Tariq Masami. I've heard about you too. There's no bounty on your head though.'

'Who gave us up?' Broekow asked, knowing he probably wouldn't get an answer.

'Listen,' began the pirate, amusement vanishing from his demeanour. 'Either you walk over here and we don't break any bones, or we'll put a few bullets in you and take what's left.'

Masami reached out and started pulling Broekow back into the *Crius*. 'Let them come, my friend. We'll have the advantage.'

As they began to retreat, two small devices flew over their heads and landed near the body back at the junction, flashing ominously.

'Afraid not,' said the tattooed pirate with a smirk.

Broekow and Masami didn't have time to think before the grenades went off. Both threw themselves back towards the tear in the hull and Broekow lost sight of the pilot as the shockwave gave his senses a jolt. When he looked up, he was lying on his back on the ice staring back at the *Crius*. The corridor they had been standing in a moment before was now a mangled mess of metal and wires. Flames were emerging from all walls and the floor too.

His ears were ringing and his vision was blurred, but he caught sight of the pistol he had given Masami lying nearby. As he made a grab for it though, a boot came down hard on his hand, slamming it against the ice and breaking more than one bone.

'It's good to see some of that old fire in your belly returning.' The half tattooed face peered down at him. 'You're going to fucking need it.'

Broekow found himself being lifted from the cold ground by two other pirates. Masami was standing several feet away, his back to the blazing *Crius* and no weapon in sight. Members of Jericho's Bold were gathering before him, throwing the occasional insult or jeer his way. They were toying with their prey.

'The name's Harz,' announced the tattoed leader. 'And I'm going to be running the fucking Expanse once Echo has been wiped out. This is where it starts.'

He nodded to one of his men, who pulled a knife and advanced on a shaky-looking Masami while the others cackled in anticipation. When the pirate swung though, Masami nimbly dodged and brought a fist up to connect under the man's jaw, sending him reeling backwards. The pilot wasn't finished and darted forward, jabbing his fingers hard into the pirate's exposed throat. As his opponent let out a gurgling groan and dropped his knife to grip his own neck, Masami scooped the weapon up in one fluid motion and rammed the blade into the man's temple.

'Next,' sniffed Harz, waving a hand and not giving his fallen man a second glance.

Another member of the Bold stepped forward, slightly more apprehensive than the last. Masami wrenched the knife from the corpse and waited for the attack. When it came, it was a feint and nearly caught the pilot in the ribs. Yet again though, Masami danced away from the aggressive strike and ducked as the pirate lashed out with his fist. He then stabbed upwards and impaled the man through the wrist. Despite the agony of the wound, the pirate was clever enough to make sure he pulled his arm away and so put the knife out of Masami's reach. He wasn't clever enough though to realise Masami's own feint as he changed direction, came up behind the flailing pirate and managed to grip the hilt of the knife protruding from the bloody wound before twisting and pulling it free.

Broekow looked at Harz, who was watching intently now. 'You don't have to do this. He'll be worth something too.'

The Bold leader regarded him with that hideous grin. 'My men need some sport before we leave this place and this one ain't worth shit.'

As he finished his sentence, Masami drove the knife into his opponent's gut and purposefully dragged the blade upwards to tear the man open. The knife emerged glistening red with viscera and the second pirate fell.

'Next.'

Masami readied himself again. Broekow wondered whether the pilot could actually make his way through the other ten standing before him.

As the third bout began, Harz sighed when Masami's knife sliced his pirate deep across the thigh. 'What the fuck are you lot doing? Do I need to step in and show you how it's done?'

'Why don't you?' panted Masami, pushing the wounded pirate away.

Harz glanced at Broekow before stepping forward, unsheathing a particularly wicked-looking blade from his belt. From his position, Broekow watched as the tall pirate loomed over the smaller Masami. He would still have put money on the pilot coming out victorious. That was, until Harz cheated.

Masami focused on the blade as it sliced through the air, stepping aside as he had done before. He failed to see the second blade appear from the bottom of the hilt though and Harz jabbed it hard into his arm. As Masami recoiled, the pirate gave a rumbling laugh that seemed to shake the very ice they were stood upon.

'You're a very skilled fighter. I need the odds to swing in my favour.'

Gritting his teeth, Masami began to lunge forward when Broekow noticed him stumble. Harz moved around him, watching as the pilot's movements seemed to slow considerably. Occasionally, Masami would lash out but his attacks were clumsier than before.

'My own concoction,' announced Harz loudly. 'I've been wanting to test it for weeks but never had the opportunity. A light coating on such a small blade seems to be just enough.'

Masami shook his head. 'Cheating bastard.'

At this, Harz stepped in, aiming to drive his knife into Masami's chest. The pilot once again surprised everyone by dodging aside then bringing his own weapon up, which caught the pirate across the chin, carving a small piece of tattooed flesh complete with beard clean off.

This drove Harz into a terrifying rage that even his men seemed frightened of. He grabbed Masami's knife hand then landed a sickening headbutt directly on the poor pilot's nose, which broke with a loud crunch. Still hanging on to him, Harz knocked the knife from Masami's hand and spun him around, placing one strong arm around his neck. As he squeezed and Masami could be heard gasping for breath, Broekow couldn't stay quiet.

'You've made your point, you sadistic fuck. Leave him be.'

Harz didn't look at him as he replied. 'Would you rather take his place?'

'Yes, I would.' Broekow was being completely honest. He would give up his miserable life for his friend and that would at least be a meaningful end.

Harz released his grip and Masami fell to his knees, choking as he desperately wiped the blood cascading from his nose.

'Noble,' muttered the pirate. 'But I haven't yet made my point.'

He reached down, gripped Masami by the hair and wrenched his head back violently before cutting his throat. Then he calmly watched the expression on Broekow's face as he was forced to watch his friend bleed out on the ice.

Broekow wanted one of them right then and there to kill him. Knife or bullet, he didn't care.

'Motherfucker,' he spat. 'Cowardly son-of-a-bitch.'

Harz wandered back to stand in front of him, wiping Masami's blood off his knife on Broekow's jacket. 'Don't worry. It's your turn next.'

With that, he punched Broekow square in the face, knocking him unconscious.

Cobb
Kalbrec system

'That's about it, boss.' Vasily stepped back to examine his work. 'Just a couple more to prime and we're good to go.'

Fuller looked across at the gigantic metal doors on the opposite side of the room. 'Good. The sooner we can bury all this, the better.'

Vasily gave the slightest of nods. 'Who actually knew what we were keeping down there? Never cared before. Guess I'm getting sentimental about leaving.'

'Not many of us. It wasn't really something I wanted people knowing about. I only told you because you were going to help me bury it.'

'And who's to say you told me everything, eh?'

Fuller scowled. 'As if I'd hold anything back from you.'

'I guess I can understand Taurus or one of the other corps wanting to get their hands on it all,' Vasily said as he wandered back to stand alongside Fuller. 'But why did you keep it in the first place?'

'Bargaining chip perhaps, should the need arise.'

Vasily knew exactly what he meant. 'A little gift for Taurus, to say thank you for marooning us all here.'

'Something like that.' Fuller didn't want to discuss it further. Soon, they would be on their way off Cobb and the bombs would be forever hidden in the depths of the destroyed bunker, along with the remains of those who died from radiation poisoning.

He cast one more look back at the sealed doors. It was never meant to be their tomb, but he had had no choice when they had become sick. He couldn't risk the rest of the survivors ending up the same way.

'Get the last ones primed, Vasily. Time to go.'

The demolitions specialist was already on his way to the bottom of the stairwell, where he had connected four sets of explosives. 'You want the honour of detonating?'

'It should be me really.'

'Well, come get the...' Vasily's voice was cut off by the sound of a pistol firing, which echoed loudly through the underground chambers.

Fuller reached for his own weapon but was too slow to react as a lone figure stepped into the dim chamber and opened fire, hitting the Resistance leader twice in the chest and dropping him.

'Sorry, old man, can't let you do it.'

Fuller could only muster enough strength to lift his head and stare in disbelief as the shooter moved to stand over him. 'Dale...what...'

Rettin shrugged, then frowned. 'Taurus didn't want you blowing this place and all your sordid little secrets sky high. Problem was they didn't want you dead either and that just pissed me off.'

'No...you can't...'

'Stop telling me what to do,' yelled Rettin. 'If it isn't you, it's Marie or one of those other pricks upstairs. Vasily used to call me *Cretin* and see where that got him. You ruined my fucking life, old man. She always listened to you when you whispered in her ear about me and then, low and behold, she flies off to Seko with my kid and next thing I know me and her are done.'

Fuller reached up with a shaking hand. 'Don't do this, Dale.'

Rettin swatted the hand away. 'Fuck you. Fuck Taurus too. *Subdue Cal Fuller and ensure no explosives are detonated before our ships arrive*. What a joke.'

'You gave up our people too?'

'Of course I did. You and your precious Resistance were just going to end up servants for those pirate bastards in the Expanse. I had to do something.'

Fuller coughed, feeling a spasm of pain ripple through his body. 'Why not...just kill me then? Why the speech?'

Rettin bristled, his face twitching at the question. 'Because I wanted you to know it was me who destroyed your Resistance and I wanted you to know it was me who pulled this trigger.'

As he aimed the pistol level with Fuller's forehead, there was a brief look of doubt on his face. There was no turning back for him now and he knew it.

'Please, Dale.' Fuller wasn't one for begging, but he needed to try buying some time, although the bullets lodged in his chest had clearly done too much damage. 'Think about this...and think about...Marie.'

Rettin's doubt vanished. 'Bye, old man.'

When the shot came, it wasn't from his gun. Kurcher fired twice, the first striking Rettin at the base of the neck and exiting messily from the front and the second taking part of the traitor's skull with it.

'Good job he was a loud, talkative fucker,' Kurcher said as he quickly moved to help Fuller.

His face confirmed what the Resistance leader already knew. 'He wasn't a bad shot though, right?'

Kurcher looked him in the eye. 'We can get you medical attention upstairs. Oakley may have something that can help on his ship.'

'Vasily?'

'Dead.' Kurcher didn't do consoling, even in this sort of situation. 'Come on.'

As he tried to move him, Fuller pushed him back as forcefully as he could. 'Vasily had the detonator. Give it to me.'

Kurcher fetched the device but hesitated before handing it over, instead casting a look around at the explosives etc surrounding them. 'Not going to bury me in here too, are you?'

Fuller managed a smile. 'Not unless you do what I say. I'm done...you know that. The least you can do is hand me that...and let me finish the job.'

'Yeah, you're bleeding out pretty fast,' said Kurcher bluntly. 'What about your people up there? They need you to lead them off this fucking planet. Those on Seko need you to help them rebuild.'

'The Resistance will live on...with your help.'

Kurcher recoiled, shaking his head vigorously. 'I've done what I came here to do. Deal with that piece of shit. It's down to you and that arrogant prick Oakley now.'

Fuller held his hand out for the detonator, then noticed another figure had entered the room. Monk stepped forward, his face ashen as he took in the scene.

'Cal, I didn't know. I'm sorry.'

'Prep the ships,' Fuller ordered the engineer. 'Time for you all to go.'

When Monk seemed frozen to the spot, Kurcher gave him a shove. 'You heard him.'

Reluctantly, the engineer turned and headed back up the stairs.

Fuller drew in a painful breath. He wished he could see or speak with Marie, but time was of the essence now in more ways than one.

'Help get them off Cobb and to Seko,' he said, ignoring the feeling of cold spreading across his chest. 'Tell Marie Butler what happened. Please.'

'I'm no escort,' snapped Kurcher, thrusting the detonator into Fuller's hand. 'Die here if you want. I'm getting the fuck away from Cobb as quickly as I can. This place can rot for all I care.'

Fuller could see the turmoil behind his eyes but chanced one last effort. 'They need someone to protect them.'

'Not me. This is the last time I'll offer to get you up top.'

Fuller collapsed back onto the floor. He could barely even feel the detonator and had to check it was still in his hand. He shook his head weakly at Kurcher.

'Suit yourself.' Kurcher turned and stalked from the room, leaving Fuller lying alone with two corpses to keep him company.

The lights in the chamber seemed to be losing power, he thought. He looked at the detonator, lifting it to examine the basic layout.

There was a part of him that always knew he would die on Cobb.

~

You should help them, Frost told him.

Let the fuckers die, said Ercko.

You're good at running away from things, commented Santa Cruz.

Kurcher sprinted through the lower halls of the bunker, putting as much distance as he could between himself and what was about to happen below. He hadn't even asked why Fuller was blowing up that part of the bunker.

He eventually found his way back to the hangar, where the remaining members of the Cobb Resistance were waiting next to the lift platform. Scanning the faces briefly, the thought crept into his mind that Rettin wasn't the only traitor among them. Something had to have brought Sapphire Nova to the Kalbrec system.

He pushed the distracting thoughts away and looked over at a despondent Monk, who was pacing behind the rest. 'Get your ships to the surface now. Fuller, Vasily and Rettin won't be joining you.'

'What the fuck are you talking about?' asked Cho angrily. 'Where the hell are they?'

Kurcher didn't have time for this. 'Look, corp ships could arrive any minute and we need to be gone by the time they do.'

'The lady asked you a question,' piped up Leeson, finding courage in front of his colleagues.

'I thought Monk here would've filled you in. Rettin was leaking intel to Taurus. He killed Vasily then shot Fuller before I could get to them. Rettin's lying with half a head below and your fucking leader is dying, so has opted to blow himself and your bunker to shit with explosives they had been priming.' Kurcher shrugged his shoulders. 'Any more questions?'

The rest of the Resistance all exchanged stunned looks before Cho took a step forward. 'You're a liar.'

Tell them what Fuller said, suggested Frost.

They won't take your word for it without proof, pointed out D'Larro.

Kurcher turned his back on them. 'Drake.'

'What?' Her response was typically sharp.

'We're leaving as soon as I get back.'

'All done then?'

He glanced back at the confused expressions. 'Not quite. We'll be accompanying the survivors to Seko.'

This started various murmurings among the Resistance members, with Cho continuing to voice her opinion on Kurcher. This time though, it was Monk who shut her down.

'It's true. I saw it myself. Cal's made his decision and given his final order. Let's go.'

This seemed to knock the wind from Cho's sails and she stared at the engineer as he made his way to the lift control. Soon, they were ascending towards the dimming light of the surface for the last time.

As the Resistance members scattered to their respective ships, with Monk offering to pilot Fuller's, Kurcher headed for the *Falcata*. Behind the sleek Echo ship sat the *Cradle's Reach*, its hull covered in dust from the surface winds.

This is a mistake, helping them, warned D'Larro.

Hedmun Oakley was waiting for him near the boarding ramp of the *Falcata*. 'What's going on?' he asked, having noticed the grief-stricken faces emerge from the bunker.

You owe it to these people to at least see them to Seko, said Frost.

Kurcher nodded at Oakley's ship. 'Will you come to Seko or return to Cradle?'

'I'll do what I can to help Fuller and his people; our allies.'

Kurcher took one final look around. The ruins of Jefferson stared expectantly back at him and he shuddered. Fucking place gave him the creeps.

Below them, the explosives were detonated. The ground shook as Vasily's blasts consumed the lower levels of the bunker, burying the man who had created and led the Resistance against all odds.

He survived everything Taurus did to him only to die at the hands of a cretin. Kurcher wasn't sure who that voice belonged to. Was it Fuller himself? Jesus, he hoped not.

He tried to ignore the screams in his head and the ghosts watching him from the ruins, turning his back on Oakley as he entered the *Falcata*.

'Cal Fuller is dead,' he called over his shoulder. 'Long live the fucking Resistance.'

Galt
Lincoln system

He was growing more nervous by the second, pacing back and forth across the VIP arrival lobby before stopping to peer out into the gloomy sky for the hundredth time.

Billings hated waiting, yet this time it would be worth it. Any moment, the ship would land on the spire's upper pylon and he could finally get away from the shitstorm that was coming. He just wished he could see Hayward's face when she realised he had already left Galt.

Below, Kingston was just waking up. The lights of the colony were beginning to blink off as another mundane day dawned on the unimpressive world. He certainly wouldn't miss the drab brown landscapes.

He had been unable to sleep so had spent most of the night considering where Sapphire Nova would relocate him to. He hoped it was somewhere verdant and free of danger. He had risked his life enough and the intel he had fed Nova was worth at least a couple of years enjoying the sun on one of their worlds out on the edge of the galaxy.

Then again, Hayward had forced his hand with the shock announcement she would be taking him back to Earth. He had no intention of letting her drag him back there; no desire to see the planet consumed by the Revenants. She didn't trust him, of course. He knew that by the way she looked at him during their meetings.

Things were so much easier when Lenaghan was still around, when Billings could rely on suspicion being deflected away from him by the pudgy prick. Rees used to come sniffing around and Lenaghan would simply distract him with some random risk to security, talking the man into submission. How things had changed though. Rees' ashes were in orbit somewhere around Straunia and Lenaghan had become another satellite of Kalvion, keeping the late Rolan Cairns company.

Billings turned away from the window. He was alone in the lobby, having arranged for all of the security forces that were usually in the upper levels of the spire to help with patrols downstairs. With Garrett and his fleet halfway across the galaxy by now too, there wouldn't be anyone left to stop him leaving.

Still, Hayward played on his mind. He never thought he would meet anyone as tenacious as Solomon Rees and yet she was more determined than the old judicial officer ever was. While Rees spent most of his time barking orders from his office, his successor was much more proactive. Mitchell had ordered her to stay on Earth, he heard, but she defied the general anyway and came to Galt just to try cleaning Taurus up. Garrett taking command hadn't exactly helped matters either, as he seemed to be a do-gooder just like Hayward. Those sorts of people had no place in politics.

Billings became aware of a soft thrumming noise and a smile played across his face when he recognised the sound as distant engines. As the lobby had windows on all sides, supposedly offering amazing views of the surrounding landscape, he quickly located the approaching vessel and watched as it swooped over the colony, circling the spire twice. It was a small ship, perfect for extracting someone quickly and quietly. It also bore no insignia and was a neutral shade of grey.

As it began descending to the upper pylon, the executive gave a loud sigh of relief and grabbed his single luggage unit. Waiting for the ship to dock, he glanced back down at the brown surface of Galt and shook his head. What a ridiculous place to run a corporation from.

He hadn't known who to expect when the airlock opened, but the temperature in the lobby seemed to dip as the man in the long black jacket stepped through. Everything about him struck Billings as strange. The face was pale, his expression blank. Dark cropped hair matched the jacket in hue and his eyes held a frightening stare, as though they were afraid to blink. Even his walk was odd, striding towards the executive with an unusual gait.

Six other men emerged from the airlock a split second later and Billings felt his mouth go dry when he saw the weapons they were carrying.

'I'm Executive Bill...'

'I know who you are,' interrupted the icy individual. 'I need you to tell me the whereabouts of the other Taurus Galahad board members.'

Billings held his nerve. 'It's just me leaving Galt. Your superiors should have explained that. I didn't catch your name.'

'No, you didn't.' The unblinking eyes scanned the lobby, even looking down at the floor at one point. 'Secure the lift.'

The other new arrivals to Kingston moved past Billings, boomers in hand. Despite the alarm bells ringing in his head, the exec calmly headed for the open airlock.

'You will tell me where I can find board members Chaldevert, Marris and Hayward,' came the oddly unique voice. 'Then you will give me your access codes.'

This stopped Billings in his tracks. 'Why do you need those?'

The man gave the faintest of sighs. 'Because I do.'

Billings tried his best to think clearly. What did it matter if he handed over the codes? He was leaving Taurus Galahad for good so it was in his best interest to appease Nova. Then again, perhaps these men had orders to capture the rest of the board and that thought made him sick to his stomach. It wasn't guilt of course. He just didn't want to share a ride with those he had betrayed. He also found it worrying that the three execs the Nova man wanted the location of just so happened to be busy elsewhere in the colony. Did he know that Tench, Kort and Pavleachenko were already in the spire?

'I don't know exactly where the others are, but Hayward has been hanging around down near one of the hangars on the ground level. Marris will be due back at the spire later today and Chaldevert has an office at the north end of Kingston.'

'Good.' The eyes were staring once more into his soul. 'Now the codes.'

The exec pulled his personal HDU out. No point delaying any longer. The sooner he obliged, the sooner he could get off Galt. He couldn't stop his hand from shaking though as he held the displayed codes out for the Nova agent to see.

There was a glint in one of the man's eyes as his app captured the data. 'Your help has been invaluable, Executive Billings. Sapphire Nova wanted you to know that.'

'Thank you. Now, can I get on board?'

Billings took a step back, aiming to swivel on his heel and march quickly onto the waiting ship. Instead, the breath caught in his throat as the agent produced a pistol from beneath the black jacket and raised it.

'Wait, I've helped you and can continue to do so.' Something warm was trickling down his legs as the fear finally took control. 'They promised me...'

The pistol fired.

~

'All this data is giving me a headache,' Hayward groaned, dropping the HDU on the table. 'I don't know whether to carry on sifting through the messages or try reading up more on the pirates. There's a lot to take in.'

Akeman nodded, his eyes remaining glued to his own screen. 'Take a break, by all means.'

'We haven't got time to take a break. I need to know who Billings has been in contact with and what that last encrypted message to him contained.'

This time, Akeman glanced up. 'I'm working on it. Should make a breakthrough shortly.'

Hayward rubbed at her tired eyes and took a walk around the long table to stretch her legs. She had barely slept since Akeman told her Billings received this message on long distance comms and was eager to uncover just who the traitorous little shit was working with. It was obviously one of the other corps and she had her suspicions which, but there was no need to keep interrupting Akeman with her thoughts while he was so diligently working for her.

The other thing keeping her awake during the chilly Galt nights was what she had been reading on both Schaeffer's Nine and Echo. She had looked into which organisations to approach and, despite the fact they were pirates with a distinct lack of morals, they could come in handy should they agree to some form of alliance. They were also already allied tentatively to one another, which could work in her favour.

Akeman had certainly made some intriguing contacts during his years as a hired mercenary. Jaffren Hewn *was* Echo and had run the organisation since its conception in 2599. After being wounded by a Sigma Royal pursuit mech in 2610, he had lain low in the Echo Expanse for seven years. It was during this time that Akeman had spoken with Hewn, as the pirate created new networks and alliances to make sure Echo were seen as major players in the galaxy. No more would they ambush corp freighters or smuggle goods for the highest bidder. When Hewn finally emerged from the Expanse complete with his new artificial arm, Echo were making good money from drug production and trafficking alongside the supply of alcohol. Hewn didn't want them to be called *pirates* any more, yet the moniker had stuck.

Schaeffer's Nine were a very different prospect. Set up long before Hewn arrived on the scene by a miscreant from Earth named Alkyn Schaeffer, they were smugglers running contraband to the systems closest to Sol until several brushes with the authorities saw them head further out to the likes of Barclay, Dalton and even Achon. Before his alleged death in 2596, Schaeffer split his organisation into nine divisions and allocated them a specific territory. Now, the individuals he placed in charge of each division ran the business like some ruthless board, not unlike the corps. One of these was Akeman's contact and Hayward was not sure she wanted to meet Ti-Jun Niang. The man was said to be a descendant of a Chinese warlord, although she expected that was a falsehood created to make him seem more important than he actually was.

She had completed two laps of the table before coming to a halt just behind Akeman. Peering over his shoulder, she could only see a variety of odd symbols displayed on his screen, all of which she assumed was coding from the hacking platform he was using.

'So you never received any response at all from Fortitude?'

Akeman gave the briefest shake of his head. 'Nothing. Did you really expect them to answer a call to meet with the Taurus judicial officer?'

'I hoped they might.' She moved back to her HDU. 'Then again, they have their hands full I guess with the aftermath of the bombings on Sullivan's Rest.'

There were other reasons Fortitude wouldn't reply, of course. Reports had reached her that they had been seen on various Sigma Royal worlds, so it looked like they were arranging new alliances of their own. Morton Hurst was a conniving, clever son-of-a-bitch and part of Hayward was thankful she wouldn't have to sit down with him.

She had not even bothered extending an invite to the Knights Templar, considering their involvement with Lenaghan's death. They denied knowledge of it, naturally, and would by now have received Hayward's message ordering them to vacate the system. She had not given a reason. The board had put up with scum like that in Lincoln for way too long, mainly due to Lenaghan's frequent visits there to sate his basic urges.

'What motivates you?' she asked Akeman bluntly.

He smiled as he continued watching the screen. 'Money. The freedom to work under the radar of everyone else. The occasional bottle of the most potent alcohol known to man for my troubles.'

Hayward picked up her HDU and chuckled. 'Fair enough. At least you're honest.'

'Why do you ask?'

'Because I find myself wondering what exactly motivates someone like Billings to betray his own people. When exactly did the human race become so corrupt?'

'Billings will be motivated by money too, only he clearly sees a way to get rich quick. He's power-hungry and obviously doesn't believe in Taurus like you do.' Akeman looked up with a smirk. 'As for the human race, it's always been corrupt. It's just taken centuries for us to hone our selfishness.'

As the two shared a rare moment of mirth, they became aware of a distant alarm sounding from elsewhere in the colony and Akeman's amusement faded.

Hayward saw the change in his demeanour. 'What is it?'

Before he could answer, there was a deafening boom and the whole room shuddered violently. The alarms rang out much louder and Hayward gripped the edge of the table to stop herself from pitching forwards. Panicked voices could be heard from the adjacent corridors.

'Kingston is under attack,' announced Akeman, leaping up. 'I need to get you to a safer location.'

'Under attack by who?' she cried, unable to hide her rising fear.

Akeman chose not to respond and instead grabbed her arm and led her swiftly out of the meeting room. It wasn't long before she could smell smoke and colonists were frantically heading in all directions.

Kingston shook again, the walls and ceiling groaning as they rattled. Hayward heard the deep thrum of an engine passing overhead.

'Where are we going?' she yelled to Akeman. 'We need to gauge the damage to the colony.'

He continued to ignore her questions, dragging her along at speed through the throng. At one junction, she glanced right towards one of the hangars and could only see flames. Then she spotted a child huddled against a nearby wall, alone and frightened, calling for her mother.

'Wait.' Hayward wrenched her arm away from Akeman's grip and ran to the girl.

The agent followed, scooping up the child. 'They've targeted the hangars so nobody can leave. I have a ship hidden on the other side of Kingston and I suggest we use it.'

'I can't just leave everyone behind,' she snapped angrily.

'Miss Hayward, the board are here and the fleet is not. This attack comes with that knowledge.'

She knew Billings had sold them out but would he have had the balls to offer up the whole of Kingston to his associates? Either way, she needed to place her trust in Akeman at that particular moment and just hope the aim of the attack was not the total destruction of the colony.

~

Rist stepped over the bodies of the security guards. Two of them had been struck in the chest by boomers and were now just a pile of smoking flesh. Dismembered limbs lay nearby, thrown clear by the explosion. The rest of the guards had taken shots to an arm or a leg and he didn't know which was a worst way to die. One man had been hit in the bicep, the following blast taking his head off as well as the arm. Another unfortunate received a bullet to the thigh which destroyed his genitals when it went off.

Despite his preference for the customised boomer he kept close, Rist found it crude of Sapphire Nova to order them to use the destructive weapons wherever possible during their hunt for the Taurus board. They clearly wanted to send a very visceral message.

'This floor, or the one below?' came the question from one of the mercs he had been placed in charge of.

Rist checked his app, locating Pavleachenko's lifesigns. 'Next one down.'

As they made their way to the lift, using Billings' access codes to bypass the secure doors, Rist glanced out of one window just in time to see the ship dive at the colony, unleashing a single missile. The reinforced metalwork criss-crossing the exterior of Kingston crumpled and twisted in the explosion. The ship avoided a retaliatory burst of gunfire from the defence turrets before soaring out of view.

Naturally, he had questioned the effectiveness and probability of success of this mission. It was a plan that would ensure there would be no turning back in the escalating war between Nova and Taurus. A single ship once used solely to carry military personnel down onto a planet now kitted out with a high quality conflector and laden with both fusion and missile weapons, crewed by just three. It seemed an unlikely choice to lay siege to a colony of Kingston's size, and yet it was agile enough to dodge the defensive gunfire while capable enough to cause significant damage.

The ship, of course, was just the distraction, allowing Rist and the boomer-wielding mercs enough time to complete their mission. The attack would leave Taurus in disarray and their board dead. In Klein's mind, it was simply an eye for an eye.

They rode one of the executive lifts down a single floor, finding themselves heading into a maze of offices. Rist kept the target firmly in the centre of his vision as he led the assault team past empty cubicles, signalling two mercs to stand watch as they approached Pavleachenko's position.

They found the exec cowering behind a desk in a locked office, which Rist had quickly opened thanks to Billings. The only illumination was from the screen before him.

'Oh god.' The terrified man raised his hands, his eyes fixed on the boomers. 'Please don't.'

'You Pavleachenko?' asked one merc.

Rist ended the conversation before it could start, his shot passing through the screen and blowing the board member backwards off his chair. There was a brief wail before the explosive detonated.

'No need to engage with them,' berated Rist as he led them back towards the lifts. 'I'd already identified the target. Don't hesitate again.'

His sensory app suddenly pinged, highlighting several lifesigns just arriving on the same administration floor. Data alongside two displayed the names Kort and Tench.

'Kill everyone getting out that lift,' he ordered.

A squad of Taurus security guards deployed as the doors opened and, much to Rist's chagrin, the mercs were impatient, firing on them too early. As boomer shots missed and detonated among the cubicles, the guards took up defensive positions. Soon, there was a destructive exchange as the Kingston men were armed with short-burst assault rifles, forcing the mercs to also dive for cover.

Rist noticed that the two board members behind the guards were not afraid to join the fray. As he crouched behind a relatively flimsy partition wall, he accessed data that Billings had provided previously on the rest of the Taurus board. Tench had once been a soldier, so knew how to handle himself. Kort had experience with firearms too and his profile showed him to be a particularly cunning individual. However, Rist had been presented with the opportunity to eliminate both men and doubted he would get a better chance.

Despite having automatic weapons, the guards soon began to fall to the unpredictable nature of the boomers. One merc missed his mark, the resulting blast forcing two of the sec team out into the open, where they were both gunned down.

As the mercs pushed their advantage and began to drive the Taurus men from cover, Rist flanked the fight, keeping low to avoid detection as he moved from cubicle to cubicle. His app was useful in situations such as these, knowing where everyone was at all times. If only he had that sort of tech in his previous life.

'Pull back,' came a cry from near the lift.

That was the moment he had been waiting for. Stepping out, he unleashed three shots in quick succession, which was a devastating trait of his unique boomer. The first struck the wall next to the lift, exploding as it ricocheted and sending the sec team reeling. The second had already struck its target before the first exploded, catching one unfortunate in the abdomen before ripping him apart from inside. The third shot missed Kort by mere inches, grazing Tench's shoulder before bouncing upwards towards the ceiling. The explosion brought panels and metalwork down around the guards. More importantly, Tench was caught by the edge of the blast and fell as he headed into the lift, flames licking across his uniform.

That spelt the end of the sec team as the mercs pushed forward. However, Kort had managed to get onto the lift. He and Tench were on their way back down the spire.

Not one to show his frustration, Rist handed his weapon to a merc and his fingers found purchase in the gap between the lift doors. The strength of the hydraulics in his left arm quickly forced the doors apart and he peered down the shaft. The lift was descending quickly. Snatching back his boomer, he leaned over the edge and fired twice.

When the explosives detonated, two things happened. Firstly, the mechanisms holding the lift in place were obliterated, plunging it into a lethal drop. Secondly, and more alarmingly, the tight confines of the shaft funneled the flames upwards swifter than Rist had anticipated. He pulled his head back just in time and stepped out the way as the heat and smoke billowed out into the room.

When he checked to see how many of the mercs he had lost, there was something worryingly familiar about the scene. Faces looked back at him, blackened by the smoke, and the crackle of flames seemed impossibly loud. The smell of charred flesh hung heavy in the air, but there was a sickly sweet aroma that occasionally hit him. The scent of Thorn's toxic plants burning.

'What now?' one of the remaining five mercs asked, giving Rist a strange look.

'We have to...' A feeling that something was amiss made him trail off.

Leaving them frowning at one another, Rist moved to the nearest window and activated his app, searching for the signature of the ship that they had arrived on. It was no longer docked with the pylon above and he eventually located it just as it disappeared into the upper atmosphere. That wasn't part of the plan.

A burst of static hissed through his head, clearing his mind and refocusing his senses.

He returned to the bemused mercs. 'We find the rest of the Taurus board.'

~

The central plaza of Kingston was a mess.

Hayward would have stopped in her tracks as they entered was it not for Akeman urging her along every few seconds, the sobbing little girl clinging tightly to him. She wondered what had happened to the child's parents and could only hope they were still alive somewhere in the colony.

Glass shards lined the floor, glinting in the light of the rising sun having fallen from windows and ceiling panels. The scent of the Galt air was noticeable through the acrid odour of smoke.

As Akeman picked his way swiftly through the glass carpet, Hayward looked up at a metal girder that had swung down, one end dislodged by the attack. It was so long that it almost touched the ground and she tried to ignore a red stain on one edge.

Hundreds of voices echoed across the concourse as colonists seemed unsure which way to flee and security guards tried their best to calm them. Medics could be seen tending to stricken men and women throughout the vast chamber, casting fearful glances upwards occasionally.

'Miss Hayward.'

She realised her pace had slowed as she took in the terrible scene. Akeman was gesturing frantically at her as he pushed past a group of colonists heading the other way.

As she followed, trying her best to keep up with the surprisingly nimble agent, she noticed flames emerging from the side of the spire several floors up. At the base, a number of people had gathered near one of the lift doors and seemed to be trying to open them. Akeman had also noticed this and his route had altered slightly to pass by them.

Hayward heard the roar of the ship engine above somewhere and instinctively ducked. Fortunately, or not so for the rest of the colony, it was focused elsewhere.

By the time she caught up with him, Akeman had just finished speaking with a guard who was among those by the spire. 'Seems there was an explosion in the lift shaft that caused it to fall. Emergency brakes managed to stop it between floors.'

She could tell there was something else. 'There are people in the lift?'

'Yes. Executives Kort and Tench.'

Hayward glanced up at the burning section of the spire. 'We need to help get them out then.'

Before she could step past him, Akeman grasped her arm. 'No, you need to get to safety.'

He had never dared lay a hand on her before, always keeping a respectful distance between them. She almost bit angrily at his response, but the expression on that scarred face stopped her from doing so. Was it concern for her in his eyes or was it concern for the money she paid him?

'They clearly need help,' she stated, gesturing at the lift doors. 'Please.'

Akeman thought for a second then unwrapped the child's arms from around his neck and handed her to Hayward, the girl almost choking the judicial officer as she clamped hold. 'Unlike the rest of us, Miss Hayward, you're not expendable.' He handed his HDU to her too. 'This shows directions to my ship along with the access codes to unlock it and start the engines. I will follow as soon as we get your colleagues out.'

She started to protest again and Akeman simply turned his back on her, running to the group at the base of the spire, where he began taking charge of the situation. When the little girl whined and sobbed against her, Hayward reluctantly headed away, checking the map on the HDU as she crossed the plaza.

~

Rist knew that Kort and Tench were both still alive. Their lifesigns had appeared in his vision as the boomer squad descended in the other lift.

The priority was clear though. They needed to deal with those who had gathered below before turning their attentions to the trapped execs.

'We're going to run out of ammo at this rate,' muttered one of the mercs behind him. 'We can't fight our way through the entire colony.'

'We should leave now,' said another. 'Get back to the ship and get the fuck off this planet.'

Rist had not divulged the fact their ride had already departed. Something still felt wrong about that but he couldn't get distracted from the task at hand.

'Two of the board are dead,' he began, looking back at the disgruntled mercs. 'Two more are injured and trapped in that lift. We do not leave until all seven are accounted for.'

The chances of being able to find Hayward, Marris and Chaldevert were of course slim, especially during the panic of the attack. If the ship had attacked the colony much later, once Rist and the mercs had managed to infiltrate Kingston properly, it would have made the mission easier. His annoyance was short-lived, as his app reminded him of the threat waiting for them below.

They had the element of surprise and, when the lift reached the ground floor, the colonists gathered nearby clearly expected some of their own to step off. A security guard was standing just before the doors waiting to usher whoever was inside away to safety. He was the first to die.

The mercs moved too swiftly into the plaza for Rist's liking, firing randomly into the horrified colonists. He knew their boomers would soon run dry and they would resort to smaller weapons, which would mean they lost their advantage. Cover was also limited down on this ground level, with the seating areas and raised plant beds the only places to duck behind.

Rist watched from just inside the lift as sec forces returned fire, trying not to hit their own people. The expressions on the faces of the colonists showed just how terrified they were. A question frequently entered his mind as he observed the slaughter.

When did I become a terrorist?

He noticed one man ushering colonists away, his voice clear and concise over the noise. He was not dressed in a security uniform but people were listening to him, even the guards. Rist tried to access any data based on the man's scarred face. Nothing was found. When he refocused on this intriguing individual, he was just in time to see him kill one of the mercs with an accurate shot to the head.

Rist moved from the lift, his aim being to remove this dangerous opponent from the fight. As he began to flank him, there was a warning ping and he dived for the nearest cover as the Nova attack ship unleashed a burst of fusion on the central plaza. Glass and metal rained down, including a girder that landed between Rist and the remaining mercs. The fusion strike had also ripped through a section of flooring, catching several of the plant beds.

When he peered out to locate the man he was determined to kill, his eyes were drawn to the burning foliage.

They've betrayed us.

He recalled the voice clearly being yelled into his right ear as everything burnt around them, the air becoming filled with the smell of the brambles.

Mikan, what the fuck do we do?

Nova's ships unleashed one last barrage before retreating. Explosions obliterated Taurus soldiers and Rist's men alike, creating a blaze that surrounded any survivors completely. Toxic fumes from the brambles stung his eyes and seared his throat as he searched for a way out.

You killed us, you bastard.

Rist found himself back in the debris of the Kingston plaza. He could still hear the final shouts of his men as they perished among the bramble forests of Thorn, poisoned or burnt alive.

He looked down at his left hand, flexing the artificial fingers that the Nova scientists had given him. He could remember the pain he felt when they scooped up what was left of him; when they cut away the charred flesh and started dissecting parts of him, only to replace them with metal and tech. He remembered trying to open his left eye when it was nothing but a raw empty socket.

'They've fucking done it again,' he muttered to himself.

Bursts of pain shot through his skull and down the left side of his body, his eyesight blurring and shaking violently. The Nova tech was trying to reassert itself; trying to force his human side back into a subservient state.

As he shook his head in an attempt to clear his senses, the sensory app pinged again. His sight returned to normal instantly and an image of a woman's face appeared at the top of his vision, linking to a highlighted figure fleeing the plaza.

Without knowing whether the boomer mercs were alive or not, Rist left the carnage next to the lifts behind in order to follow Karin Hayward.

~

The closer she got to Akeman's ship, the quieter the colony became. His directions had taken her into a part of Kingston populated by storage bays connected by wide hallways. The alarms from the rest of the colony could still be heard behind her, and she hadn't felt any explosions since the last fusion strike on the plaza. She hoped that meant an end to the attacks.

The little girl still clung tightly to her, but she had at least learned her name. Rose hadn't spoken much since they came across her on the other side of Kingston and was clearly traumatised. The child had finally quietened down and Hayward was extremely thankful for that. She had been close to losing patience with the incessant sobbing.

She looked down at Akeman's HDU. 'Nearly there.'

She hoped the agent was still alive. There had been the sound of gunfire as she fled before the ship blew another hole in Kingston. As much as she wanted to go back and help, ensuring Rose's survival was more important at that moment in time.

Ahead was a crossroads and she began to veer right, remembering the directions more easily now that there were no distractions. As she approached the junction, there was a strange sound from behind her, like a muffled pop of air. She glanced back before disappearing round the corner, only to see a man at the other end of the hallway.

Something fizzed past her head and struck the wall, then she was blown forward by an explosion. Her face hit the floor hard and she heard Rose scream. Her ears were ringing and her vision swimming as she tried to get up. Her shoulder felt as though it was on fire.

By the time she had pushed herself up into a kneeling position, the man she had seen was standing before her. In one hand was Akeman's HDU, whilst the other held an odd-looking weapon. She tried to focus on his pale face but her eyes were watering by that time.

When she heard a gentle sobbing again, she felt some semblance of relief.

'Rose?'

'The girl will live.' The man's voice was cold, almost devoid of emotion.

'Who are you?' she demanded. 'What do you want?'

He was staring intently at the HDU screen. 'Who am I?'

Hayward noted a complete change in the voice, as though it was someone else talking. The question was tinged with uncertainty.

'Just let the girl and me go. Please.'

His face twitched, as though he had felt a twinge of pain. 'No.'

She was suddenly staring down the barrel of his weapon and closed her eyes, realising that there was nothing she could do to stop the inevitable.

A shot echoed along the hallway and Hayward tensed. However, it was the distinct sound of a pistol and, when she opened her eyes, her assailant had turned away and was stalking back the way they had come. Her jaw dropped when she noticed that one of the man's ears was missing, metal gleaming from the wound. It dropped further when she spotted said ear lying on the floor, next to the HDU.

The assassin began shooting, his bullets exploding further down the hallway just as the one that barely missed her had. It was then she saw Akeman, the agent managing to dance away from one blast and returning fire. Another explosion sent him reeling backwards and all he could do was fling himself around the corner of the junction at the other end to avoid being seared.

Two more boomer rounds destroyed sections of the wall and then the assassin came to an abrupt halt, looking down at his weapon and shaking it. Seeing this, Akeman swung from his cover, pistol ready to fire. He managed to get off a single shot. Hayward's heart missed a beat as she realised the assassin had feigned a problem just to lure Akeman out and had somehow managed to pull his own pistol with his free hand. Akeman's shot struck the man's shoulder with a metallic thud. The assassin's shot hit Akeman square in the chest, knocking him onto his back.

When the killer turned and looked back at her, Hayward realised that she had been transfixed by the exchange with her would-be saviour. She jumped up, her legs responding painfully slowly, and ran as fast as she could for Rose, who was lying stricken in a foetal position.

'We have to go,' she yelled at the child. 'Now.'

As she tried to rouse the girl, Hayward looked up and once more froze as the assassin was returning, his pistol trained on her. The vicious boomer had been discarded. When he was close enough, she could see that the bullet to his shoulder had produced no blood, same as the ear. Only tech was visible within. As her vision had cleared slightly, she could see that the man's eyes were aglow with data. Still, there was a look akin to confusion or fear on his face now and his arm wavered.

'Please...' she whispered, as the barrel of his pistol was placed against her forehead.

His voice this time was edged with sadness. 'I must complete my mission. Thorn *must* belong to Sapphire Nova.'

Hayward wanted to frown but the cold metal pressed against her skin stopped her brow from crinkling. 'Thorn?'

'No, they...left me to die...again.' He suddenly lowered the pistol slightly, still keeping it pointed at her, and picked up the HDU from next to his shredded ear. After gazing at the directions to Akeman's ship for a moment, he looked at her with distant eyes. 'I was once Mikan Rist.'

With that, he was gone, sweeping past her and away in the direction she *had* been heading. Hayward's knees felt weak and her stomach couldn't knot any tighter. Her body aching and sore, she picked Rose up and carried her as quickly as she could to where Akeman lay, his breathing laboured and his face ashen.

'Don't move,' she told him. 'I'll call the medics.'

'I think they might be quite busy elsewhere,' he said, managing a weak smile.

She could see blood pumping from the wound in his chest, seeping through his clothes and pooling on the floor beneath him. 'I can't just let you die.'

Akeman waved a hand over the bullet hole. 'I'll bleed out quickly so you'd better work fast, Miss Hayward. I'll guide you as best I can.'

She put Rose down and crouched down, ready to do what was needed. 'Best call me Karin from now on.'

Seko
Miller system

He had waited long enough for his bombshell to sink in.

'Everyone understand?' Kurcher asked them, purposefully sounding impatient.

Hedmun Oakley nodded, his eyes firmly fixed on the new leader of the Cobb Resistance. Marie Butler had her back to the rest of them, her hands covering her face and her head bowed.

Kurcher glanced at Drake, who rolled her eyes and shrugged. Fischer was standing alongside the pilot wearing the same frown he had greeted them with just a couple of hours previous.

The other two people in the room had hardly uttered a word since they arrived. Monk had his broad arms crossed and looked wholly uncomfortable, whereas Cho still seemed as angry as she had been on Cobb before they departed.

Fuller was a father figure to a lot of these people, noted Frost.

There is a time and a place to grieve, added Santa Cruz.

'Kurcher's right.' It was Oakley who took the lead finally. 'All of the Resistance is now here on Seko, ready to start over and rebuild with help from Echo and ourselves. You have to take the reins and guide them.'

Butler turned to face them. When her hands dropped, her eyes were red from tears. '*All* of the Resistance? The most important person isn't here. Vasily and Dale aren't here. Those who were intercepted and taken by Taurus aren't here.'

'They were taken because of Dale.' Monk had plucked up the courage to speak. 'Cal and Vasily are dead because of Dale.'

'And Dale is dead because of Dale,' said Kurcher. 'Look, you can dwell on what might have been but the father of your child was a traitor and a murderer. He's gone. Time to move the fuck on.'

Tactful as always, remarked Frost.

'Amen,' mumbled Drake.

Butler regarded Kurcher with a look of pure disdain. 'You just happened to be the last one to see Cal and Dale alive. How do I know you're telling the truth?'

'Monk was also there,' sighed Kurcher. 'The message is simple. You're in command of the Cobb Resistance now and, by working with your new allies, you can thrive on this planet.'

'Seko is a damned sight better than your previous home,' spoke up Fischer. 'You have resources here and we'll support you where need be.'

'As will we,' Oakley was quick to add.

Kurcher's head was beginning to pound. It was times like this he wished he could still activate his boost app and feel the Parinax surge through his veins. That tech was defunct now and his drug reserves empty.

She'd stab you right through the fucking heart if she could.

Ercko was right. Butler was still glaring at him and he had clocked the pistol at her side the moment he had entered the room. She knew he had killed Rettin and her suspicious gaze told him she also thought he might have had a hand in Fuller's death too.

As they waited for her to respond, Kurcher took another quick look around the room. He had expected to land at some makeshift camp, where the remaining members of the Resistance were living in tents or on board their crusty old ships. Finding a relatively modern base of operations already being built had come as a surprise. They had Hewn and Fischer to thank for that.

It just means Hewn will ask her for a big favour one day, said D'Larro.

Pirates don't do anything for free, commented Frost.

'So what about those who Taurus captured?' Butler asked the room. 'Surely they would have extracted the intel that we were coming here.'

'Without a shadow of a doubt,' replied Fischer, stepping forward. 'Taurus aren't about to come storming into the Expanse looking for you though. They know we own these systems and I don't think you'd be high on their list of priorities right now. No offense.'

'That's true, Marie,' piped up Cho. 'Taurus and Nova had been kicking the shit out of one another in Kalbrec. Sounds like they are doing the same all over the galaxy.'

Fischer continued. 'The corps all have their hands full with power struggles or Kindred bombings. You're safe here on Seko, I assure you.'

'And what of Libra?' Butler asked, raising an eyebrow at Hewn's second. 'You're still working with them, right?'

Fischer gave a curt nod. 'Our alliance with them is a mutually beneficial one.'

She sniffed and looked away. 'I know. Drugs.'

'I'm sorry for your loss,' Fischer told her, trying to sound sincere. 'We all are. Contact me if you need anything.'

As the pirate headed for the door, Kurcher noticed a flick of the head at Drake. The pilot followed Fischer out, a bored expression plastered across her face.

'You...' Butler was addressing him once more. 'I should throw you in a cell to rot for what you've done, or just execute you now.'

For a moment, Kurcher thought Oakley had gone back on the promise to keep his past from the Resistance.

'I vouch for him,' the old officer said, snuffing out that thought and drawing looks of surprise from the others. 'If anything, he saved your people.'

Monk stepped forward, casting a derisive glance at Kurcher. 'I'll second that.'

Butler's eyes were beginning to tear up again as she looked across at Cho, who gave a reluctant nod.

'Well, as humbled as I am by the love in the room, I'll leave you to it.' Kurcher tried to stride away nonchalantly, but the idea that Butler might pull her pistol at any time made his exit slightly more clumsy than he would have liked.

It was a simple route back to the temporary landing pads and he passed several engineers busily working on their new home, choosing not even to look their way. The door leading outside was partially open and a gentle Seko breeze stroked his face as he approached. It also brought with it a familiar voice.

'I'm not asking for much,' Fischer stated. 'Just the facts.'

'I've given you the facts.' Drake's response was as sharp as ever. 'We did the job Hewn sent us out there to do, plain and simple.'

'Yeah, but you didn't actually see what Kurcher was up to, right? He was down in the bunker and you were above in the *Falcata*.'

'What the fuck has that got to do with anything?'

'Hewn trusts him way too much.' Fischer had lowered his voice. 'He's a junkie, a murderer and an ex-Taurus goon.'

This fucker clearly has a hard-on for you, laughed Ercko.

Kurcher shuffled nearer to the door, straining to hear the conversation as some of the engineers behind him yelled to one another.

'You jealous, Vance?' mocked Drake.

'Of that prick? Listen, I've got one request. Keep a close eye on him. He's bad news for Echo. For all we know, he *did* kill Fuller.'

'Why the fuck would he do that?'

'To save his own skin.' Fischer's tone was full of contempt. 'He could go back to Taurus with the news he had iced the leader of the Cobb Resistance and hand over a shitload of data stolen from their bunker. He could lead them right here, just to get back in their good books.'

This guy really is a piece of work, noted D'Larro.

He's going to cause you more problems, remarked Santa Cruz.

'Kurcher is a seriously fucked up individual.' Drake paused, most likely to take a drag on one of her cigarettes. 'He's not stupid though. Sure, he has delusions of grandeur. Don't we all?'

'*You're* vouching for him now? You fuck him or something?'

'Yeah, I did. Next question.'

Kurcher smiled as he imagined the look on Fischer's face. Was Drake actually standing up for him or was it simply her usual abrasive nature?

'There are a lot of people in Echo who don't want him around,' Fischer said a moment later. 'I thought you'd be one of them.'

'You just worry about you,' came Drake's distant call, indicating that she had walked away from the conversation.

When Fischer stepped back inside the colony, Kurcher wanted to pass him without speaking and yet there was a burning question he needed to ask.

'Any news on Broekow yet?'

Hewn's second looked him up and down, clearly biting back both his anger and envy. He was also trying to work out whether Kurcher had caught any of his exchange with the pilot.

'Nothing so far.'

'And you're not concerned?'

'Are you?' The reply was swift and harsh. 'Not many in our organisation tend to make reports on the fly. They wait until they're standing in front of Jaffren.'

'Sounds like a shit way of doing it. Masami seemed like the sort who would check in.'

Fischer gave a purposefully loud sigh. 'The *Crius* often has trouble with comms. Masami has been trying to repair it, but his assignments have been coming thick and fast of late. He told me recently that he would gather any intel and hand it all over once he was back.'

'They should be back by now,' Kurcher observed.

'Maybe.' Fischer made to step away from him. 'Maybe not. They're probably still investigating. It's pretty important we find out what happened to the *Magnussen*, for the benefit of our alliance with Libra. So, unless you have some fucking valid points to make, you need to get back to the *Glaive*.'

Kurcher couldn't be bothered arguing with him and they parted ways. He stepped outside and breathed in the sweet air of the verdant world. All around the edge of the colony, tall trees waved in the wind that was slowly picking up, their green and red pod-like foliage rustling as they danced.

He made his way to the *Falcata*, which Drake had set down as far from the new base as possible. The *Cradle's Reach* loomed on the opposite side of the clearing, blotting out the slowly dipping sun, and Kurcher wondered why Oakley didn't leave it in orbit rather than insisting on landing such a large vessel.

He found Drake in the cockpit, feet up on the console and staring at the colony as she lit yet another cigarette.

'Those things will rot your lungs,' he mumbled as he fell into the other seat behind her.

Truth be told, he was getting used to the aroma.

'And I suppose Parinax was good for your brain?' she shot back.

That made him smile. 'It kept me focused. Gave me the boost I needed to get the job done.'

'You should have the implant removed. Tech like that will fuck you up.'

He wished he could have all the Taurus apps removed. The sensory app helped him locate targets and avoid unnecessary risk. The comms app had kept him in close contact with Frost even when he was on the ground and she was up in the *Kaladine*.

I miss her, said Frost.

Now, the sensory app lay dormant, its tech burnt out by Echo, and the altered comms app gave him headaches. He would have jumped at the opportunity to have everything surgically removed was it not for the risk such a procedure carried. The boost app itself would have been simple to remove. It was the miniscule vial that once held the Parinax and the feed direct to his veins that would prove tricky to disconnect. Besides, he didn't much like the idea of someone digging around behind his eyes for the sensory app.

'Jesus, do you ever shut the fuck up?'

He realised he had drifted off with his own thoughts again. At least they *were* his own.

'Fischer said we're to go back to the *Glaive*,' he mentioned. 'We're done here.'

'We'll go back when I say we will.' Drake took an abnormally long drag then let the smoke slowly seep from between those blue lips.

'I guess there are shitter worlds to visit. Good place to take some time out.'

‘Fuck Seko.’ The pirate rose from her seat, revealing she had unbuttoned her shirt.

Kurcher made a point of staring at her breasts. He knew she liked that. His eyes roamed across the tattoo that covered her left breast; some hybrid beast looking like a wolf crossed with a bear. One day, he would have to ask what it was supposed to mean. Then again, when he had asked about the one on her thigh, she punched him in the cock.

Drake lowered herself onto his lap and wrinkled her nose. ‘You need a shower.’

He grinned and ran his hands up her hips. ‘So do you.’

Every time they had sex, it was always on her terms and this time was no different. The cockpit of the *Falcata* wasn’t exactly the most comfortable place to do it, but she didn’t care. The pleasure outweighed the pain.

An hour later, she was done with him. As always, she left him alone without any departing words. This time though, she had also left him with several bleeding welts. Maybe that was why the beast on her breast. She was a fucking animal.

He took the shower he so desperately needed, stretching his aching limbs as the tepid water tried to wash him clean. He was starting to feel older than his thirty-seven years, especially when he knew that Drake was nearly ten years younger. He realised at that moment he had actually had a birthday during the *Falcata*’s journey to Cobb. He was thirty-eight.

Fuck.

By the time he had dressed, Oakley was waiting for him just inside the airlock. Drake was nowhere to be seen.

‘Butler wants to see you,’ he told Kurcher, clearly disgruntled at being her errand boy.

‘I haven’t really got anything else to say to her.’

Oakley’s mood darkened. ‘I’ve just spent the last hour explaining your worth so don’t make me look like an idiot.’

‘I didn’t ask you to.’

Don’t forget he could screw you over at any time, Frost reminded him.

With a frustrated shake of the head, Kurcher headed back to the colony, not even bothering to wait for Oakley, nor checking whether the old man was actually following.

The sun had dropped below the horizon and the clearing was lit by lamps supplied by Echo. Above, the stars were revealing themselves and Kurcher tried to ignore just how serene Seko seemed to be.

Butler was still in the same room as before, although this time she offered him a weak smile instead of execution. For several seconds, there was only silence as she found the courage to speak.

'Maybe I jumped to conclusions too hastily. I would never have believed Dale to be capable of such betrayal.' She bowed her head slightly. 'If anyone is to blame, it should be me for pushing him away.'

Do we really have to listen to this bullshit? asked Ercko.

'He was weak and clearly blamed Fuller for what happened, so you need to move on.'

There was another flash of anger across her face. This time, it dissipated quickly.

'You have to understand that I've lost the only two men I ever truly loved so it's difficult thinking about them lying dead thousands of light years away from here.'

Kurcher glanced around the room, avoiding eye contact with her. He had left corpses in most corners of the galaxy and even some outside it. The whole Milky Way was becoming one vast graveyard.

'I have to return to Hewn shortly,' he said bluntly. 'What was it you wanted?'

Butler's vulnerability dissolved. 'You came to us back on Cobb asking for help in fighting Santa Cruz. It was an unfair request considering the size of our operation and the quality of our ships and weapons. Even though Rane was with you, using that silver tongue of his, Cal chose to help because he saw just how important the cause was and knew the benefit of an alliance with Echo.'

The mention of Rane still fuelled some furnace of hate within him. The manipulative prick had been plotting to use the *Grail* against Sapphire Nova even as they persuaded Fuller to join them, all the time knowing that the Resistance would likely be wiped out during the distracting battle in Flint.

'So now I ask for your help.'

Kurcher gave a nonchalant shrug. 'Echo will help you as much as they can. They've already given you a new start on a peaceful world.'

'No, not Echo.' She stepped closer to him, a steely look in her eyes. 'You.'

She thinks you owe her, D'Larro noted.

'What do you want with me?' he found himself asking.

'We are still the Cobb Resistance,' she said proudly. 'However, we lost a lot of people fighting your battles and because of Dale's actions so we must grow again. We need to become a force to be reckoned with in our own right, so that nobody will take advantage of us again.'

'You're not answering my question.' Kurcher sounded impatient and yet his heart was starting to beat much quicker than it should.

'You're an enlister. You may not have the official title any more but let's not mince words. The only difference to before is that you now do Hewn's dirty work, either bringing people on board with Echo or blowing their heads off. I want you to enlist people to *our* cause.'

Since he first carried out his orders on Cobb during the war, those who died because of his actions had haunted him, their wails and cries for help threatening to drive him mad. Suddenly, they were all laughing at him.

If only she knew the truth, said Santa Cruz.

'I don't want anything to do with this.' He turned to leave.

'Why?' Her question made him hesitate. 'What is it that you dislike so much about the Resistance?'

'I was there.' He was surprised by his own admission. 'When Taurus chose to make an example of your people.'

Don't burn this bridge too, warned Frost.

Tell her, yelled the voices of Cobb.

Butler was regarding him with a look of both confusion and suspicion. 'In what capacity?'

'I don't want anything to do with this,' Kurcher told her again angrily.

'We helped you and now you need to repay the favour. If you were truly there during the war, you know how the colonists suffered. Help us rebuild.'

You were the one making them suffer, Santa Cruz reminded him.

'I know.'

Without looking back at the leader of the Resistance, Kurcher stalked from the room. As he returned to the *Falcata*, his mind was reeling. The voices argued among themselves, the odd word stinging his brain.

Murderer.

Torturer.

Redemption.

Unnamed vessel
Callyn system

Even lifting his head was an effort.

Broekow's eyes would become accustomed to the darkness of the room, only for Harz or one of his men to turn on the lights. Sometimes they came in after doing so, sometimes they were just playing with him.

They wouldn't let him sleep either. Whenever exhaustion took hold and he drifted off, one of them would wake him up with a loud siren or, more often, a punch to the stomach.

He had no idea what day or time it was. He didn't know how long it had been since he had been forced to watch Harz murder Masami. He certainly didn't know where the hell they actually were now. All he knew was that he was a prisoner on the Bold's ship and that, so far, they hadn't even asked him anything.

The torture had started lightly, focusing on his already broken hand. Then they started the cutting and slicing, targeting a different part of his body every time they returned. The last cut they gave him was across his forehead, allowing the blood to run into his eyes. With his hands bound, Broekow couldn't wipe it away. As he had closed his eyes tight though, the pirates had set to work punching him from various angles. Some of his ribs were no doubt broken and his body was covered in dark bruises.

He looked up to the chains holding his arms aloft. The shackles had cut into his wrists, turning the metal crimson. His arms too were stained where the rivulets of blood had made their way down.

His body was numb now, as was his brain. The last session had involved them using a blowtorch on him, searing the skin just enough to make him cry out before stopping. The pain of the burns took a long time to dull and now he was just waiting for the next time the door opened.

Truth be told, he was ready to die. There was nothing to go back to; nothing to look forward to. The only person who could have been labelled a friend was lying dead on a frozen moon, his body slowly being buried beneath snow and ice. Everybody who got close to him ended up dead. Perhaps he and Kurcher were more similar than he had first realised.

His body needed to rest and his head dropped once more as sleep took hold. Seconds later, the only door to the room was thrown open with a loud grind of metal.

'No time for that,' boomed Harz, turning the lights on and slamming the door shut behind him. 'We have a lot to talk about.'

When Broekow mustered the strength to lift his head once more, he found the pirate's grotesque tattooed face unnervingly close to his own. He couldn't help but focus on the section of missing beard that Masami had sliced off. New skin had already started to form across the wound.

Harz pulled that wicked knife from his belt. In his other hand, he held a blowtorch.

'Thought it was about time you and I had some quality time together.'

Broekow wanted to spit in the man's face but even his saliva glands seemed to have given up. Instead, he looked away, unwilling to engage with the sadistic brute.

'It's best you pay attention.' The blowtorch burst into life and Harz held his blade under the roaring flames. 'This is the chance to show your worth.'

When there was no reaction, Harz placed the red hot blade against Broekow's chest and grinned at the pained cry it evoked.

'What's the name of Hewn's flagship?'

Broekow took a deep breath, trying his best to ignore the smell of his own seared flesh. 'I'm sure you already know the answer to that,' he muttered.

'I do,' shrugged Harz. 'But I want you to tell me nonetheless.'

'Fuck you.'

Harz calmly heated the blade again, then placed the blowtorch down and grabbed Broekow's right hand. With one savage cut, he severed the index finger halfway down.

The pain that shot through Broekow's body was excruciating and he pulled against the shackles as he spasmed.

'That was your trigger finger, right?' Harz said, gleefully. 'The finger that killed fuck knows how many men.'

Broekow daren't glance up at his butchered digit. 'Just cut my throat and be done with it,' he managed to mumble.

'What's the name of Hewn's flagship?' came the question again.

'Fuck. You.' Broekow wanted to believe he was being brave, knowing that the Bold would gladly cut off every part of him piece at a time to get what they wanted. He wasn't sure there was anything courageous about it though.

Harz placed the tip of his blade just beneath Broekow's eye. 'You've still got an app implant in there. Either you answer my question or I'll go in through your eye socket and remove it.'

'It'd do me a favour. Can't stand having Taurus tech in me anyway.'

Harz gave an amused snort, then gave the knife a sharp jolt. Broekow felt it break the skin, the blade pushing in far enough to tap the bone. Then the flood of pain washed over him as blood began running down his cheek to drip off his chin.

'One flick of the wrist and you'll be able to see your own dick without even looking down.' Harz leant forward, his breath pungent. 'What is the name of Hewn's flagship?'

Broekow hesitated. When he felt the blade start to move around though, he gave in.

'The *Glaive*.'

Harz wrenched the knife back, shredding some of the skin around the wound. 'Good. What system is the *Glaive* in?'

'Could be anywhere.'

Broekow regretted his instinctive reply the moment the words left his lips. Harz grabbed hold of his jaw and squeezed hard. When the pressure made Broekow open his mouth, the pirate swiftly stabbed the knife into the exposed upper gum, taking not only a tooth but also the root, nerves and skin. Warm blood gushed over his tongue, out over his lips and some down his throat, making him choke.

'What system is the *Glaive* in?'

'Miller,' gasped Broekow. 'It was in Miller.'

Harz released his grip, allowing his prisoner to spit out the blood. 'Very good. Now come the *really* important questions.'

Broekow wanted the wipe the tears from his eyes. He wanted to get out of the shackles. He wanted to take that knife and ram it deep into Harz's black heart.

The pirate picked up the blowtorch once more. 'Which planet is Hewn's family on?'

Minerva
Berg system

Fleeting moments of consciousness. He had no idea how long they lasted, but each time he found himself afloat in silent darkness. The void surrounding him gave comfort, as though he belonged in limbo. Being alone seemed right somehow and yet it always felt as though something was waiting out there beyond the blackness of oblivion.

He became aware of the peculiar sound first; a thousand unintelligible whispers with a distant wail constant behind them. Then he began to *feel*. A numbing cold seeped through him, followed by discomfort behind his eyes and an odd sensation of pressure within his skull.

His heart raced as panic set in and instinctively he tried to move his arms and legs to no avail. A moment later, the comforting void gave way to a dull light that grew slowly in intensity until it threatened to blind him. His eyelids were reluctant to close, just as the rest of his body seemed unwilling to respond.

This was all wrong. He knew he shouldn't be feeling anything, and yet he did not know why exactly. There were no memories; no recollection of what had come before.

As his vision went from a bright blur to a softer grey, he realised he wasn't alone after all. Vaguely humanoid forms moved around somewhere in the haze, the occasional noise emanating from them. He couldn't understand them, especially with the distant wail echoing in his mind still.

He managed to close his eyes and fell out of consciousness immediately. He was unsure how long it was before he came to again, but this time the wailing was softer. The whispering was still there, yet now he could hear clearer voices over the top of them.

'I'm at a loss.'

'Why the hell is he awake?'

'What's going on up there?'

There was an intense throbbing pain now in his stomach. When he tried to move, again he found himself restrained by something. His eyes tried to search for the culprit, but they still couldn't focus. An annoying itch had also started behind his eyes – it felt like his optic nerves were twitching relentlessly.

'Can you hear me?' The female voice was closer than expected and a slim silhouette hovered just in front of him.

'There's no telling whether he will be able to use his vocal chords, doctor,' came a second voice, also female but with a higher pitch.

'Can you see me?' asked the woman standing before him.

He wanted to respond. It was painful when he tried though.

'I'd say he can both hear and see me. Amazing.'

The whispering suddenly intensified, accompanied by a very different voice that sounded like it was calling from the other end of a long tunnel. He knew it wasn't a human voice, yet it was possibly more familiar to him than the others.

There was a burst of sound that overloaded his senses and he slipped into darkness again.

When he awoke the next time, he found his vision had cleared somewhat. Seated directly in front of him was a woman dressed in grey, her dark hair tied back and a pensive expression on her narrow face.

'Hello again.' She tapped at the device resting in her lap. 'You look more coherent this time.'

His eyes were drawn to the emblem on her uniform. When they lingered on the image of the blade, his stomach began to hurt once again.

'Recognise this symbol?' she asked, having seen his gaze. 'Can you tell me what it is?'

He understood her, but was not even sure he could answer. Instead, he glanced around the small sterile room they were sharing. Was this where he was last time? Where were the others he could hear before?

'Your reactions tell me you can both hear and understand me. That's good.' She tapped at her device again. 'Do you remember anything?'

When he looked at her, he noticed a strange haze had appeared around her entire body. The whispers returned, this time telling him where her major organs were located. Her heart, brain, kidneys, liver and lungs all glowed a soft blue. For a moment, this reveal seemed normal, until his own mind warned him something was severely amiss. As he continued to stare at her, certain points around her body were highlighted. Points to exploit when the time came.

She became uncomfortable beneath his glare and looked down at the device. 'Let's start with your name or perhaps the last thing you remember before you woke up here.'

'Last...' He could only utter the one word before his throat closed up.

The woman stood and walked behind him. He couldn't turn his head far enough to see where she was, and yet he knew her exact position. When she returned, she had a thin plastic container in her hand. The genetic make-up of the liquid within told him it was water.

She tentatively put it to his lips and tipped it slowly. At first, the water stung his mouth and his tongue, burning as he swallowed it. Then the thirst kicked in and he quickly drained the rest.

'Your body will have forgotten many things,' she told him. 'It's been receiving nutrition intravenously for quite some time. Although I have to admit I'm more interested in exactly what you are seeing right now.'

'Where am I?' His voice sounded disembodied. He didn't recognise it.

She gave him a cold smile, as though surprised he had managed to say anything. 'You are on Minerva, at the Hayes colony. Can you tell me what system?'

Star maps swam through his mind, not all familiar. 'Berg.'

'Very good.' She retrieved her device and eagerly tapped at the screen. 'Can you tell me what you remember?'

'Nothing.' He tried to move his arms, finding them held down by secure clasps.

'What about this?' She pointed to the emblem on her shirt.

Whenever he looked at it, pain gnawed at his stomach.

Seeing his discomfort, she tried something else. 'Do these words mean anything to you? Taurus. Requiem. Nova. Earth.'

His brain processed each word like a machine, displaying the resulting data in his mind's eye. 'They all do. Why am I restrained?'

'For your own safety,' she smiled. 'My name is Lynn White. I'm in charge of the research facility at Hayes. Do you recall your name?'

'No. I can't remember anything before I woke up here.'

'It may take some time for your memory to return, although you don't seem to have any problem accessing certain other bits of information.'

Another intense burst of noise reverberated around his skull, but this time he didn't pass out. Instead, he could hear the same voice calling to him as before and the wailing accompanied it. He flinched as a piercing scream lanced through his head, followed by a number of cries for help.

'The colony,' he muttered.

White frowned. 'What about it?'

An alarm suddenly rang out, startling her. Seconds later, a door opened and a man's ashen face appeared.

'We've got a real problem above,' he announced nervously.

‘I’ll be back shortly,’ she promised, before following the man out.

The alarm continued, but he barely noticed it. Instead, he focused on the various noises that only he seemed to be able to hear.

He wasn’t sure how long he was on his own in that room. White still hadn’t returned and he needed to get free somehow. The clasps holding his wrists and ankles were starting to chafe. When he looked down at them, he could see the wiring within and realised they were activated somewhere else. It didn’t dawn on him until a moment later that the wiring was hidden beneath the metal casing. No man should’ve been able to see it.

A woman’s scream came from just beyond the door. He knew from the pitch that it wasn’t White. Then the sound of a gunshot rang out, slightly muffled. If someone was attacking Hayes, he didn’t want to be incapacitated when they worked out where he was.

Without hesitation, he mustered all his strength and wrenched his right arm upwards, snapping the clasp open. He gave no thought to the fact he should not have had the power to break the lock and instead freed his other arm. The leg clasps seemed easier to escape.

It was the first time he noticed he was dressed in gleaming white clothing. It was the sort worn by patients in hospitals on Earth. Perhaps White was correct about his memory.

The door was not locked. Beyond was a larger chamber fitted with a number of very uncomfortable-looking beds and a variety of medical equipment. He swiftly made his way across to the next door, his eyes searching for something he could use as a weapon.

He entered a long corridor and came to a sudden halt when he saw the bodies littering the floor. All of them were wearing the same grey uniform as White, although most were now covered in blood stains. Strange noises were coming from one of the rooms at the far end; tapping, clicking, whispering.

He went in the opposite direction, stepping over bodies. He recognised the man that had opened the door to interrupt his involuntary session with White. One lifeless eye stared up at the ceiling. The other eye had been violently shoved deep inside the skull, pushed directly into the brain. He noticed alarmingly similar wounds on many of the others lying at his feet.

He found the pistol beneath one of the bodies. Only one shot had been fired. It was a pleasant feeling to be holding a gun and memories of firing such weapons shot through his mind so quickly he barely had time to take them all in.

Sounds of movement from the other end of the corridor drove him to dive for cover through the nearest door. He found himself inside a restroom. No way out. When he peered back, he should have been shocked to the very core and yet his heart didn't race, nor did his palms sweat or his legs go weak.

The creatures moved so quietly on their six legs despite their size. They looked like nightmarish shadows come alive, traversing the smooth floor with an almost insect-like grace. As they passed beneath the lights, their chitinous bodies displayed shades of brown, dark green and black. Two rows of eyes resembled tiny sunken pools of dark water that glistened as they moved.

Most of the creatures were carrying devices of varying sizes, each glowing with a neon blue light. Jagged tendrils clutched the artefacts securely against their bodies. The last one to emerge into the corridor was not holding an inanimate object. It was dragging a body behind it. When the body flailed, he realised they hadn't yet killed that one. The others had been disposed off so quickly and efficiently that there must've been a reason for taking someone alive. He wasn't sure he wanted to know that reason.

The alien convoy turned off the corridor and vanished into the complex, their tapping footsteps resounding off the walls. As the last one disappeared from his view, he saw that the unfortunate being taken was in fact White, her face bloodied and her previously tied back hair now matted and wild. He wanted to feel sorry for her, but there was no emotional reaction. Just curiosity.

After waiting for some time, he realised that the whispering and wailing had stopped in his head. He was certain he was alone down in the research facility below Hayes. The only thought he had now was to find a way off Minerva and to get to Earth. He knew it was his home. Perhaps there would be answers there.

Questions on what he had just witnessed swirled around his mind, and yet there was a part of him that knew the answers already. He *knew* those creatures were not some lifeform indigenous to Minerva. He *knew* they were there for the devices. He *knew* they were intelligent beings, driven by a need to survive and determined to eradicate their tainted kin. He *knew* that their presence spelt disaster for the human race.

Stepping back into the restroom, he decided to wash his face. The cool water felt good on his skin, but his eyes still itched. He also drank his fill, trying to quench the unbelievable thirst he was now experiencing.

When he turned the faucet off and glanced up into the mirror over the sink, he found a familiar face staring back at him. Other memories began to stir from their slumber, this time rousing his emotions and causing him to question just what he was seeing.

He leaned forward, his nose nearly touching the mirror. Ice blue eyes looked back, asking how he was alive and, in the pale irises, silver flecks glistened in the artificial light.

Sapphire Nova Assault Ship Harbinger Geraint system

'Fifty-eight ships.' Bavelli whistled. 'Looks so fucking impressive.'

The three officers stared out at the fleet, drinking in the scene. It was the first time in decades that Sapphire Nova had gathered so many assault ships together in one place. Only twenty were not present. Some of those were under repair after the battles in Haskell, Wagner and Kalbrec. The rest had been left with skeleton crews to help protect Nova's key systems alongside the guardians they had at their disposal.

Klein had considered having the transports, explorers and mining ships kitted out with heavy weaponry. Bringing them to the battle would have been logistically difficult, but they could have drawn fire away from the *Harbinger* and her fleet. In the end, he had decided against it. Time was not something they had in abundance since the events on Galt.

'How long have we got before they arrive?' Fletcher asked.

'Half a day,' Klein replied. 'Perhaps slightly longer.'

Bavelli chuckled. 'They took the bait like hungry fish.'

'Bait?' Klein raised a meaningful eyebrow at his colleague. 'Garrett isn't as stupid as Mitchell was. He'll know we're here. The distress call from Carson, the blocked comms...we should have had a better plan.'

Fletcher and Bavelli gave each other a baffled look.

'Why do it then?' asked the latter. 'We should've just taken Lincoln from them and battered their fleet when they arrived.'

'You make it sound so easy.' Klein shook his head. 'Take our fleet into Lincoln and we would've been hit from all sides. At least here, we know they are only coming from one direction.'

His eyes turned to the odd one out among the fleet; the fifty-ninth ship. If they had time, he would have ordered the *Victory* painted in their own colours, just to piss Taurus off more. However, its presence at the battle and the fact they would use it against those who created it was much more significant.

Perhaps he should have brought Ishlan along too and given Garrett cause to hesitate when realising he would be firing on his own people. Then again, that's exactly what Klein would tell the opposing general.

‘Any news from Rist?’ he asked.

‘Fuck all,’ grumbled Bavelli. ‘He’s dead for sure. Not even he could’ve got off Galt once Taurus knew they were there.’

‘Pity,’ sniffed Fletcher. ‘He was pretty handy.’

Klein had to agree. Rist had gathered all the codes they needed from the other corps, assassinated the executive targets and led a meagre handful of mercs into the lion’s den to kill the Taurus board. Reports they had managed to intercept told them that Billings and Pavleachenko had been killed, plus the two thorns Tench and Kort had been badly wounded, although he was certain the resilient old fuckers would survive. There was no word on the rest, but Kingston had been hammered by their ship and the casualties were numerous.

Their plan to draw the attention of the Taurus fleet had worked well enough. Fletcher and Bavelli had both escaped their respective target systems without significant losses. It was just a pity that they had lost Rist and the ship they sent. Truth be told, he had never expected Rist to return. The man had been of great use but there was something about him Klein had never liked, even aside from the fact he was part machine.

‘Time to return to your ships,’ he announced. ‘Make sure they are all ready. This is the end game and we’ll celebrate at Flint once the battle is won.’

‘Next time, I’ll command the *Harbinger*,’ grinned Bavelli. ‘Not some boring shitty little assault ship. I’d say stay safe, but you’ve got all that reinforced fucking armour surrounding you.’

As Bavelli strode away, Fletcher sighed. ‘I don’t expect him to survive this.’

‘Me neither,’ agreed Klein. ‘As soon as he sees Taurus colours, he’ll wade in like a bloody berserker.’

‘See you on the other side, Tomas.’

Klein gave his friend the warmest smile he could and shook his hand. ‘You will.’

Once he was alone, he couldn’t stop the deluge of thoughts as to the potential outcomes of the battle entering his mind. If Taurus brought more ships than expected to Geraint, the *Harbinger* would be the key to success.

Trying to second guess Mitchell had been simple, as the man had been impatient, rash and greedy. Garrett was the total opposite, even acting sensibly when news reached him of the attacks in their systems. He wouldn’t bring his fleet to Geraint without something up his sleeve and it was Klein’s job to make sure there were no unexpected surprises as well as ensuring that Sapphire Nova were victorious. It was a bold move, taking the largest corporation on like this, but it was time to stop striking from the shadows and put Taurus to their own sword.

His eyes once again were drawn to the *Victory;* his ace in the hole.

Rikur
Almaz system

Devlin grimaced as he watched the pirates approaching.

Ever since taking over as head of security, he had tried his best to ensure the flotsam of the human race didn't find its way to Harper. The murder of Portman had unsettled his entire staff and produced a wave of rumours that spread to the other colonies, stating that Harper was a haven for criminals of all kinds. It had taken the best part of the following year to get a grip on the situation, although it still didn't sit well with him that they had pinned the late head of security's murder on a known deviant instead of the real culprit. The people needed someone to blame.

Now, here he was, receiving a gang of Jericho's Bold. He was just glad he had ordered them to land well out of the way of prying eyes.

Devlin counted how many were trudging towards him. Ten tattooed pirates and their prisoner, who was being carried by the two at the back. The leader of this particular crew cut an especially forboding figure and had a wild stare in his eyes.

'I'll do all the talking,' Devlin told his sec team. 'Just keep a close watch.'

He didn't trust Jericho's Bold in the slightest. However, the message from them had intrigued him and, if the opportunity was genuine, he couldn't pass it up. He also doubted they would come to Harper just to pick a fight.

'You Devlin?'

It took a moment to realise the voice belonged to the pirate leader, as the man's thick beard covered his mouth. Devlin did note the strange patch of missing hair on his chin however.

'I am. I take it you're Harz.'

The pirates stopped several metres from the sec team, weighing them up. Their hungry glares lingered on the two female members.

'We don't want to be here any longer than we have to,' Harz stated. 'You got the bounty?'

'It's ready to transfer as soon as I get a look at him.' Devlin glanced to the man being carried, but the face was covered by a crude hood. 'Tell me again how you happened across him. Whereabouts was he?'

Harz grinned, then gave an amused snort. 'Never could stand the way you corp fuckers talk. Pompous and arrogant. Making demands.'

Devlin didn't share the amusement. 'Let's not get off to a bad start here. I know it's the nature of the Bold to throw insults, but the sooner I know what I'm paying for, the sooner you can go back to wherever you came from.'

Harz shared a look of utter contempt with the head of security. 'Picked him up on the edge of the Echo Expanse. We received reliable intel on his location and just had to wait for him to arrive.'

'Intel from who?' Perhaps there might be a lead to help him track the others down too.

'That's not part of the deal.'

'Nobody else with him?'

Harz gave his men a look, drawing a few sniggers. 'Yeah, a pilot. Just some Echo runt. A nobody.'

Devlin didn't want to ask too many questions. The Bold weren't known for their patience. 'So he was working with Echo?'

'With. For. Let's get this over with.' Harz signalled to his two men and they hauled the limp body forward before dumping it unceremoniously on the hard floor grating. 'There. Take a look for yourself.'

Devlin didn't hesitate, moving to crouch next to the prisoner. He could hear the man's ragged wheezing breaths and wondered just how much fun the Bold had with him during their journey to Rikur. When he removed the hood, he couldn't help but show his dissatisfaction. *Fun* was probably the last word that should've been used to describe what this wanted criminal had endured.

'Hard to recognise him in this state,' Devlin snapped. 'You'd better not have removed his tongue too.'

'He can talk. When he's conscious.'

Devlin shook his head at the mess that was Sieren Broekow. He could tell it was him by the features, despite the swelling and dried blood. Some wounds were obvious; the two missing fingers, the burnt skin and the clearly broken wrist and ankle. When he examined the beaten man more closely, he found snapped teeth, sliced gums and a number of smaller wounds that together must have caused him severe pain. No wonder he was unconscious.

'How do I know he isn't brain damaged? Looks like you worked every possible part of him. If he dies from his wounds...'

Harz gave an impatient grunt. 'He won't. We know how to fucking torture someone so they don't die on us. He won't be able to walk properly and he'll have to have his food liquidised for a while, but he'll be coherent enough to answer your questions.'

Devlin gave his team a nod and they moved to pick Broekow up. 'Fine. You come across his associates and there will be more money in it for you.'

He made the transfer. Best to get rid of Harz and his unwashed crew as quickly as he could. There was no further exchange of non-pleasantries and he stayed to make sure the Jericho's Bold ship had launched, watching it disappear into the upper atmosphere.

The medical team worked on Broekow for hours. During the whole operation, Devlin stood with arms crossed waiting to hear when he could start his interrogation.

It was nearly an entire day before Broekow regained consciousness. Even then, his eyes struggled to focus and he flinched with every slight movement.

Devlin had listened to his drugged-up muttering to start with, intrigued by the way the ex-sniper kept apologising. He heard the occasional name too. Hewn. Tariq. Justyne. Eventually, he grew tired of waiting and ordered the medics to rouse Broekow properly, giving him a shot of adrenaline to clear his senses as best they could.

'Welcome back to Harper.' Devlin kept his voice low and calm. 'The good news is your friends from Jericho's Bold are long gone. The bad news is it's my turn now.'

Broekow glanced around the medical bay and groaned softly when he saw he was restrained. When he tried to speak, saliva dripped from the side of his mouth and into his beard. 'I know you?'

'You murdered several of my men nearly a year ago and I've been looking for you ever since.' Seeing the blank expression, Devlin continued. 'Your new friends in the Bold could've turned you over to Taurus Galahad or to those idiots in charge of Nova. Instead, they brought you here. I was less likely to fuck them over.'

Broekow looked around again, his confused gaze settling on the emblem mounted behind his new captor. 'But you're Nova.'

Devlin gave a curt nod. 'You remember your last visit to Rikur? You shot down my guards, with help from Davian Kurcher, before managing to get off the colony with two others you just happened to pick up here. It seems that the four of you then made quite a name for yourselves on various other worlds.'

'So now I'm back.' Broekow's tone became sharper. 'Just execute me. You'll be doing me a favour.'

'Those pirates really did go to town on your mouth. I can hardly understand you.' Devlin began pacing before the stricken criminal. 'I'm not going to execute you. Yet.'

Broekow's eyes became more distant. 'I've got nothing to say to you.'

'The Bold are sadistic bastards,' stated the head of security. 'I have to admire their interrogation methods though. Coarse, yet effective. However, I do things differently.'

He walked across to one of the tables at the back of the room, scanning across the options available to him. Various drugs to provoke a multitude of reactions.

'I could turn you into an addict were you not one already. Although I bet you haven't had a drop of alcohol for quite some time. How does it feel?'

There was only silence from Broekow so he headed back, standing close to his prisoner and examining the man's face intently. There was only sorrow and shame behind Broekow's eyes. It would be a challenge to break him after the torture Harz had put him through.

Devlin heard his comms crackle to life, calling him back to work. Something about a dispute between two traders. With a tut of annoyance, he headed for the door, deciding to leave Broekow with something to think about while he was gone.

'When I get back, you'll tell me where I can find Davian Kurcher and that murderous fuck, Edlan Rane.'

Echo flagship Glaive
Miller system

Kurcher always felt nervous when Hewn asked to see him alone. He still expected the pirate to seek revenge for what happened at his drug facility on Tempest. After all, it was Kurcher who allowed Rane and Ercko free rein to cause the distraction. How could he know the two would kill so many, both Echo and Libra personnel?

Because they were the two sickest freaks on the Kaladine, answered Frost.

I did love the smell of blood, among other things, Ercko remarked.

'You seem more distant than usual.'

Kurcher realised Hewn was offering him a beer and snatched the bottle with a grim nod of thanks. 'Just thinking about Cobb.'

Hewn settled into an adjacent seat and swigged his beer as he gazed out at Seko. 'Cobb's done and dusted finally. There may be a few survivors dotted around here and there but they'll be dead soon and it really will be a ghost world.'

'You've no fucking idea,' Kurcher snapped. 'You never saw what was left of it after...'

We don't need to drag this up again, Frost told him.

He had to agree. 'What will happen to the Resistance now?'

'They'll rebuild and settle quietly on Seko.' Hewn's eyes darkened. 'Until I need them again.'

'Butler isn't like Cal Fuller. She's one tough bitch, mourning the loss of her father figure and coming to terms with the fact her ex-lover betrayed them all. She won't help you unless they get something in return.'

'They have our protection,' growled Hewn, angrily. 'If they won't become part of Echo, I'll have them turfed out and watch as the hungry wolves prowling our borders feed on them.'

Kurcher could tell the pirate had something weighing heavy on his mind. 'They need people to join them. They want the Cobb Resistance to grow and flourish on their new world.'

'In memory of their great leader?' Hewn snorted. 'The man was weak.'

'He fought Santa Cruz for us and led their fleet.'

He led them to their deaths, Santa Cruz reminded him.

'Joining us was the only option he had to save his people. If I hadn't offered them solace here, the Resistance would have been wiped out within a couple of months. Once Taurus have finished this feud with Nova, they'll be quick to return to Cobb and claim it back.'

'Feud?' Kurcher shook his head as he gulped down the cool beer. 'They're kicking ten shades of shit out of each other. I doubt either will stop now until the other is buried.'

Hewn couldn't disagree with that. 'I guess the attack on Galt was the last straw. Reports place most of the Nova assault fleet in Geraint, and Taurus will be there shortly. I expect whoever loses that fight will turn tail and vanish into the outer systems, leaving a shitload of worlds open to conquest.'

Kurcher saw the glint in his eye. 'And creating a shitload of opportunities for Echo.'

Hewn shrugged. 'Maybe. We've been focusing too much lately on distractions from our key objectives. Echo has been built on maintaining a supply of drugs and alcohol out into the galaxy, and needs to turn its attention to technologies and weapons too.'

'Echo was built on the graves of those you crushed underfoot to get to the top of the pile,' corrected Kurcher. 'You're pirates, not a fucking corp.'

'Not much difference.' Hewn downed his beer. 'We have to expand into all markets if we hope to survive the coming onslaught. We have a lot of obstacles in our way though.'

Sounds like your hands are going to be full, noted D'Larro.

You're no pirate so tell them to get fucked, suggested Angard.

'Go on then.' Kurcher sat back and waited, purposefully plugging his mouth with the bottle so he didn't blurt out something else unsavoury.

Hewn fetched another two beers. 'I'm not sure whether you even care about this, but we've lost contact completely with Broekow and Masami.'

That wasn't what Kurcher was expecting. 'Fischer said the *Crius* had comms problems sometimes so he wasn't worried.'

'It did have shit comms. Masami told me he was getting it fixed so I hoped he had done so. Either way, they've been gone too long and we can't pick the ship up anywhere in Galen. I should've sent others with them.'

'You think they've been destroyed, like the *Magnussen*?' He despised what Broekow had become and yet the thought he was dead didn't sit well. 'You want me to go out there?'

'No.' Hewn was quick to reply. 'I'm sending a small fleet out there to find out what the fuck is going on in that system. Someone is clearly trying to establish themselves in my territory, and they'll pay if they've destroyed one of my ships.'

Kurcher watched the pirate's expression for a moment, trying to gauge what he was thinking. Perhaps he thought Broekow had overpowered Masami and fled. Perhaps he didn't like the idea of his valuable alcoholic bargaining chip disappearing into the void, leaving only the bitter, angry killing chip as collateral.

'So what else?'

'The Kindred.'

Kurcher wasn't expecting that either. 'What about them?'

'You've encountered them before, right?'

'Yeah. Last one I saw was on Sullivan's Rest. Put several bullets in the fucker. Never said a word, just stared like he was stoned out of his mind.'

'Was he easy to identify?' asked Hewn, fully engaged with what Kurcher had to say.

'Yeah, my sight app was working then.' When the pirate gave him a look devoid of amusement, Kurcher shrugged. 'I'd say they'd be easy to identify in a crowd. Blank gaze, dirty, stinking, pretty shitty clothing, mute.'

Hewn thought for a second. 'When they attacked those stations recently, their actions directly affected my business. I had people on Grade working for both Libra and Echo, so I can keep an eye and ear on what's happening out there. It's where a lot of my intel on Libra is sourced. When those bombs went off, one of my agents died. The others got spooked and have been demanding more danger money.'

'I thought they only used firebombs to destroy the wiring across Grade,' frowned Kurcher.

'The man who died was installing some new tech in one of the ducts to amplify our comms link without raising suspicion,' Hewn explained.

'Wrong place, wrong time.'

Hewn drank deep from his bottle, some of the liquid dripping into his beard. 'The Kindred are getting closer to us and that gives me cause for real fucking concern. I don't want one of those freaks walking into our brewery on Warren and blowing it sky-high.'

Mainly because that's where he hid his family, Frost pointed out.

Kurcher hated beating around the bush. 'So why tell me your concerns? Obviously you have some task in mind.'

'As you know what members of The Kindred look like, I'm going to want you to help us identify them before they can sneak into the Expanse or before they find one of our facilities elsewhere. Just not yet.'

Here comes the real reason you're sitting drinking with him like an old friend, said D'Larro.

Never trust a pirate, warned Santa Cruz.

'I need you to come with me to Kismet.'

This stopped Kurcher's arm as he went to drain his beer. 'Why the holy fuck would I go back there? You've already sent me to Cobb and now you want me to go back to the place where I killed one of Sigma Royal's best enlisters, blew up his ship and murdered his crew?'

'Yes.' Hewn's expression was stoic. 'Ever since Trystan Hengeveld came here demanding I hand you over to him, I've been keeping track of that arrogant prick. His orders were to start hitting some of Sigma's outer colonies, claiming their less protected worlds while the poor old Royals tried to regroup after the deaths on Meta. True to form though, he overstepped the mark and took his soldiers to Kismet, believing that the military presence there was depleted. Turned out Sigma had been gathering a force secretly.'

'He was captured.'

'Yes. Put up quite the fight apparently. Lost most of his men and the *Erudite* fled Genesys before any Sigma assault ships showed up. One of the commanders in Monarch City sent a message to Libra showing Hengeveld alive, saying that no other corp would ever take them for granted again.'

'So I'll repeat my question. Why the hell would I go back there then? Especially if Trystan fucking Hengeveld and an army of Sigma soldiers are there.'

Hewn slammed his bottle down hard with his artificial hand, the glass shattering violently. 'I always knew Libra would fuck me over. They're threatening to break our alliance unless Echo rescues Hengeveld. They don't want to risk all-out war with Sigma when we could get onto Kismet without being noticed.'

'Cowards.'

'With Libra personnel in a number of our facilities, ending the alliance now would be a disaster. Everything I have worked to create would crumble.'

Kurcher knew he shouldn't ask but he enjoyed the questions that provoked an angry response. 'Didn't you realise that's why they allied with you in the first place, to infiltrate your facilities and be ready to seize control when the time came?'

Hewn's eye twitched. 'I'm going to lead the rescue mission myself. My reasons for taking you along are threefold. Firstly, you know Monarch City well.'

He's got you there, muttered Frost.

'Secondly, I've received intel that this prick, *The Luminary*, has mechs on

Kismet using that new app. We need to bag ourselves one and see whether we can learn more about this guy.'

'You hate mechs,' Kurcher stated abruptly.

Hewn glanced down at his arm, watching as the metal fingers flexed. 'I really do.'

'And thirdly?'

The pirate's eyes rose to meet his. 'I need to utilise your disregard for human life.'

Sapphire Nova Assault Ship Harbinger
Geraint system

Klein had to admit that he hadn't given Garrett enough credit.

Mitchell had been a very direct man, if not predictable, and it had been easy enough to lure him into the trap on Straunia. Within seconds of the Taurus fleet arriving in Geraint, Klein realised he had underestimated the new general.

He wasn't surprised by the fact Garrett had brought such a major percentage of the fleet with him. Seventy-five assault ships displaying the colours of Taurus Galahad now approached his Nova fleet and a niggle of doubt had crept into his mind as he reviewed which specific vessels they would be facing.

Behind the enemy fleet came ten explorer-class ships, no doubt there for support as they could manoeuvre easily around the flanks of the imminent battle. They would not be a concern.

It was the hulking metal oval at the centre of the Taurus force that worried him most. A ship they had thought destroyed months ago when Santa Cruz had used it as protection. Klein had read about the way it cut through Sigma Royal assault ships and the fact it had been purposefully reinforced to withstand an onslaught from fusion weapons and even missiles. Taurus had brought the *Sentinel* back to life and the guardian would need to be removed from the fight as quickly as possible.

He passed orders through to Bavelli and Fletcher, telling them to task a number of ships under their command to hit the *Sentinel* as soon as it was in range. But something told him that it would take the additional firepower of the *Harbinger* to break that monstrosity.

Klein shifted uncomfortably in his command chair. So this was it. After years of skirmishes and increasing bad blood, Nova and Taurus were about to engage in the largest battle recorded since the five corporations came into existence.

It was time for a shift in power. Taurus had been dominant for decades, boasting the biggest fleet and the most systems. They acted like they were a caring corp, looking after their colonists and providing a strong future for the human race. They even refused to leave Earth, despite the fact the Revenants were killing the planet. However, the events on Cobb showed them for what they were, and Klein was certain the Taurus board knew more than they let on about Santa Cruz and his insane mission.

He had reviewed the events leading up to the attack on Straunia over and over again. Some in the Taurus hierarchy may have had a conscience, leading them to try stopping the rogue fleet. Solomon Rees' conscience got him and his enlisters killed of course. It was the absence of the rest of Taurus that played on his mind , along with the way Mitchell refused to lead his own ships against those of Santa Cruz. The decisions made by the Taurus board had signed their own death warrants.

Pride suddenly seeped through Klein's entire body. He would lead Sapphire Nova into a new era as the controlling power in the galaxy and avenge those who were killed so mercilessly.

'Sir?' His comms officer interrupted the thoughts of a Milky Way ruled by Nova. 'There is a request from General Garrett to talk. Private channel.'

Klein bit his lip. His military background had taught him not to engage the enemy in idle conversation when the outcome was set in stone. However, there was a part of him that wanted to face his opponent and gauge the man's resolve.

He granted Garrett his private conversation, settling in front of his personal console.

'General.' His greeting was curt but respectful.

'Commander,' came the reply. 'I'm offering you the opportunity to remove your ships from Geraint.'

Straight to the point. Klein liked that. 'I should've just invited you here and not wasted my time with a lure.'

'You wouldn't attack Carson,' Garrett said. 'Would've been a bad move on your part and I get the impression you're not stupid. In fact, quite the opposite. Your plans to dismantle the board were barbaric and arrogant, yet clever. Then you savagely overstepped the mark.'

'Oh, let's not get into who overstepped which mark.'

Garrett took a deep breath before continuing. 'Your attack on Kingston claimed the lives of innocent men, women and children. That can't be ignored.'

'Quite right, general. That's exactly why we're here. We all lost someone when your wayward commander Santa Cruz used that weapon on Straunia. How many innocents died then?'

'Jorelian Santa Cruz was a very disturbed individual who acted on his own in the attack on Straunia. Taurus Galahad had no idea just what he was capable of.'

'Then it worries me what sort of people you allow into your ranks.' Klein applied a small amount of venom in his response. 'Mitchell was a greedy dictator who knew exactly what was happening and did nothing to stop it. Lenaghan was a fat, corrupt bastard with zero morals and a penchant for power. Those lapdogs who followed Santa Cruz...Byrne, O'Brien and even poor old Neri Ishlan.'

Garrett glared angrily through the screen. 'So you killed them all just to make the galaxy a safer place to live?'

'I didn't kill anyone,' Klein corrected. 'In fact, I'm sure you've noticed a very familiar ship among our fleet. Commander Ishlan and her crew are on the *Victory*. They were...'

'I'm not here to banter with you, commander,' interrupted Garrett. 'Withdraw your forces from our space immediately or we will open fire.'

Klein studied the general's image, finding no tells in the man's stoic expression. 'We are here to eradicate those who threaten the survival of our corporation.'

'As are we.' Garrett severed the comms link.

Klein was quick to contact Bavelli and Fletcher. 'When they're in range, don't hesitate. Make sure you fire first.'

It was Bavelli's ship, the *Grosvenor*, that opened the initial exchange. When the Taurus fleet arrived, led by the *Ravenedge*, fifteen Nova assault vessels had positioned themselves for the first barrage. Fusion beams sliced through the darkness. A split second later, a formation of missiles were heading for the Taurus ships on the front line.

From his position, Klein found it hard to see exactly what damage Bavelli's lead attack had wrought. There was a reply from Taurus as twenty of their ships broke to engage.

The *Sentinel* loomed into view, approaching with a sinister silence that made Klein want to shudder. Flanked by a number of assault ships, it would be the modern version of a siege weapon, laying waste to its enemies from afar.

When he saw Fletcher's *Rothwell* leading twenty of their fleet towards the guardian, Klein turned to his command crew.

'Long range strike on the *Sentinel* now.'

The *Harbinger* opened fire, its fusion beam flashing past the throng of assault ships and striking the guardian, which held firm. There was no slowing the ominous hulk as it continued to approach the battle. A second strike from the *Harbinger* removed some of the outer hull plating but didn't penetrate beneath.

The two fleets finally came together. There would be no turning back now.

Rikur
Almaz system

When he closed his eyes, he could see her. Sometimes he remembered her sitting at the *Kaladine*'s controls, cigarette hanging from her lips, or the wicked smile she gave only to him when they were alone. Most of the time though, he saw her bravely fighting to keep control of her beloved ship as it was pulled in by Cerberus, her legs crushed and bleeding. He remembered her voice in his ear as she whispered her final words, telling him that he was a good man and to make sure he started over somewhere quiet. He knew she loved him, but she would never have said that at such a difficult time. It would've made him want to stay with her in that smoke-filled cockpit. He wished he had.

'It's not time to sleep again yet.'

Broekow didn't want to return to reality. Opening his eyes would mean having to deal with the pain as well as the guilt eating away at his soul. He wanted more time with Frost, trying to remember her as she was. Meeting her had helped ease his troubled mind after having been forced to kill those officers and having found himself hunted down by enlisters. Even when he discovered just why he was on the *Kaladine*, he couldn't bring himself to hate her. She was torn between her loyalty to Kurcher and what her heart was telling her.

'Open your eyes or I'll have them opened for you.'

This time, Broekow complied and found Devlin's scowling face before him. He knew he was frustrating the head of security, but just didn't care.

'The sooner you give me Kurcher and Rane, the sooner I can let you rest. It really isn't the time to protect them.'

'I'm not protecting anyone,' mumbled Broekow, his voice hoarse. 'I've already told you that Kurcher is working with Echo and I have no idea where exactly he might be. Rane vanished months ago.'

'So you say.' Devlin began pacing again. 'After the three of you tried to stop Santa Cruz from attacking Straunia. You expect me to believe someone like Edlan Rane actually cared what happened to the people on that planet?'

'Believe what you will.'

'What happened in the Flint system has sent shockwaves across the entire galaxy and yet I had you brought here to answer for the murder of my men. Once I have what I need, you can tell the new Nova board all about how you tried to save Straunia, although I doubt they will believe you either.'

Broekow turned his head, focusing on the door on the other side of the room. He could just about recall the layout of the maintenance tunnels he and Kurcher had used to gain entry to the colony. If he could get free, he could hide there for a while. Then again, it would just be easier to step through the airlock and into the inhospitable atmosphere of Rikur, letting it choke him to death. It was what he deserved.

'Sieren Broekow,' yelled Devlin, clearly trying to rouse his prisoner. 'Born in 2586 on Galt. Father killed in action on Cobb. Mother worked at military hospital on Galt and still alive, although unwilling to discuss her son who she understands is a cold-blooded murderer.

In 2604, you enlisted in the Taurus Galahad military, becoming a sniper in 2611. In 2616, you killed your superior officers and fled, eventually being captured by Jed Cooke. For reasons unbeknownst to us, Cooke let you go on Sullivan's Rest, where you met Davian Kurcher. You came to Harper looking for Maric Jaroslav and ended up slaughtering a number of my security personnel alongside Kurcher and Rane before managing to escape Rikur.'

When Broekow didn't so much as blink, Devlin continued.

'When my medical team saw to your wounds following your time with those Jericho Bold maniacs, they found that you had two old gun shots to the chest. I could tell what the pirates had done to you as that was blatant, so who shot you?'

Broekow didn't want to be reminded about Harz and his torture techniques, nor about the amount of information he spilled during that interrogation. Did he really care whether Jericho's Bold acted on that? What was it to him if Echo was destroyed?

'Santa Cruz. He shot me on the *Grail*.'

Devlin tilted his head slightly, clearly intrigued that Broekow had offered him something new. 'They were serious wounds. Who saved you?'

'Kurcher.' Broekow finally locked eyes with the head of security. 'Hewn.'

'And Rane?' Devlin asked.

Broekow allowed himself a wry smile. 'He stayed behind on the *Grail*.'

Devlin shuffled closer, a confused frown appearing on his brow. 'Are you telling me that Rane died that day?'

Fuck it. What did it matter now if he told the truth? He would at least get some pleasure seeing the shock on Devlin's face.

'Rane managed to escape the *Grail*, but only after using it to wipe out

Straunia. That's right, Nova's homeworld was destroyed by Edlan Rane, not Santa Cruz.'

Devlin's jaw couldn't have dropped further open. 'Nova have gone after Taurus for what happened. Why should I believe you? According to you, Santa Cruz shot you and left you for dead.'

'Why would I lie? What do I possibly have to lose?'

As Devlin hesitated, his mind reeling from the revelation, there came a low booming noise followed by a violent rumble that shook the entire room. Alarms immediately sprang to life.

As the head of security turned away to check his comms, Broekow could still feel the vibrations coming up through the floor. A few moments later, there was another boom, although this time it was accompanied by a horrific screeching sound.

The door opened and one of Devlin's team stepped through, her face glistening with sweat. 'Sir, it's the rig.'

'Tell me.'

The sec officer glanced at Broekow before answering. 'Major malfunction has led to explosions in most sectors, including electrical fires. The rig shifted and pitched, breaking part of Harper apart. Initial reports are that we've lost a number of people but we can't know how many yet. Rig workers, maintenance, sec and civilians all among the casualties.'

Devlin had gone extremely pale. 'How the fuck can this happen? We had procedures in place to avoid another accident.'

Broekow remembered Harper had suffered a planetbore rig incident before. It had taken them years to rebuild it. How long would it take this time?

'Your orders, sir?' asked the sec officer, her voice panicked.

'Get everyone over there and secure any breaches in Harper's exterior. Make the colony safe and then we can gauge the extent of the damage caused by the rig. I want fire crews from all sectors working together and prep the medical bays for an influx of patients.'

Again, her eyes were drawn to Broekow. 'Including this one?'

'Of course,' barked Devlin. 'I'll secure this room before joining you. Now go.'

Harper continued to vibrate as Broekow watched Devlin pace before him, the man clearly devastated by the news. It meant he now had more urgent priorities.

'At least place me in a cell so I can rest.'

'You'll remain here,' snarled Devlin, an almost feral look in his eyes.

The head of security checked the restraints were locked firmly in place, trying his best to tighten them just to make sure Broekow couldn't somehow wriggle free.

'Why don't you just execute me then? One less worry on your mind.'

Devlin stepped back, pulling out his HDU. 'You've got a lot more to tell me, I'd wager. For now though, shut the fuck up.'

As Broekow watched the officer flicking through reams of data coming through on the situation Harper faced, he heard the door open again.

'Sir, you're needed out here.' This time, it was a man's voice.

With one last glance at Broekow, Devlin made for the exit. 'Why aren't you with the others? I gave an order to...'

There was a grunt, followed by a muffled gurgle and the door closing. When Broekow turned, he saw Devlin slumped against the wall. Blood was pumping from a savage wound to his throat and the head of security was gasping for breath.

'Not my usual standard but time is of the essence.'

Devlin's attacker stood tall before Broekow, dressed in a full security uniform. A broad grin could be seen beneath the helmet visor.

'What..?' was all Broekow could utter.

'You've seen better days, Sieren,' said Rane. 'Best you come with me.'

Sapphire Nova Assault Ship Harbinger
Geraint system

Klein felt numb.

The broken husks of Nova and Taurus ships filled the screen, their lifeless corpses displaying just how relentless the battle had been. Nova had lost thirty-one, Taurus thirty-six.

Despite being badly depleted, the Taurus fleet still outnumbered them. Nova had suffered the loss of well over half their ships, including the *Rothwell.* He recalled how he had held his breath when one of the *Sentinel*'s lethal beams punched a hole through Fletcher's ship. There had been a split second of hope his friend had survived before the *Sentinel* finished the job. Fletcher and his entire crew were incinerated in the explosion as the *Rothwell* disintegrated before Klein's eyes.

He shifted his attention to the ginormous guardian spinning slowly beyond the ocean of dead ships. A glow could still be seen from it and he could take some solace from the fact it was the fires burning inside. After it had destroyed the *Rothwell*, he had given the order to focus the entire fleet on taking the *Sentinel* down. It had taken time to even break through its hull but, once they had, it had allowed the *Harbinger* a pinpoint strike that rifled through its softer interior, causing widespread havoc throughout the guardian. It hadn't fired a single shot since and had slowly drifted away from the battle. Klein was not about to pursue it though.

Bavelli had fared better, the wily commander keeping the *Grosvenor* moving and proving a difficult target to hit. He was still out there, fighting on for their cause.

Klein checked his tactical data. Much to his chagrin, the *Ravenedge* was still active. Garrett had ridden his luck, leading his fleet into battle like a general of old. He must've felt invincible.

As he studied the screen, another Nova ship was destroyed and two more reported serious damage that was affecting their systems.

'I need comms open to every commander in our fleet.' It was time to change tactics.

As he waited for the link to be established, the thought crossed his mind that reports would say they had lost the battle. He had hoped the *Harbinger* would've been able to give them an advantage with its longer range strikes and reinforced hull. He hadn't foreseen Taurus using the *Sentinel* and that had been the difference. Maybe he should have taken Garrett's warning more seriously.

'This is Commander Tomas Klein,' he began solemnly. 'All remaining ships are to pull back and jump to the Flint system to regroup. The Taurus Galahad fleet will not pursue us there.'

It didn't take long for the surviving assault vessels to start their retreat. Taurus seemed to hesitate when they realised what was happening.

As he expected, Bavelli contacted him via his personal comms.

'With the *Sentinel* gone, Tomas, we can take them. We're so close.'

'Close to being wiped out,' Klein responded. 'If we continue fighting here, Kam, they could bring in reinforcements to flank us and then we're screwed. I know it's in your blood to continue fighting but we pull back. It's not over yet.'

'Arys is dead, Tomas.' Bavelli's voice was pained. 'Retreating will feel like we're leaving him behind.'

'Understood. Consider this though. We have destroyed a significant percentage of the Taurus fleet here today, depleting their resources and making them vulnerable. They will want to slink off to lick their wounds, giving us time to regroup and plan our next steps. This is the beginning of the end for Taurus. Besides, you don't think I'd leave Geraint without one final *fuck you*, do you?'

There was a moment of silence as he waited for Bavelli's comeback. 'See you in Flint then.'

Taurus ships allowed the Nova fleet to retreat, only edging forward very slowly to watch as their enemy left the battlefield.

'Take us to the jump point,' Klein ordered his navigation officer, as he rose from the command seat. 'Follow the rest to Flint and get us into orbit around Straunia.'

As the *Harbinger* turned, he made his way to his personal console. He needed to be alone for the final part of his battle plan. The *Victory* was right where he had left it, devoid of any crew whatsoever. Those who had piloted it to Geraint had transferred over to the *Harbinger* before the battle began. The shots it fired on the Taurus fleet were remotely activated by Klein himself, giving the impression it at least had a command crew on board.

He connected with the *Victory*'s automated system easily, which was testament to Nova's technicians, and gave two final commands.

The engines of the former flagship kicked into life, propelling it forward and towards the waiting Taurus fleet.

By the time the *Harbinger* had vanished into the darkness, and by the time Garrett and his remaining commanders had realised what was happening, the *Victory* had self-destructed in a frightening explosion of volatile fusion energy, taking two Taurus vessels with it and damaging others.

One final *fuck you.*

Minerva
Berg system

Jacobs thought he had seen it all. Ships carrying exotic minerals exploding in glorious multicoloured displays, acidic rain melting through green jungle canopies, whole colonies disappearing as the very ground opened up beneath them to form adolescent chasms. Then he came to Minerva.

The distress signal had reached Hecton Station several days previous. Jacobs and his crew just happened to be out near the jump point in Pendium so he volunteered them for the mission without hesitation. The *Farlane* was fully kitted out and he already had three medics on board so it was a no-brainer. An assault ship and an explorer-class had also been dispatched from Hecton but were a couple of days behind.

Intel had been sparse on the reason behind the signal. They knew it came from Hayes. They knew it had been an automated alarm, designed to be sent out by the colony systems in the case of a major incident. They knew it had stopped almost as quickly as it had begun. Jacobs' first thought was that it was a false alarm from some overzealous piece of corp tech, however all efforts to contact Hayes had failed.

When they arrived, the whole crew had fallen into a stunned silence, which he never recalled happening before in all the years he had worked with them. Even the new medic, Ablett, was at a loss for words, and she had been a pain in his ear since joining.

Minerva was being orbited by a thick layer of debris; a mishmash of fragments that could only have once belonged to assault ships and guardians. There was no sign of the shipyard Jacobs had heard so much about. It had apparently been a confidential project to help build and maintain the fleet of exploration vessels Taurus wanted to send into Coldrig. Information accumulated from several visitors to Hecton though had spread the rumours fast.

Berg had long been a system cut off from the rest of Taurus, to which only those with a special clearance could travel. Until now, such clearance had evaded Jacobs. Then again, all he knew was that Hayes was a scientific community with a technically advanced research operation.

Their initial thoughts on the destruction surrounding Minerva was that

Nova had managed to sneak into the system somehow and lay waste to the key scientific site. With the war escalating dramatically, it was certainly a possibility. Then again, it could have been a pirate raid. Maybe Jericho's Bold had opted to head out to the darkest edge of known space.

Both ideas were ruled out quickly once they began scanning the debris. There were no signs of fusion weapons being used to destroy the ships and no scarring or scorching from missile impacts. It was almost as though they were simply smashed by some hammer of the gods or wrenched apart. *Dismantled* was a word he had heard one of his crew mutter.

Hayes was still illuminated when they landed, with its docking systems in check. The only thing out of place on the surface was the assault ship, which was sitting in the dark on a vast pad on the south side of the colony. Jacobs recognised her straight away. He had thought the *Requiem* destroyed or lost, especially considering who her last commander was, yet here she sat.

He couldn't have begun to imagine the horror they would discover inside Hayes. The colonists were dead; men, women and even children. A security force had fallen together, clearly defending the colonists from whoever had attacked. Families had been murdered while cowering in one of the mess halls. Those in charge of the colony operations hadn't even made it out of the admin block.

When the medics examined the corpses, they were unable to give an answer as to who could have inflicted such barbaric violence on innocent people. Many looked as though they had been stabbed with a jagged or serrated blade, and yet the sheer brutal trauma inflicted from the strike couldn't have been achieved by human hand. The revelation from Ablett had been that the killers must have employed mechs to do their dirty work. He had heard of mercs using mechs fitted with knives. Their hydraulic pressure delivered lethal wounds that would often propel their victims back several feet. Still, he didn't see other glaring signs of mechs. No bent floor gratings or dented walls.

It was the children that bothered them the most, naturally. It would've taken a particular cold and emotionless individual to slaughter them as they huddled against their mothers. Another piece of evidence pointing towards the possible use of mechs, of course.

Jacobs looked around at his team as they worked to access the colony logs. They had cleared the admin block of bodies and he had assigned Ablett, Oberman and Surimoto the rank task of tagging every corpse, to account for the whole population of the ill-fated Hayes. The three medics would be kept busy while the rest of them tried to find out just what happened.

He hadn't like splitting the team up, fearing that the attackers could still be lurking somewhere in the shadows. They had searched the entire upper level and he had set up sensors at the entrances to the sub-level. But they had all agreed that whoever had wiped out the colony was long gone, knowing that Taurus would eventually get someone out there.

'We any closer?' he asked the room. 'I don't want to be down here any longer than we have to. Gives me the fucking creeps.'

Six ashen faces glanced in his direction and he could see just how badly the find had affected his team. Hardly a word had been uttered since they found the first body sprawled just inside the main airlock.

Jacobs gave an exasperated sigh, his breath swirling out into the freezing air. 'And someone get the damned heating on.'

He left them to their job, heading back into Hayes to find the medics. He could hear Surimoto and Oberman long before he entered the central hub of the colony. The two were arguing over the wounds on one young woman, with Oberman certain she had been dragged a fair distance after being killed. Surimoto believed it was before her death however.

'Is that really cause for raised voices?' Jacobs' question startled them both.

'It would help paint a picture as to what happened to her,' replied Oberman. 'Why would someone kill her and then drag her body round with them?'

Jacobs looked down at the lifeless face. She was no more than twenty-five, he guessed. The Taurus Galahad emblem was hard to make out on her torn jacket as it was right where the puncture wound was.

He turned away. 'Let's just get this done. Where's Ablett?'

Surimoto shared a disapproving look with Oberman, before pointing at one of the southern corridors. 'She went that way.'

Jacobs wasn't impressed. 'You let her wander off on her own? What the fuck's wrong with you?'

Both medics gave a shrug that made him want to bang their heads together. Instead, he went to find Ablett, cursing beneath his breath that two of his more experienced team could be so stupid. None of them were exactly thinking clearly since arriving at the colony so perhaps he needed to cut them some slack.

He found Ablett standing at the top of a stairwell. The young medic seemed lost in thought and jumped when he called out to her. She pressed a finger to her lips as he approached, indicating he needed to be quieter. When he arrived next to her, he peered down the centre of the stairwell before giving her a baffled look.

'Thought I heard something,' she whispered. 'Maybe someone moving around down there.'

'Sensor alarms haven't gone off yet,' he told her. 'We didn't detect anyone alive.'

'Not yet.' Ablett nodded towards the stairwell. 'Can we check it out?'

'Let's get sorted up here first and try to get to the bottom of what actually happened. Then we can conduct a final search.'

'Even if the sensors didn't pick anything up, it doesn't mean there isn't someone alive, possibly wounded, down there.' The medic looked up at him, her eyes wide. 'It *is* our job to rescue people, after all.'

Jacobs pointed back towards the hub. 'Go back to helping Surimoto and Oberman. No more wandering.'

'But...'

'No.' He knew she would protest so cut her off sharply. 'That's an order. We'll head down to the sub-level once you've tagged all the bodies.'

'There's no point.' The new voice made them both freeze. 'There's nobody else left alive.'

Jacobs pulled his pistol and swung to face the stairwell again. The man was dressed in standard colony garb, his hands raised as he walked slowly up towards them.

'Who are you?' The question Jacobs wanted to ask was why the hell his sensors hadn't alerted him. 'Are you hurt?'

The colonist seemed to stagger slightly on his ascent. 'The name's Saul. I heard your voices and knew it was safe to come out. Can't stop shaking, I'm afraid.'

Jacobs squinted, trying to make out the man's face in the dim light. The only thing he could make out clearly were the piercing light blue eyes.

'Not surprised you're shaking,' piped up Ablett. 'You've got a gun aimed at you.'

Jacobs lowered the pistol and gave him an apologetic smile. 'Sorry, but considering what we've found here, I can't be too careful.'

Saul tripped as he neared the top step and Ablett rushed forward to offer support.

'He's no doubt in shock and freezing cold,' she told Jacobs. 'Need to get him warmed up quickly.'

Jacobs looked him up and down now that they were so close. There was something off about the way he was standing and the shakes were a concern. He gave a nod to Ablett.

'Okay, get him to one of the empty mess halls.'

Saul gave a cough and clutched at his chest. 'Not to sound ungrateful but

I'd rather not remain inside the colony. I've been on my own here for days with only the dead for company. Please.'

Jacobs glanced at Ablett, then at the stairwell. 'You say nobody else is alive down there? That would make you the sole survivor, which seems a little odd.'

'I was sealed in a research lab conducting an experiment alone. I heard screams and people dying. By the time I dared to come out, they were all dead and whoever did it had gone.'

Jacobs tried looking into Saul's eyes but couldn't hold the strange gaze. The man didn't come across as someone who had just found out all of his friends, colleagues or family were slaughtered. Of course, shock was a potent and complex condition.

'I'll take him to the *Farlare*,' Ablett said, starting to lead Saul away. 'Treat him there.'

Reluctantly, Jacobs agreed and gave his own support as they returned to the hub, where the other two medics blinked in surprise at seeing the survivor. After ordering Oberman to tell the rest of the team what had happened and to keep trying to access the colony data, Jacobs steered Saul in the direction of the landing pad.

Once on the *Farlare*, they led the colonist directly to the med bay, where Ablett draped a heat blanket around him.

'The old-fashioned equipment is the best, I find,' she smiled, displaying her dazzling bedside manner. 'I'm going to need to examine you shortly though, if that's okay.'

'And I have questions for you,' added Jacobs, leaning against the doorway.

Saul gave a nod as he shuddered beneath the blanket. 'Happy to oblige. However, I haven't eaten anything but spoiling or spoilt food so would you mind?'

In the light of the med bay, Jacobs could see the man's features much more clearly. His skin had a clammy white hue, giving him a sickly appearance. There was a darkness beneath his eyes that was not down to exhaustion. It looked more like bruising. There was also scarring near his temples on either side. Apart from that, he had an excellent physique and seemed in good health.

'I'll go get you some food, Saul,' Ablett said, giving him a reassuring pat on the shoulder.

Once she had left the room, Jacobs stepped closer to their patient. He wanted to get a closer look at the man's unusual eyes. It was almost as if there was something reflective in them, occasionally catching the light.

‘You don’t use apps?’ asked the colonist, looking down suddenly under Jacobs’ scrutiny.

‘Never have. Some rescue teams swear by them. We tend to prefer the human touch.’

Saul had stopped shaking. ‘I haven’t thanked you for coming here. Your ship seems perfect.’

Jacobs frowned. ‘What do you mean?’

Before he could even reach for his pistol again, Jacobs found himself staring down the barrel of Saul’s own weapon, the colonist having risen so swiftly.

‘I’m afraid I’m going to have to take the *Farlare*. I’m sure another ship will be along soon enough to pick you and your crew up.’

‘Wait...’ Jacobs needed to think fast. He should’ve expected this. ‘Look, we were going to take you out of Berg anyway. If you need to go somewhere specific, we can take you there.’

‘You really can’t,’ Saul said sadly.

Jacobs was trying to remain as calm as he could. ‘Well who the fuck are you then? Is your name even Saul?’

‘It was.’

Jacobs found himself being marched from the *Farlare*. Ablett was persuaded easily enough to join him, as she was coming back with the food she had promised. Saul still thanked her for it.

As they stepped back into Hayes, Jacobs turned on the lone survivor before he could close the airlock. ‘Can you at least tell me where you’re taking my fucking ship?’

Saul regarded them with his icy reflective gaze. ‘Straunia.’

Echo flagship Glaive
Miller system

'Their actions can't go unanswered, Jaffren.'

Kurcher found Fischer's angry outburst quite amusing. Whenever they were all together, Fischer might as well have pulled his dick out and pissed everywhere.

'They won't,' snarled Hewn, his rage obvious for them all to see. 'I'll crush Harz's skull until it fucking explodes for what he's done.'

Kurcher looked down at his HDU again, reading through the message Hewn had transferred. There were no clues as to who had sent it, but they seemed to know a lot about what Broekow had been through since he left the *Glaive*.

'Possibly another ruse of some sort,' he told the other three. 'Could be someone wants you worrying about an attack from Jericho's Bold just to see how you react.'

'Really?' Drake gave him an incredulous look. 'That's your genius response to this shit?'

Kurcher had seen her mood change significantly since reading the message. Something to pry into later when they were alone.

'This is no ruse,' Hewn said, tapping his own HDU. 'There have been whispers for a long time about the Bold, saying they have been gearing up for something. I just didn't think that something would be declaring war on us.'

'You know this Harz?' Kurcher asked.

Hewn grimaced as he nodded. 'Vicious motherfucker. He's been pushing to lead Jericho's Bold for years. I guess this is his way of getting elected.'

Kurcher glanced back down at the scrolling text. Masami murdered on Vir, Broekow captured and tortured by Harz before being shipped to Rikur. Devlin found dead, stabbed through the neck.

So where the hell is Broekow now? pondered Frost.

Dead most likely, answered D'Larro.

If he did survive, he certainly won't come back to the Expanse, Frost added.

Kurcher shook the voices away. He didn't need them sounding off when he was still trying to wrap his head around what had happened.

'Surely this last part is cause to take a look at your entire operation,' he found himself saying to Hewn. 'Broekow and Masami were sold out by someone in Echo. Do I have to hunt down another fucking traitor?'

'If it's true,' Hewn muttered. 'We'll have to deal with it once everything else is taken care of.'

'Surely this has to be the priority,' yelled Fischer. 'As much as I hate to agree with Kurcher, we can't have someone leaking intel to Jericho's Bold. Jaffren, we have to show we will not tolerate traitors in...'

'Enough.' The room shook under Hewn's roar. 'I know what we have to do and we'll fucking do it, but I don't want the Bold walking freely into the Expanse and taking their pick of targets.'

'Broekow didn't know much,' Fischer reminded them.

Hewn turned on his second. 'He knew enough. Harz will have been looking for a weakness in our operations. A place to hit us.'

Kurcher knew what that meant. As he himself had heard through whispers among the crew, Broekow was also aware Hewn's family were allegedly on Warren. No wonder the Echo leader was raging.

'Vance, I need you to speak with Marie Butler and Hedmun Oakley again.' Hewn moved to his map of the Expanse. 'We need their help patrolling our borders. We're going to be stretched thin as it is.'

'How many ships *do* you have available?' Kurcher had never asked before.

'Twenty-seven. Maybe two more if we can get them repaired quickly.' Hewn nodded at Drake. 'The *Falcata* isn't included in that number.'

'Nor the *Crius* I hope.' Kurcher regretted saying that as soon as the words left his lips.

Hewn ignored the comment and returned to Fischer. 'Get the Resistance and the Oakley fleet on board. I'll send you the systems I want patrolled and the operations I need increased security at. I want those ships out there yesterday.'

'Understood.' Fischer shot a glance across at Kurcher. 'Perhaps our enlister should come with me. He seems to know them all well.'

Kurcher gave him a smile. 'Oh yeah, we're all great friends.'

Keep tweaking his tail and he'll bite, Frost said.

He needs a boot in the fucking balls, suggested Angard.

'You two need to go prep for our trip to Kismet.' Hewn waved his artificial arm at Kurcher and Drake. 'We're leaving soon. Need to get that shit out the way.'

Fischer gave him a curious look. 'You're still going? Surely that can wait, with the Bold lurking out there somewhere.'

‘It’s in our best interest to keep Libra on our side and going after Hengeveld will strengthen that alliance.’ Hewn pointed at the Genesys system on the map. ‘We need Libra for security on Tempest and a number of other ops outside the Expanse, plus they can help deter Harz and whatever plans that fucker has.’

Drake spun on her heel and stalked off towards the door. Kurcher wondered whether he could get through her attitude for one last fuck before they left the *Glaive*.

‘All the best with your mission, Vance,’ he called. ‘Give my regards to Seko.’

With a nod to Hewn, he jogged after Drake. They walked in silence back to the *Falcata* and, once back on board, Kurcher ran a hand around her hip, stroking the soft skin on her belly.

She pulled away. ‘Fuck off, prick.’

Your charm must’ve worn off, laughed Espina.

‘Something bothering you?’ he asked, trying to catch her before she vanished deeper into the ship.

‘Clearly you’re not bothered,’ she replied bluntly.

‘I’ve never seen anything get to you before. Why now?’

Drake gave him a scathing look, her eyes wild. ‘You fucking kidding me? Jericho’s Bold have destroyed the *Crius*, killed Masami and tortured a shitload of intel out of your alcoholic friend which could damage everything Echo have worked to achieve. Meanwhile, Taurus and Nova are at war, and we’re being sent to Kismet to help Libra rescue some arrogant fucker from Sigma. How are you *not* affected by any of this?’

Kurcher dared a step closer. ‘I learnt not to care a long time ago. Broekow’s life has been fucked up since he murdered those officers and I should’ve left him to die on the *Grail*. He’s certainly not my friend. Hewn should’ve had Masami put a bullet in his brain before now but I’m starting to realise Echo’s supposed pirates have a conscience. You’re not the ruthless dickheads I was led to believe for so many years.’

Drake’s knife appeared at his throat, point first. ‘And you’re not always right. Like it or not, Broekow *is* the nearest thing you have to a friend in this universe and you really don’t give a shit about him. Sure, you saved him. Big fucking deal. Now he’s a drunk and has been carved up by Harz and those bastards he commands.’

Kurcher lifted his hand slowly and pushed the blade carefully away from his skin. ‘Broekow makes his own choices. I made one for him and it was wrong. As for Taurus and Nova? They’ve been sparring for decades, building up to that battle taking place in Geraint.' He saw Drake reach for one of her cigarettes. 'I don't want to go to Kismet any more than you do. I can understand why Hewn wants to do this though.'

'I never said I didn't want to go,' she growled, almost throwing the cigarette into her mouth. 'You seem to think you know me. A few fucks here and there don't make us close, and I sure as hell am nothing like that last pilot you had.'

Kurcher glanced at the knife still clutched in her other hand and chose his words as carefully as he could. 'Well you know a lot about me. You know I was born in Geraint. You know I lost both my parents in very different ways. You know Taurus took me in when I was fourteen and that I was part of a special unit sent to Cobb during the civil war. You know I was addicted to Parinax and that I'm responsible for activating the fucking *Grail*, leading to the deaths of millions. How am I doing? Missed anything?'

'I'm not interested in talking about my past,' she said, her voice barely a whisper.

Don't push her too much, warned Frost.

She has a lot of secrets, enlister, said Santa Cruz.

'You got some old link to Jericho's Bold?' It was a question that might get him skewered.

Drake pursed her lips around the cigarette. 'Fuck you.'

She walked away, leaving Kurcher wondering whether he had hit a nerve or was a long way off said nerve. He hadn't considered the possibility before, but the fact she chose to paint her lips blue every day now played on his mind. Maybe it was just coincidence she used the colour preferred by the Bold.

Maybe she's feeling guilty about Masami, D'Larro considered.

Surely Drake isn't the one leaking intel to Harz, said Frost.

You don't know who she used to work for, pointed out Santa Cruz.

Kurcher shook his head and made for his quarters. He needed to get his mind straight for the mission to Kismet and doubts about the pilot would only get in his way or get him killed.

He just couldn't shake the feeling that the shit was about to hit the fan.

Carson Freight Station
Geraint system

The journey from Galt to Carson had been nerve-racking. Despite being on a steady, fast transport, Hayward had spent most of the trip glancing nervously out of the broad viewports, hoping not to see Nova ships descending on them.

The station was completely surrounded by the remnants of the fleet. Some assault ships were docked, while others orbited Carson keeping their sensors tuned for any sign of the enemy.

She still didn't feel particularly safe when she was walking through the station's wide hallways, on her way to the meeting rooms. Knowing that The Kindred had bombed Carson so recently as part of their maniacal plan made her look warily into every darkened nook and cranny. It didn't matter where she went. Threats waited at every corner. Seeing Garrett's face would ease her nerves, she hoped.

The general stood as she entered the room. 'I'm glad you made it. How's the shoulder?'

Hayward gave it a rub for effect. 'Sore. At least I'm in one piece though, same as you.'

Several of Garrett's officers had been in conference with the general and took their leave, each offering a greeting to Hayward as they passed. She didn't feel like sitting and walked across to the window. It offered a view of the *Ravenedge* and she noted the damage to the hull.

'You read my whole report?' Garrett asked, joining her at the window with two glasses of something warmly familiar.

She wanted to down the vodka in one go. 'Thanks. Yes, your report was difficult to read. So many lost in such a short space of time.'

'We're arranging a memorial service to honour all those who lost their lives in the recent events.' Garrett's eyes were distant as he sipped his drink. 'Not just the men and women in the battle here.'

'What of Nova?'

'Off licking their wounds. As you saw, they lost a significant portion of their fleet. They won't be back in a hurry, although I have a decision to make. Push our advantage and take the fight to their own systems or let them think on their actions and hope they make the right choice to end this war.'

'Your ship took a beating I see,' she said, nodding at the flagship. 'Nova's general also survived?'

'Unfortunately. Tomas Klein is a cagey son-of-a-bitch. The *Harbinger* was key to them surviving the battle. Tough ship to break. It had a hand in taking down the *Sentinel*.'

'Is it salvageable?'

Garrett gave the slightest of head shakes. 'She's done her duty. Time to let her rest in peace.' He gazed out at his ship. 'We took heavy losses, Karin. It's going to take a long time to get over that.'

Hayward studied his face. There was the slightest waver in his strong jaw. She couldn't think what to say to console him. He'd watched ships blown apart and officers die, all at his command. She couldn't fathom the turmoil there must be in his head.

'Did you get a chance to read *my* report?'

He smiled, although it was clearly not easy for him to do so. 'Not all. Tell me how the rest of the board are faring.'

She relished the burn of the vodka for a moment. 'Tench was badly wounded by a boomer and has been having treatment for his burns. He's a tough old bastard though, as you know, so was already back working when I left.

Kort is okay too, although won't stop going on about how he saved Tench. Both men are devastated that so many were killed, as we all are, but they are keeping a brave face on for the rest of the colony.

Marris and Chaldevert were lucky enough to be in a part of Kingston that wasn't attacked so they're looking after the whole clean-up operation.'

She took another long sip, knowing what she needed to bring up next. The images she saw from the medics had made her sick.

'They found Billings at the top of the spire, brains blown out. He was packed to leave.'

Garrett grimaced. 'Traitorous little fuck got what he deserved. If he was still alive, I'd have had him thrown off the spire by now for what he did.'

She wasn't sure she would have let him. 'Which just left Pavleachenko. What was left of him we found in his office, plastered all over the walls and floor...and ceiling.'

They stood in silence for a moment, letting that sink in.

'How's Akeman?' Garrett asked her, his voice echoing inside the glass as he drained the last drop of vodka.

'Alive. Just.' She shuddered at the memory of trying to stop the agent bleeding. 'In fact, I'd like to request he works for me once he recovers.'

'I thought he already did.' Garrett gave her a sly sideways look. 'Of course. He'll get a medal for what he did, I'll see to that.'

'He wouldn't like that. Not one for the limelight.'

'Fine.' He turned to face her. 'Tell me what happened with this Mikan Rist.'

Hayward sighed before finishing her drink. 'He was there to kill me and yet he was struggling to do so. The man was part machine. I'd never seen anything quite like it before. After he and Akeman fought, Rist looked lost. Then he let me be and fled Galt in Akeman's ship.'

'I'm trying to find out who he is. I don't like the idea of someone like that still being at large. If Nova have people like that in their ranks, it's yet another problem for us to worry about.'

'Before I left, Akeman said he remembered Rist's name and he would look into it once he was fit to do so.' She shrugged. 'Something tells me the man...machine... whatever he is, won't come after me again.'

Garrett signalled for her to sit down as he took a seat. 'We both need some time to rest, Karin. Just tell me what's happening with your other priority plans, then we can break for a few hours and get some sleep. Or get drunk. Both sound good to me.'

Hayward gave a slightly nervous laugh. 'Fine by me. I was due to have a meeting with Jaffren Hewn of Echo, but he postponed saying he had something he urgently needed to do. He was very apologetic and polite though.'

'Hmm. Probably had to go sell drugs to colonist kids somewhere in the outer systems. What else?'

'I still plan on meeting with a representative of Schaeffer's Nine and, despite not agreeing to meet, Fortitude did offer some interesting information as a goodwill gesture. They said they have been dealing with a new app designed to make mechs much easier to control, especially in battle situations. These mechs, they believe, could help us against the Revenants.'

'By help, they mean slaughter them?' asked Garrett, raising an eyebrow.

'Control them, repel them, push them back. We need something to help take back Earth, general. That's why I'm also suggesting we look at allying with Libra, Sigma and Impramed. It's time to bring the corps back together to fight a common threat.'

He stared at her for a few seconds, making her slightly uncomfortable. 'None of these organisations can be trusted. They would try to use the situation to gain a new foothold on Earth.'

Hayward nodded excitedly. 'Exactly. That's why I'm suggesting we meet with them on Earth. Bring them there so they can see just what the Revenants have done to our beautiful homeworld.'

'I'm not sure it would work,' he told her, being as honest as always. 'They would be more likely to come to Earth armed to the teeth and try removing Taurus so they can swoop in and claim it. They could turn the Earth into their own warzone. Don't forget Libra and Sigma are hardly on good terms.'

She could see the extreme doubt in his eyes and so chose to be as honest as he was. 'The corruption that was rotting Taurus Galahad from the top has been eradicated. Lenaghan, Billings, Mitchell, Santa Cruz. All dead. Nova have been battered and driven back to their systems. This is the perfect time for us to form new alliances.'

Garrett thought for a moment, tapping the table. Then he lifted his hands. 'Okay, you have my blessing to proceed, but I want to be in the loop all the way. I need to make sure you're protected during any meetings you arrange. Agreed?'

She grinned. 'Thank you. Any more vodka?'

The general grabbed the bottle and refilled both glasses. 'I'm impressed that you never gave up on Earth, even after everything that has happened to you on Galt. I thought you'd be arranging to move somewhere else permanently. Somewhere quieter.'

'Earth's my home,' she stated. 'Always has been. If we can't take back our original homeworld, what hope do we have for the future?'

He spun the glass slowly in his hand. 'Plus I assume you have family back there too?'

Hayward looked down into her drink, her smile fading. 'I did. They died in the Revenant attacks.'

Garrett looked like he had been slapped. 'I'm sorry, Karin. I didn't know.'

'My son. He was just five.' She downed half the vodka. 'Now you know why this means so much to me.'

They sat in silence for some time. Garrett clearly didn't know what he should say to that revelation. She actually felt glad she had told him. It was a relief finally telling someone.

'Well then.' He leaned forward and raised his glass. 'Here's to your son and to our new imminent alliances.'

Her smile returned. Now that was a toast worth making.

Sapphire Nova Assault Ship Harbinger Flint system

Klein couldn't tear his eyes away from Straunia.

Had he made a terrible misjudgement in his plans? The trap he set in order to tempt the other corporations into Flint, sending Rist to Galt, attacking Haskell, Wagner and Kalbrec. He had arranged it all just so they could chip away at Taurus before the hammer blow. He regretted taking the fleet to Geraint. It was too soon. He should've had more patience.

'Valen, Armstrong, Ixxis, Karstad.' Bavelli held the HDU up in front of his friend's eyes, trying to get his attention. 'We should regroup at one of those, not here. It won't be long before the rest of the corps focus their attention on Straunia.'

Klein surveyed the data on the screen. A list of systems alongside the remaining roster of assault ships. The fact that the *Rothwell* was missing just made him doubt his decisions even more.

'Valen is the obvious choice,' he said, finding his voice. 'We should gather all of our forces there.'

'Not all.' Bavelli scowled and shook his head. 'We need to take stock of our guardians, transports, explorers and mining ships. Then we need to look at how many soldiers we have available.'

Klein finally wrenched his gaze from Straunia to look at the commander of the *Grosvenor*. 'Soldiers? We have men and women on many of our worlds. You want to bring them all together?'

'Maybe. We shouldn't just run away and huddle out of sight in the farthest edges of the Milky Way. We should hit some of Taurus' smaller colonies. Keep some form of momentum, in this case ground attacks.'

'No.' Klein wouldn't risk losing more people so soon after the losses suffered in Geraint. 'Kam, we lost the battle. No point pushing when Taurus have the upper hand.'

Bavelli gave a derisive snort. 'We didn't lose the war. Taurus took a massive loss as well, don't forget.'

'My orders...' Klein glanced around at his command crew, who were all trying their best to ignore the conversation. 'My orders are to take the fleet on to Valen, where we will form a new war council led by the both of us. You and I won't make the decisions alone any more.'

Bavelli was lost for words for all of several seconds. 'Tomas, Nova is still alive because of us. Our people believe in this war and they believe in us.'

'Are you sure?'

As Bavelli went to reply, the comms officer called out. 'Commanders, you need to see this.'

They made their way to his console and Klein had to blink hard to make sure he wasn't seeing things. There was a weak signal coming in and it seemed to be coming from Straunia.

'Can you source it?' Klein asked the officer, leaning over his shoulder.

'I can already tell you that it is coming from a ship, sir. I should be able to tell you the designation shortly.'

'How so?' Bavelli was leaning over the other shoulder.

The comms officer tapped his display. 'The ship is coming through the upper atmosphere so we should be able to get a visual soon too.'

Klein and Bavelli shared a look of disbelief. No ship had returned from Straunia since the *Grail* went down. All the technical issues they had had on fly-bys which stopped them scanning the surface had led them to believe the teams had been lost.

Klein felt a renewed hope stirring in his chest. 'Well?'

The officer was quiet as he waited for the data. 'It's the *Cognis*, sir.'

'One of ours, right?' Bavelli looked to Klein for the answer.

'Yes. One of the investigatory teams we sent down there. Lost contact just like the rest.'

The comms officer looked up at Klein. 'Want to hear the message, sir?'

He gave a nod before standing straight and returning his eyes to Straunia. He couldn't yet see any sign of the small craft.

'This is Manders. To any of the Sapphire Nova assault ships in orbit, I've managed to jury-rig the *Cognis* engines and escape the surface, but they won't last long under this pressure. I need permission to dock.' Silence for a couple of seconds. 'Plus, I have urgent intel to share on events that have occurred on Straunia.'

Klein managed to shake off the funk he had been experiencing since Geraint. 'Get that ship docked with the *Harbinger*. Kam, we'll be there to meet Manders.'

The *Cognis* managed to break free of Straunia's gravity despite its spluttering engines and was steered towards the flagship. It looked like it would collide with the extended pylon of the *Harbinger* and Klein was glad to see its pilot managed to correct the trajectory at the last minute to avoid a disastrous approach.

Klein and Bavelli rushed eagerly to the airlock, keen to lay eyes on the only man to get away from the doomed planet. Behind them, a small squad of soldiers tried in vain to keep up.

'Let's hope he's got something worthwhile to tell us,' Bavelli said, his breathing heavy after the run through the ship.

Klein, who was slightly fitter than his colleague, stayed focused on the airlock door. *His* hope was that the intel Manders was about to deliver to them would give them a new edge; something to work with following the deaths of so many.

The door slid open and a very sorry-looking individual stepped through. His Nova uniform was torn and almost black with grime. His skin was streaked with dirt, hair matted and greasy. His eyes though were bright and almost shone in the light.

'Welcome back,' greeted Klein, stepping forward to meet him.

Manders regarded him with a strange smile before shifting his gaze to Bavelli and the soldiers standing ready behind. 'Thank you, sir.'

Klein's own smile disintegrated as a mass of dark bodies pushed through the airlock behind Manders, surging into the *Harbinger* and reaching out for the commander with nightmarish tendrils of black and silver.

See the Antecedent series (scan with a smart phone, click on the message):

See more Science Fiction books from GBP:

www.ingramcontent.com/pod-product-compliance
Lightning Source LLC
LaVergne TN
LVHW091048080826
845145LV00002B/669

* 9 7 8 1 9 1 2 5 7 6 4 9 4 *